Praise for The Laird's Willful Lass:

"*The Laird's Willful Lass* was a sexy introduction to Anna Campbell's new *The Lairds Most Likely* series." **Kathy's Review Corner**

"Anna did a fantastic job of giving us a story to remember! Such a fabulous read from beginning to end!" **5 stars *Rose Is Reading***

"I lost myself in the beautiful Scottish highlands with this wonderful romance. Two fascinating characters, intense passion and a story that flowed wonderfully and held my attention from beginning to end. A great start to a new series." **Annie West, *USA Today* Bestselling Author**

"How wonderful! We have two strong willed, confident and poised people looking for, and finding, love without knowing it. They drive each other crazy with their dictatorial assertiveness, which turns into, "Me thinks thou dost protest too much." Watching them each learn the art of compromise was charming! I completely enjoyed this story. Once again, Ms. Campbell brings us characters that we can get behind, cheer for and enjoy." **Buried Under Romance**

"Anna Campbell brings her amazing talents from the London ton to the Scottish Highlands. The chemistry between Fergus McKinnon, the Laird of Achnasheen, and Marina Luchetti, an artist from Florence is amazing." **5 stars *Amazon Review***

"This is the first book I've read by this author but it won't be the last! Her writing is magnificent, taking you where the characters are with her brilliant descriptions!" **5 stars *Amazon Review***

"A wonderful new book from Anna Campbell, she pours such emotion and power into her characters, it's hard to put her books down once started, but would you really want to with such a stunning backdrop of the Scottish Highlands to keep you amused." **5 stars *Amazon Review***

"*The Laird's Willful Lass* is another winner with the author's ability to layer in historical details while creating strong female characters that get happily ever afters." ***Night Owl Reviews***

"A romantic and satisfying read with plenty of steam and heart." ***Roses Are Blue***

"My suggestion to Ms Campbell is put Regency England on the back burner for a while, and welcome (fáilte) to bonnie Scotland! As Scottish romance readers like myself are absolutely exhilarated and thrilled! This book is an absolute masterpiece from start to finish!" **5 stars *Celtic Barb's Tartan Book Reviews***

"Anna's writing is witty and emotionally satisfying. The sensual attraction is hot! She will keep you enthralled from the first page to the last. I am a fan and will be adding this one to my keeper shelf with all my other Anna Campbell Historical Romances." ***The Reading Wench***

ALSO BY ANNA CAMPBELL

Claiming the Courtesan

Untouched

Tempt the Devil

Captive of Sin

My Reckless Surrender

Midnight's Wild Passion

The Sons of Sin Series:

Seven Nights in a Rogue's Bed

Days of Rakes and Roses

A Rake's Midnight Kiss

What a Duke Dares

A Scoundrel by Moonlight

Three Proposals and a Scandal

The Dashing Widows Series:

The Seduction of Lord Stone

Tempting Mr. Townsend

Winning Lord West

Pursuing Lord Pascal

Charming Sir Charles

Catching Captain Nash

Lord Garson's Bride

The Lairds Most Likely Series:

The Laird's Willful Lass

The Laird's Christmas Kiss

The Highlander's Lost Lady

The Highlander's Defiant Captive

The Highlander's Christmas Quest

The Highlander's English Bride

The Highlander's Forbidden Mistress

The Highlander's Christmas Countess

The Highlander's Rescued Maiden

The Highlander's Christmas Lassie

A Scandal in Mayfair Series:

One Wicked Wish

Two Secret Sins

Three Times Tempted

Christmas Stories:

The Winter Wife

Her Christmas Earl

A Pirate for Christmas

Mistletoe and the Major

A Match Made in Mistletoe

The Christmas Stranger

His Christmas Cinderella (in the anthology A Grosvenor Square Christmas)

Other Books:

These Haunted Hearts

Stranded with the Scottish Earl

The Laird's Willful Lass

The Lairds Most Likely Book 1

ANNA CAMPBELL

My heroine, intrepid watercolor artist Marina
Lucchetti, was inspired by a real-life female
photographer who traveled all over the Western
Highlands and Islands in the early 20th century,
recording a way of life that was even then starting
to become part of history. So I'd like to dedicate this
book to Mary Ethel Muir Donaldson (1876-1958)
whose beautiful, haunting photographs first caught
my attention at the excellent Mallaig Heritage
Centre when I was on my way to stay on Eigg in
2017. I'd also like to thank Helen at the Heritage
Centre for helping me to research M.E.M.
Donaldson's life in more detail when I decided that
she'd make a wonderful model for a Regency
painter.

PROLOGUE

Western Highlands of Scotland, April 1802

"I think we're lost," Diarmid said, trudging along the narrow path a few feet behind Hamish.

Hamish could hear how hard his eleven-year-old cousin fought to stop his voice trembling with fear. He was frightened, too, and he was only ten, but as was his habit, he hid his disquiet beneath humor. "We can't be lost. My mother will kill me if I'm not home for breakfast."

The weak attempt at a joke didn't do much to lighten Diarmid's mood. "You said you could guide us by the stars."

"I could until the moon came up," Hamish retorted, wrapping his arms around his chest to contain a shiver. The day had been warm for April; the night turned bitterly cold.

"I can't even see the moon anymore."

No, damn it, he couldn't either, and then the blasted mist had risen, as well. Although his mother wouldn't like him swearing, even if only in his head.

On a bright, clear night, he and his cousin had set out to stargaze. They'd sneaked out of their tower bedroom in the rambling hunting lodge their parents had rented for a few weeks. The trip offered a chance for the two families to get together, for the Macgrath sisters to catch up on gossip, and for the children to play.

The moment he heard about the plan to stay in the hills outside Plockton, Hamish had been ecstatic. His cousin Diarmid, a whole year older, always struck him as the finest fellow in the world. And any masculine company made a nice change from a household shrill with three older sisters, and now the addition of a baby girl in arms.

When he'd climbed out of the high window and down the old oak tree, an excursion in the open air had seemed a great lark. Now thick mist rose about them, the temperature dropped toward freezing, and the slopes were so steep and rocky that if he or Diarmid stumbled on the path, a plunge to the death surely awaited.

"We should wait here," Hamish said. "It's too dangerous to go on. I brought a tinderbox to make a fire."

"I doubt we'll find any dry kindling," Diarmid said. Hamish began to find his cousin's habit of looking on the negative side rather grating.

"We're still better off stopping." Hamish turned back to Diarmid, who formed an indistinct black shape against the looming rock. "It's too dark to see our way, and the mist is getting worse."

"If we stay in one place, we'll freeze to death." His cousin stood a few feet away, and Hamish felt him staring back through the murk.

"If we go on, we'll fall off a cliff."

"Is that any better?"

Diarmid had a point. But Hamish was tired of fumbling around in the dark, especially as he had a horrid suspicion that for at least the last hour, they'd gone around in circles.

A grim silence descended. Hamish shivered again and curled his toes against the soles of his boots to try to restore the circulation. When he left the hunting lodge, he'd been snug in his thick coat and woolen socks and stout boots. Now he was colder than he'd ever been in his life. His home on the coast at Glen Lyon was much gentler country than these wild northern climes.

"Hullooo!"

At first, the sound seemed a trick of the gusting wind.

"Hullooo, up the brae!"

"Is that..." Hamish asked, turning his head, though mist and darkness prevented him seeing anything.

Diarmid lifted his head and shouted. "We're up here!"

"Are ye in trouble?" This time there was no mistaking that the sound was human, although it was difficult to tell from which direction it came.

"Aye. We're lost."

"Then dinnae move."

"Should we keep shouting so you can find us?" Hamish called out.

"Aye," came the ghostly reply.

"What shall we shout?" Hamish asked.

Over the last acrimonious hour, Diarmid's hero status had lost some of its shine, but Hamish had never admired his cousin more than when he broke into a stirring tune.

"Scots, wha hae wi' Wallace bled,
Scots, wham Bruce has aften led;
Welcome tae yer gory bed,

Or to victory."

Hamish laughed with a shaming trace of relief and joined in the song. Now that rescue was on the way, their scrape turned back into a grand adventure.

They were into their second reprise before two figures emerged from the mist on the path ahead of him. One was a large, black dog of indeterminate breed. The other was...

"But you're just a boy, too," he said, his brief hope vanishing and all his earlier fear rushing up in a choking wave.

"I'm all of fourteen," the lad said huffily, lifting the lantern he carried to reveal Hamish and Diarmid shivering on the ledge. Under a long leather coat, their rescuer wore a rough linen shirt and a red and black kilt. A brace of dead hares dangled from his wide black leather belt. "I'll have ye ken I'm up to bringing a pair of brainless Sassenach laddies down a brae. You're lucky I was out chasing some game and heard your voices on the wind."

"My cousin didn't mean—" Diarmid said.

"I'm no Sassenach," Hamish interjected. "I'm as Scots as you are. I'm going to be the Laird of Glen Lyon one day."

"Och, is that so?" The newcomer sounded skeptical as he peered at Hamish through the flickering light and clearly found nothing noteworthy. "Yet here ye are, sounding like ye live in Mayfair and take tea with King George every afternoon."

This time, Hamish was grateful for the unreliable light. It hid his blush. His father might be hereditary master of beautiful Glen Lyon, but he'd worked for years at the War Office in London, and Hamish had spent the last two years at Eton.

"I mightn't sound Scots, but it's what's in your heart that counts," he muttered.

The tall, thin boy with dark red hair subjected him to a searching regard, then smiled with sudden, surprising charm. "Well said, laddie. I beg your pardon. I'm Fergus Mackinnon, and I am the laird of this glen. I'm guessing you're staying in the hunting lodge beside the loch."

"Aye," Diarmid said, and Hamish noted his cousin made an effort to sound Scots, too, even though he went to Harrow and his school was as much a bastion of the English establishment as Eton was. "I'm Diarmid Mactavish, and this is my cousin Hamish Douglas. We're devilish glad to see ye, Master Mackinnon."

Mackinnon arched an eyebrow and rested his free hand on the dog's shaggy head as it sat at his side, observing the conversation with intelligent yellow eyes. The boy's manner was altogether superior, and Hamish wasn't sure he liked him, although he was deuced thankful someone had come along to lead them down the mountain. "I suppose you're a wee laird as well?"

Diarmid pulled himself up to a full height that was impressive for an eleven-year-old, if not equal to Mackinnon's. "Not yet, but I will be. My father is the Laird of Invertavey, down on the coast by Ullapool."

"Then it's a gey distinguished gathering we have indeed." More irony. "What I want to ken is why two bairns are out so late, wandering the hillsides of Achnasheen on a dreich night that promised mist."

Hamish bit back an objection to being called a child. He mightn't approve of Mackinnon, but he wasn't stupid enough to offend him. If their rescuer abandoned them, he and Diarmid would be stuck out here the rest of the night. However, he couldn't help pointing out a salient fact. "You're out wandering the hillsides, too."

"Aye, well, it's different for me. Even if I was a blind man, I'd find my way over every inch of this glen. A wee bit of Highland weather doesn't change that."

A pang of envy sharpened Hamish's hostility. While he loved Glen Lyon, the family only spent a few weeks there a year. He was a stranger to his inheritance in a way that Fergus Mackinnon wasn't.

"We came out to look at the stars," Diarmid said.

"Aye?" Mackinnon's single word communicated endless wonder at Sassenach stupidity, despite these particular Sassenachs claiming to be Scots. "I dinna see the stars for the mist, but then I am a dim-witted Highlander."

Hamish would wager a year's allowance that this boy wasn't dim-witted at all. "They were bright as diamonds before the moon came up. I've never seen Arcturus so clear."

"Hamish knows all the constellations," Diarmid said eagerly. It was very like his cousin to try to smooth over any antagonism. "He's going to be Astronomer Royal one day."

"Is that so?" Mackinnon didn't sound any more impressed, now that he'd heard Hamish's credentials. "Yet the next Galileo wasnae clever enough to ken that once the full moon came up, the stars would fade to invisibility?"

"I did. But we were headed home before that happened, and I thought we could find our way using the moonlight. Then all the hills started to look alike, and the mist came down, and we got lost," Hamish snapped, uncomfortably aware that tonight's debacle was mostly—well, *all*—his fault. "So will you take us down the mountain?"

Mackinnon shook his head. "No, that I will not, my fine laddie."

"I say, that's a bit rum," Hamish began hotly. "Just because I don't sound like I live on top of Ben Nevis and have haggis for breakfast every morning—"

The older boy broke into Hamish's tirade. "The mist makes it too dangerous. I'll no' be risking my neck, let alone yours."

"Then what are we to do?" Diarmid asked. "It's getting colder."

"There's a cave nearby that will get us out of the wind, not to mention the sleet that's on the way. We can wait there until the mist clears."

"And when will that be?" Hamish asked irritably.

"Hamish," Diarmid said in a reproving tone. "Master Mackinnon is kind enough to help us. He deserves our courtesy."

While he laughed up his sleeve at both of them, Hamish wanted to say, but he didn't. "I'm sorry, Master Mackinnon," he said grudgingly, more for Diarmid's sake than his own.

"Aye, well, follow me, and I'll make sure ye get back to your parents in one piece." Mackinnon clicked his fingers to the dog, who was regarding Hamish and Diarmid with an expression only a little more disdainful than his master's. "Come, Bailey."

Mackinnon set out ahead, the dog trotting beside him, while Hamish and Diarmid did their best to keep up with his long-legged stride. Hamish had to admit that the young Laird of Achnasheen trod these mountains as if he owned them. His familiarity with this rugged landscape made Hamish feel depressingly feeble and...*English.*

Hamish mightn't much like their brusque rescuer, but he liked what their rescuer accomplished. Within an hour, the three boys were hunkered down beside a roaring fire at the mouth of a cave that kept them out of the howling wind. They'd all enjoyed an excellent supper of roast mountain hare. Mackinnon had even managed to conjure up some dry bracken for bedding. Prickly, but better than the bare rock.

Hamish struggled to stay awake with the older boys to prove he wasn't a useless Sassenach, but warmth, hot food, and safety all conspired to put him to sleep.

He had no idea what time it was when he stirred. The fire had burned down low. He was deliciously cozy, and it took him a minute to realize that the scruffy black dog was curled up against his chest, breathing in soft snores.

The flickering light threw strange shadows across the faces of the two boys sitting up and talking in low voices. It highlighted Diarmid's gypsy dark looks. The black eyes, long bony nose, and thin cheeks. Hamish and Diarmid might be cousins, but nobody would know to look at them. He was as fair as a Norseman, with a sheaf of wheat-blond hair and eyes the bright blue of his mother's.

The flames turned Mackinnon into a young Scottish warrior. Hamish loathed admitting it, but their rescuer looked much more at home in this stark, magnificent setting than he or Diarmid did. The rich red hair, the cleanly cut features, and some indefinable air of authority marked him as prince of this domain.

Still half-asleep, Hamish lay concealed in the shadows back from the cave mouth. He curled his fingers in the dog's soft coat, loving the pungent canine smell and the knowledge that a living creature rested up against him. He'd begged his parents for a dog of his own, but his silly sisters were afraid of them.

Cocooned in physical comfort, he didn't immediately realize what the other lads were talking about. To his surprise, it wasn't hunting or sport, but their ideas about the girls they might one day marry. This struck Hamish as ridiculously premature, but curiosity kept him quiet as the soft voices, one with a musical Highland lilt and the other clipped and precise and English, murmured across the dying fire.

"Och, aye, bonny. Who wants to look at a sour-faced besom over the supper table?" Mackinnon leaned forward to prod the fire with a stick, and the flare of light revealed the face of a boy not far from manhood. "It would put me off my taties."

"All right, I suppose I'd like her to be pretty. But there's more important things than how a girl looks."

The comfortable note in Diarmid's voice indicated he was enjoying the company. Hamish felt an unworthy prick of jealousy, only partly mollified by knowing that after tonight he'd never have to see that rude sod Fergus Mackinnon again.

"Aye, like being willing to recognize her lord and master and do what she's told. If there's one thing I cannae abide, it's a pert lassie who doesnae ken her rightful place in the world."

"I hope you're so lucky." This time Diarmid's laugh held an edge. Hamish could imagine why. Both their mothers, the famously beautiful Macgrath sisters, gave as good as they got when it came to family decisions. "No, I was talking about qualities like honesty and loyalty, and maybe a bit of spirit to keep things interesting."

"Och, aye, if ye must have those things. Remember, a lassie wants a man to protect her and smooth her path in life, while a man wants a woman who sees a hero when she looks at him. And by God, whatever ye say, any wife of mine is going to be bonny."

"It's not always easy to love a beautiful woman," Diarmid said somberly, and something in his voice made him sound older than his eleven years.

Hamish frowned. He ignored family politics, as long as they left him free to pursue his astronomical interests. But over the last few weeks, even he had picked up the tension bristling between Diarmid's parents.

"I'll keep her in line."

"You're very confident." It was spoken more as a question than a compliment.

Mackinnon shrugged. "I took charge here five years ago, after my father died. My mother was prostrate with grief, and my two sisters were only six and seven. They all appreciated a strong hand on the tiller."

Part of Hamish's mind marveled at—and unwillingly admired—Mackinnon, if he had been master of his estate since he was a mere nine years old. Perhaps there was some justification behind that insufferable self-assurance.

"And you exerted this influence at nine?" Diarmid asked with a hint of disbelief.

"Aye, I did. I was old enough to know that a woman's like a horse. A man needs to keep a firm grip on the reins and show her who's in control, and she's all the happier for it."

"I want a good Scots lass who makes sure nobody ever calls my children Sassenachs," Hamish said, before he thought to stop himself.

"And do ye think a good Scots lass will have ye, my wee laird in the making?" Mackinnon asked, looking in his direction, and Hamish went back to hating him. How could such a nasty brute have such a nice dog, when some very nice boys couldn't have a dog at all?

"Why not? Glen Lyon is a fine estate, and I'll treat her well."

"When you're not watching the skies," Diarmid said.

Hamish sat up, disturbing Bailey. He was getting ready to punch his cousin for his lack of loyalty, when he looked out the cave mouth. "Does it seem lighter to you?"

The others turned toward the opening. "By God, I think the mist is clearing," Diarmid said.

All three boys scrambled to their feet, and Mackinnon began kicking dirt over the fire. "At last. I'll have ye both back at the hunting lodge before breakfast."

"We can find our own way," Hamish said ungraciously, wanting this stranger gone and Diarmid to himself again. The dog rose with a groan, had a good shake, and stretched.

"Maybe. But having saved your necks, I dinna want ye tumbling down the next brae, once I leave ye to your own devices."

Diarmid ignored Hamish fuming beside him and extended a hand in Mackinnon's direction. "Master Mackinnon, I'd like to thank you for saving our lives. I dread to think what would have happened if you hadn't come along. We'd have frozen to death, if we hadn't fallen down a cliff first. This adventure will always unite us."

Devil take Diarmid, Hamish hoped not.

A hint of a smile hovered on Mackinnon's face. "Given I've just saved your thin southern skins, ye should call me Fergus."

"I think so, too. I'm Diarmid."

As the young Scotsman shook his hand, Diarmid cast his younger cousin a disapproving glance. "Hamish?"

"Oh, aye," he said in a sullen tone and stuck out one grubby paw. "Thank you for saving us."

To his surprise, Mackinnon shook his hand and laughed—not nastily either. "No' as eloquent as your cousin, but, aye, I'll take it."

Hamish felt a pang as Bailey wagged his tail and trotted back to his master. "I like your dog."

"Aye, Bailey's a braw creature, if not the bonniest. He's just fathered a litter of puppies, if you'd like one."

"Would I?" Hamish responded with a rush of enthusiasm, then native caution revived. "Why on earth would you give me a dog?"

The boy's expression turned mocking, as if he read the epic battle between pride and yearning in Hamish's heart. "Every good Scotsman needs a good Scots hound by his side."

Diarmid gave Hamish a surreptitious kick. "Don't cut off your nose to spite your face, cuz," he whispered.

Hamish looked at Bailey with a longing that was so sharp, he could taste it. "I'm not allowed to have a dog," he mumbled. "My sisters don't like them."

Mackinnon clapped him on the shoulder and picked up the lantern. With the sun coming up, he didn't relight it. "I imagine once I bring the two lost lambs back to the fold, a small request like a home for an unwanted puppy willnae be turned down."

"Is he unwanted?" Hamish asked. He tried not to look down the mountainside. The brightening light made it clear that if he or Diarmid had fallen while they picked their way along the path, they would have broken their necks.

"Well, ye want him," Mackinnon said, striding away with the black dog trotting at his heels. "Come down the brae. I'm ready for something more than hare to eat, even if ye two laddies want to stay up here to enjoy the fresh air."

The fresh air was icy. The sun hadn't had a chance to warm things up yet. Hamish realized that he was hungry, too, and dead tired, despite his nap. When Diarmid set off after Fergus, he didn't hesitate to follow.

The promise of a dog of his own was so exciting that he almost didn't mind the admiration in Diarmid's eyes when he looked at Fergus. The kind of admiration, Hamish couldn't help noting with some mortification, that he was in the habit of directing at his older cousin.

The three boys and the dog left the cave and followed the path over the ridge.

CHAPTER ONE

*Achnasheen, Western Highlands of Scotland,
September 1817*

The smart yellow carriage careered wildly along the steep, rutted track that snaked down into the glen. Fergus hauled Banshee to a stop on the bend of the road. Horror churned in his gut, as he watched the vehicle speeding toward the burn, swollen to river size after the rainy summer.

"Bloody hell," he muttered, digging his heels into Banshee's sides. The mare set off through the twilight at a gallop, while his dogs Macushla and Brecon ran barking at her heels.

The coach horses were running in a blind panic, out of control. As the carriage veered closer, he saw that the coachman had lost his grip on the reins. There was no way that the driver would negotiate the sharp corner at the base of the mountainside to keep the vehicle on the bridge and clear of the water.

Fergus had reached the stone bridge when the inevitable happened. The horses swerved at the sudden appearance of the burn in front of them. There was a crack as an axle broke, then another louder crack followed by the tinkle of shattered glass as the carriage rammed into the sturdy pillar supporting the end of the bridge.

The coachman screamed as he hurtled through the air to land on the grassy verge of the road. For a sickening moment, Fergus was sure not only that the driver was dead, but that the carriage must overturn into the burn. His heart lodged in his throat, as the vehicle teetered on the crumbling bank above the rushing brown water.

Fergus flung himself from the saddle and rushed over to the prostrate man. Banshee shifted uneasily, agitated by the other horses' terrified whinnying, but bless her, she stayed put. As if things weren't bad enough already, it started to rain.

"Are ye all right, laddie?"

Praise heaven, the man already started to stir. By the time Fergus got to him, he was sitting up and groggily rubbing his skull. His high-crowned hat lay upside down on the wet grass beside him. "Ma heed, ma heed."

Even through the shrill neighs of the carriage horses and the thunder of the rushing burn, Fergus noted the Glasgow accent. "Can ye move?"

The man's resentful look told Fergus that any injuries he'd sustained weren't too serious. What a miracle. "Aye, if I must."

"Then do something about the horses." They'd both broken free and shied all over the bridge, trailing tack on the ground and showing the whites of their eyes. "Before they kill themselves or someone else."

Fergus helped the man up, made sure he was in fact unhurt, then turned his attention to the wrecked carriage. With each second, it appeared more unstable, Fergus guessed because the passengers moved around inside it.

"For God's sake, stay still," he called out, as he dashed toward the vehicle. Out of the corner of his eye, he saw the coachman stagger across to the jittery horses.

When Fergus reached to tug the door, a woman in a rich crimson cape poked her head out of the shattered window. "Good. You can help."

Could he indeed? He bristled at her imperious tone, while common sense insisted that he had no time for pique, if he meant to save these travelers from a dousing. "Are ye hurt?"

She raised one slender, gloved hand and pushed back the hood on her stylish cape. He found himself under the regard of calm, dark eyes in a face that was striking for its hauteur.

Not at all his sort of woman, he could already tell. Too high-handed by far. Nonetheless, despite the urgent circumstances, he couldn't help taking a split second to admire her. While the lassie mightn't be to his taste, she was a prime article.

And by heaven, she was brave. Most women he knew would be in hysterics after that crash.

"No. Just a little shaken," she said steadily. "But I fear Papa has broken his leg."

To confirm this, a groan and a stream of curses in Italian emanated from the coach's shadowy interior.

"He'll end up in the drink if we dinnae get him out. So will ye. Is there anyone else in the carriage?"

"No, only the two of us."

For a brief moment, Fergus wondered why she wasn't traveling with a maid. The carriage was expensive, and so was that cape. Discreet jewels sparkled at her ears and throat. Whoever the lady was, someone had spent money on her appearance and comfort.

After months of rain, the bank was all mud and not the most reliable foundation. To help anchor the carriage, he stood on the step. "Can ye get out alone, or should I lift you?"

When she shoved uselessly at the door handle, the coach gave an ominous creak and tipped closer to the rushing water. "I think—"

"For pity's sake." Fergus wrenched open the jammed door with a grunt of effort, and hoisted her free.

He had a brief impression of lily fragrance and a tall, nicely curved body, before he set her on her feet on the road. She clutched a worn leather satchel that seemed too big for a lady.

"Well, that was decisive." In the rain, she looked as ruffled as a wet hen, but he didn't have time for politeness.

"Stay there and dinnae move."

He turned to shout at the coachman who was hauling the horses up the bank, away from the bridge. "Are the horses hurt?"

"No, my lord, only frighted." The man edged away from Macushla and Brecon who approached him, more out of canine curiosity than aggression, Fergus knew.

"Then get down here and help me," he said, blinking the rain away from his eyes.

"But the horses, my lord—"

"They willnae wander far, if they wander at all."

Fergus returned to the step and stuck his head into the carriage. The lady's father turned out to be a portly gentleman huddled in the far corner, just where he was most likely to tip the vehicle. The light inside was dim, but not too dim to hide the unnatural angle of the man's left leg as it dangled in the well between the seats.

"*Maledizione.* I told Marina this *viaggio* was cursed, but does she ever listen to her papa?" the man said in a thick Italian accent. "No, not that one. She always knows best."

"Papa, stop complaining and come forward so we can pull you free," the woman—she was no ingénue, but at least in her middle twenties—said from beside Fergus's shoulder.

He stifled a growl of annoyance. No wonder she hadn't objected to his orders. She'd decided to ignore them instead. At least when she added her weight to his on the step, it helped counterbalance the tilting carriage. Even if things were a wee bit cozy for strangers, with the two of them sharing the narrow metal platform.

"My leg, she hurts," her father groaned, shifting further away.

Fergus bit back a curse. If the coach slipped now, all three of them would end up in the burn.

"The rest of you will hurt if you fall into the river," the woman said, edging closer to Fergus. The scent of lilies mixed with the fresh smell of the rain. When she reached inside for her father, the carriage gave another alarming creak.

"Get out of the way, lassie. This is nae place for a woman," Fergus snapped, catching her by the waist again. He'd already rescued her once. He shouldn't have to do it twice. "And mind the broken glass." Jagged shards littered the seats and floor.

"Oofff," she gasped as, with little ceremony, he hauled her off the step.

"And stay there, ye wee besom," he said, plopping her back on the road with no great expectation she'd heed him. She hadn't yet.

If he had time, he might call her unwomanly. If he had time, his appreciation for those fine eyes might convince him she was very much a woman after all. "You're getting in the way."

"My father isn't a small man," the woman said breathlessly, as she staggered to keep her feet. He noted that, unlike her father, she spoke English with the clipped accents of the upper classes. Perhaps once they were out of this blasted mess, he'd find out why. "You'll need help."

"I'm sure I can manage, madam." He didn't delay to make sure she was all right. Using his sleeve to brush the glass shards from the seat, he leaned in to assess what he needed to do. "Can ye slide across to the door, *signore*? It will be easier on your leg that way."

"I can't move," the man moaned, pressing against the far door. When the shift in weight set the carriage rocking, Fergus's stomach twisted in dread.

"*Si*, you can," the lady said. She was back peering over Fergus's shoulder. Just his luck to be stuck with a woman unable to recognize the voice of authority, not to mention good sense. "I know it hurts, Papa, but if you use your good leg, you can do it."

The man's terrified gaze sought out his daughter, and Fergus recognized paralyzing fear. So far, the older man showed considerably less fortitude than his offspring. "You're *una ragazza crudele,* and the angels despair of you."

"We dinnae have time for this," Fergus said between his teeth.

"Papa, if you don't come out, I'm coming in to get you. Then it will be your fault if we both drown."

"*Per pietà*, this won't work."

"Try, Papa. *Per favore.* You don't want to be buried in Scotland."

"*Certo,* I do not! Even for a dead man, this country is too cold."

"In that case, you have to move."

Fergus was about to tell the woman to be a bit gentler with her father's fears, when to his surprise, he saw determination seep into the plump features. "For you, then, *figlia mia.*"

"Take my hand," Fergus said on a surge of hope, reaching in, while still trying to use his weight to keep the carriage level.

"You, Coker, come and hold the broken shaft to keep the coach steady," the woman said sharply behind Fergus. Coker must be the blockhead of a coachman.

Grunting in pain, the Italian began to shift gingerly in Fergus's direction. Halfway along the leather seat, he stretched out a shaking hand. Fergus lurched forward to grab the man's wrist as he felt the carriage settle further into the mud. Coker must have at last decided to lend his aid.

The next few seconds became an agonizing nightmare of suspense. It seemed to take the older man an hour to get into position. Beside him, Fergus heard the woman's unsteady breathing and what he thought was a whispered prayer or two.

She wasn't quite as unemotional about her parent's plight as she pretended. He liked her better for the hint of vulnerability, and for her courage in keeping it to herself.

This time, he didn't waste his time telling her to stand back, although if the coach went into the burn, it would take half the bank. The mudslide would carry her away with it.

"That's it, Papa. *Bravo.*"

"Give me room, madam," Fergus said curtly.

"Of course." Before he had an instant to remark on her sudden cooperation, she went on. "I'll hold you steady while you bring him out."

Fergus didn't have the breath to consign her to Hades, although he wanted to. When she stepped down, the coach gave another alarming wobble. As Coker struggled to keep a grip on the shaft, he swore in some incomprehensible Glaswegian patois.

"*Coraggio,* Papa." Fergus heard how she strove to keep her tone bright. "You won't be in there much longer."

"Try and maneuver yourself out. If I pull ye, I might damage your leg." If only he'd had the luxury of splinting the break before bringing the man out, but the carriage was too close to going over.

"Don't let me go, *per favore*," the man said shakily, struggling to stand on one foot. The movement set the coach shuddering again.

"Coker, hold on!" the woman shouted.

Fergus reached in, trying not to upset the vehicle, then felt surprisingly strong hands grab his waist and ground him from behind. The Italian fellow gave a broken cry of agony, as he made a clumsy hop toward Fergus. There was no time for niceties. With every second, the carriage tilted at a steeper angle.

"I willnae let you fall, sir," Fergus said.

"Papa, listen to the man," the woman said.

"Let me go, lassie. I need to step back if he's to get out."

"Very well," the woman said. Despite the fraught circumstances, he noted that for the first time, she did what she was told.

Praying the carriage wouldn't tip over without his weight to hold it steady, Fergus retreated backward onto the muddy road, hauling the Italian as he went. Inch by inch, the older man advanced, then with an awkward movement, more stumble than step, he toppled through the door.

Fergus lurched forward to catch him before he put any weight on his broken leg. As the man popped free of the cabin, the yellow traveling coach pitched to the side, then slid into the flood, taking a great slice of the bank with it.

"Oof," Fergus grunted, as he took the injured man's weight in his arms.

"Hell's bells," Coker gasped, jumping back. He only just avoided the shaft knocking him into the water, too.

The carriage bobbed like a cork on top of the rushing water, then with a loud creak, it sank up to its shattered windows, and the current swept it away. Macushla and Brecon barked and dashed down the bank in pursuit, finding all of this a great adventure.

Bracing his booted feet against the slippery ground, Fergus shifted his grip on the groaning Italian. The injured man was as tall as he was and twice as wide. His bulk made it no easy task to keep him upright. Straining to balance under his burden, Fergus hardly looked up as with a crash, the wrecked carriage jammed on a rocky islet about five hundred yards downstream.

The woman slid her shoulder beneath her father's arm, mercifully taking some of the weight off Fergus. "Papa, are you all right?"

Gasping for breath, Fergus shifted to the other side to prop the Italian up. Even with two of them supporting him, the man's weight was crushing.

"*Porca miseria*, my leg hurts." Under thick gray hair, the man's face was as white as new snow on the mountains. He, like the woman, was dressed in the height of fashion.

After much grunting and groaning, and some savage swearing from Papa that Fergus didn't need translated, they managed to swing the older man onto the grass verge.

"Can ye hold him up?" Fergus asked her.

"Papa, lean on me and balance on your good leg," she said calmly. By God, Fergus had to give her credit, she was cool in a crisis.

He swept his greatcoat from his shoulders and laid it over the grass, then helped the woman lower her father onto the thick wool. That would at least keep the injured man from the worst of the damp.

The woman unfastened her red cloak and placed it over her father. Fergus bit back a protest that she exposed herself to the elements. There was no particular reason for her to heed him, apart from the fact that he was a man and in the right. But every atom of his masculine soul protested at leaving a lady to shiver on a hillside that belonged to him.

She sank down to cradle her father's head on her lap. "How is that now, Papa?"

"Better." The man's lips twisted as he attempted to smile. "If I cut back on the spaghetti, it will be easier to hoist me about like a bag of wheat."

She managed a smile in return. Not a very convincing one. All three of them must be aware that leaving him on the wet, rough grass was a temporary solution.

Now that the immediate threat to life retreated, Fergus realized how cold he was. He wasn't wearing a hat—he'd expected to be sitting beside his own fireside by nightfall, with a glass of the local spirit in his hand. His hair was sodden, and icy rain trickled down the back of his neck.

The woman must be freezing, too. Beneath the cloak, she wore a blue traveling dress that clung close enough to reveal a bonny, if not overly plump bosom, and a hint of curved hips and long legs. Her black hair was tied up in some folderol around her head. Or at least that must have been the plan. The persistent rain weighted her coiffure and sent tendrils snaking down around that fascinating face.

"You, coachman, get your bony arse over here and give your coat to the lady before I boot ye into the burn."

Sullenly, the man approached and unbuttoned his coat. In the rain, Fergus couldn't be sure, but the man didn't smell of drink. Rank incompetence rather than drunkenness must be to blame for this accident.

With visible reluctance, the woman accepted the coat and fumbled until it covered her shoulders. "Thank you, Coker."

"My pleasure, miss." He couldn't have sounded less sincere, and Fergus fought the urge to shove him into the burn anyway.

The man trudged back to the horses. By now, the poor beasts were so cowed, they'd forsaken all urge to bolt. They didn't raise their heads when Macushla and Brecon wove around their legs in a canine game.

"He's my servant, not yours," the woman said.

"He's utterly useless is what he is," Fergus muttered, straightening the coat to offer her better cover from the rain. "I fear his coat's none too clean, and it might have fleas, but you'll freeze wearing nothing but that becoming gown."

"I'm glad you admire my style," she said drily.

Fergus hunkered down and drew a folding knife from his pocket. With a couple of economical movements, he sliced away the older man's trouser leg. More muttered Italian curses that lacked the earlier vitriol. Pain and exhaustion were taking their toll on the older man.

"Is it broken?" the woman asked Fergus, with more of that unfeminine composure.

It struck him as almost unnatural. These circumstances would leave the ladies of his acquaintance, including his mother and sisters, completely overcome. He wasn't sure how to deal with a woman who took calamity in her stride the way a man would.

"Aye." The man's shin was misshapen and swollen, although thank God, the skin remained intact. "At least it seems a clean break."

"That's something." The rough garment draped around her should lessen that air of cool control, but she still looked like a duchess.

"There's a grove of rowans across the bridge. I'll go and cut a stick to make a splint, then I'll fetch help." Fergus closed his knife and slipped it into his pocket again. He passed the lady his hip flask. "Ye might need to give him some of this while I'm gone."

Those snapping black eyes settled on him with an unreadable expression. He was surprised when she said, "Thank you. You've been very kind."

Something about that assessing gaze made him feel as awkward as a boy at his first ball. Ridiculous, really, when he was master of all he surveyed. Because he didn't know what to say, he nodded, then stood and left in search of a suitable piece of wood.

Upon his return, he discovered the woman had ripped her petticoat into strips to hold the splint. He gave her credit for initiative, although some devil inside him regretted that he'd missed a glimpse of her ankles.

Achnasheen was well away from the fashionable world, and the advent of an attractive woman was a nice surprise. While she was a wee bit too willful for his taste, this lady was intriguing and easy to look at. He mightn't want to deal with her long term, but short term he was man enough to enjoy the view.

Even in this deplorable situation.

"Give me the splint," she said. "I can look after that while you get help. It's too cold to keep Papa out here long. It's better you go straightaway."

Fergus struggled to ignore her managing tone. "Are ye no' coming back to the castle with me?"

"Someone has to remain with Papa."

Her father's eyes were closed, and his lips were starting to turn blue. Fergus hoped to hell that the man was all right.

"There's nae need for you to stay. Let the coachman freeze out here."

She shot a dismissive glance at the fellow who stood a few feet away, huddling miserably in his sodden shirtsleeves and holding the two coach horses. "I wouldn't trust him with my worst enemy."

Then why the devil did you hire him? Fergus bit back the question. Something in him hankered to put this outspoken female in her place, but not when the weather was closing in and they had an injured man to get to safety.

"I'll no' be leaving a lady out in the rain."

Her lips tightened. In the circumstances, it was perverse to notice that they were the color of crushed cherries and just as luscious. "I'm not made of icing sugar. A little water won't kill me."

Fergus had already decided she was more spice than sugar. "Very well, then, if ye insist."

"Thank you."

Fergus turned to the coachman. "Take the horses along this road to the gatehouse. I'll be ahead of ye, and I'll give them instructions about what to do when you arrive."

"Aye, my lord," the man mumbled.

Fergus waited for the woman to complain about him appropriating her authority again, but she was busy wrapping her father more securely in her cape and helping him to sit up. The man gave a groggy moan, and his eyes no longer seemed to focus as his head lolled against her shoulder.

"I'll be as quick as I can," Fergus said. "Dinnae be frightened."

The minute he spoke, he wanted to wince. Frightened? This lassie didn't look like she'd tremble at the crack of doom.

"I willnae be long." He caught Banshee's bridle. The mare whinnied and sidled away, but settled at a quiet word. Further along the road, the coachman led the horses toward Achnasheen.

"That's good," the woman said. "Here, Papa. You'll need this before I'm done."

As she held the flask to his lips, the injured man curled his shaking hand around hers. He jerked away. "*Basta!* This is vile stuff."

Despite their plight, Fergus hid a smile. "It's Bruce Mackenzie's finest."

"Not brandy?"

"No. *Uisge-beatha.* We call it the water of life." Not quite legal in the eyes of a Sassenach exciseman, but the best drop of whisky produced across ten glens.

"*Dio*, I'd rather be dead."

The man had more courage than Fergus had credited. Perhaps he and his daughter were more alike than he'd thought. "Aye, you'll do," he murmured.

Fergus whistled up his dogs and mounted Banshee. He wheeled the mare in the direction of the castle and set off through the rain at a gallop.

CHAPTER TWO

y the time the high-handed Scot with the long legs and impressive shoulders rode back into sight, Marina was soaked and close to frozen solid, despite her coachman's thick and pungently scented coat. Her father had lapsed into a restless doze, fueled by whatever filthy spirit the silver flask contained. Darkness had descended, and the rain settled into a steady drizzle.

"Are ye all right?" the man asked from the saddle. That voice retained its quality of command, even when he expressed concern. "How is your father?"

"He's drifted off." She was relieved to see the Scotsman again, although she'd known he'd come back for them. Men with chiseled jaws like his tended to be true to their word.

Behind the gray horse looming out of the murk, she saw lanterns bobbing along the road. Their rescuer, whoever he was, had summoned an army to their aid. She felt so shaky and upset, the sight of the approaching lights made her ridiculously emotional.

The two big black dogs trotted up and sat on either side of her like sentinels. Holding her breath against the odor of wet dog, she reached out and patted both of them.

The man dismounted. Her eyes had adjusted to the darkness well enough to appreciate the powerful, liquid grace of the movement, despite her current predicament. Her rescuer was annoying, but handsome and strong. His strength, if not his good looks, was welcome. However much she might bristle under his autocratic manner, she appreciated his efficiency. And his speed. He'd only been away about half an hour.

"I've got a wagon coming. We can lie him flat, and it will be easier for him than a carriage. It will be a bumpy trip home, I'm afraid."

She stumbled upright on legs that felt as if they were made of wet string. Cold, wet string. "Then it's a good thing he's near unconscious," she said, struggling to keep her voice steady.

Marina knew she hadn't succeeded, because the Scot cast her a worried glance, visible even through the gloom. The lanterns came closer, and when she wiped the rain from her eyes, she saw a flat-bedded cart with a canvas roof, drawn by two draft horses. Beside it strode half a dozen brawny Highlanders who should have no trouble coping with her father's bulk when they lifted him.

The red-haired man tugged something from the saddle and passed it to her. "This might suit your dignity better than the coat ye have on. And it's dry."

She had to admit he was thoughtful. Her independent air discouraged most males from trying to look after her, which was the way she liked it. She told herself that she was capable of standing on her own two feet, however wobbly, but when she discarded the coachman's coat and wrapped the soft woolen cloak around her, she almost wept in gratitude. "It's very kind of your wife to lend me her clothes."

The man's grunt of amusement was brief. "It would be, if I had a wife, but the cape belongs to my sister Clarissa. She left it at the castle last time she went back to Edinburgh."

He wasn't married. Not that that should be of any consequence. Then she realized what he'd said. "Castle?"

"Aye. I told ye that's where I was going."

She supposed he had. Through her fear for her father and her need to hide how much she hated staying behind on the bare hillside, she hadn't paid close attention.

Any chance for private conversation came to an end. Everything turned to action under the authority of the tall man with hair like flame and eyes like gray ice. She mightn't appreciate him giving her orders, but right now, she appreciated the way he gave orders to other people. Orders that resulted in her father gently lifted and placed on a wagon bed lined with furs and blankets.

Marina sagged with relief now she transferred her father's care into capable hands. Her overwhelming concern for Papa had kept her panic and pain at bay. She hadn't been injured in the accident, but she'd been bruised and tossed around. Her legs turned to jelly, and she fought against collapsing in a heap and bursting into tears.

Then she caught her rescuer's eye. Although she had no clue why she refused to betray any weakness, she straightened her spine and raised her chin.

"Would ye like to come up with me on Banshee, or travel in the wagon with your father?" he asked as the procession was set to go.

Some reckless part of her, the part that she'd spent most of her life struggling to suppress, wanted to ride like a rescued princess behind this handsome man on that high-spirited horse. But she was old enough to know that in the end, only one person could rescue her—and that person was herself. And her father needed her. "Thank you for the offer, but I should go with Papa."

"Ye willnae be very comfortable, lassie, and it's unsuitable transport for a lady."

"I'm sure it will be fine." It wasn't the first time he'd tried to treat her as if she was too delicate for this mundane world. He seemed to labor under the misconception that females were made of gossamer and butterfly wings.

"Aye, well, if ye insist." He didn't seem too disappointed with her refusal, blast him. "It's only a wee way, a mile or so."

First she had to climb into the cart. Her traveling gown with its stylish military frogging was *à la mode,* but its narrow skirt wasn't designed for getting in and out of farm vehicles. Dismayed, she surveyed the gap between road and wagon bed. Then hard hands closed around her waist, she rose into the air, and she was sitting on the back of the wagon with her booted feet dangling in space.

Her heart set off on a wild swoop. Partly from shock. Partly from foolish feminine pleasure at a strong male hoisting her about, as though she weighed no more than a feather.

This quivery feeling was utter nonsense, but something about knowing her autocratic rescuer could pick her up without effort made her pulses race. He had a penchant for grabbing her and putting her where he wanted. She needed to stop acting like a silly goose and tell him she was capable of moving under her own volition.

"I need my portfolio," she said, sounding disgracefully breathless as she pointed to the leather satchel lying on the edge of the road.

Without a word, the man collected it and passed it to her. The brawniest of the brawny Highlanders also brought over the lovely red cape she'd bought in Venice. When she'd put it over her father, she hadn't given it a thought, but now she felt a pang of regret that it would probably never recover from its rough treatment.

Her eyes followed the Scotsman as he crossed to the big gray horse that stood in place, awaiting her master. Marina was sure he appreciated the beast's perfect obedience.

At a careful speed, the cart began to trundle along the road. Even with all the padding under her, Marina felt every rut in the road. She hoped her father wasn't in too much discomfort. Before they lifted him, they'd given him more of the spirit with the outlandish name. To her surprise, he hadn't protested at all.

At least it had stopped raining. She glanced away from the dark landscape to find her father had regained consciousness. He watched her from where he lay stretched out upon a pile of pillows and rugs. Already Papa looked more comfortable, and in the lantern light, she saw that the pinched look faded from his lips.

"Papa, how are you feeling?" she asked in English.

"I'd rather be at home, taking the air in the Piazza della Signoria," he answered in the same language. When in private, they tended to speak in an idiosyncratic mixture of the two tongues.

She smiled, relieved to hear him sounding more like himself. "I'm sure. Is the pain still bad?"

"I'll be glad when we get to wherever we're going."

So would she. She was cold, despite the luxurious cloak, and every bump reminded her that she'd rattled around inside the runaway carriage like a dice in a cup.

For a few minutes, they traveled in silence, then her father spoke in a musing tone. "He's a handsome devil."

"Who is?" Marina asked, although she knew exactly who her father was talking about.

"Our rescuer. The gallant Scotsman with the woeful taste in liquor and the brisk way with an emergency."

"Is he? I hadn't noticed." Through the wagon's open sides, she regarded the man who rode at the head of their cavalcade.

"Then you should have."

She directed a cranky glare at her father. "I would have thought you had other things on your mind."

Papa's lips twisted in something approximating a smile. He really must be feeling better. "Some things are impossible to ignore."

She supposed she should be glad he had the energy to tease her. Waiting with him on the roadside, she'd been sick with worry about the way he wandered in and out of coherence. "You know I don't like pushy men, and he acts like he's master of the world."

The man walking beside the wagon, a thickset Highlander with a magnificent black beard chuckled. "Aye, he does at that. But then in this corner of the Highlands, the Mackinnon *is* master of the world, lassie."

"I didn't mean—" She blushed at her lack of discretion. She should have stuck to Italian.

However autocratic the red-haired man might be, she owed him a debt of gratitude. It hadn't missed her notice that apart from him and the people he'd summoned, not a soul had come along the lonely track. Without his help, she and her father would be in serious trouble.

The man marching beside the cart laughed again, a bass rumble, while his big hairy legs under his kilt ate up the ground beneath him. "Och, aye, ye did. The laird's inclined to give orders and expect them to be obeyed. We're used to his ways."

In which case, his retainers should be downtrodden shadows. She saw no sign of that in the impressive crowd of men escorting them back to the castle.

"You'll get used to it." The man went on in the same lilting local accent that lay so attractively on their rescuer's deep voice. "It helps that he's always right."

Marina bristled under the comment. "I doubt I'll be here long enough to need to get used to it, Mister..."

"Och, everyone calls me Jock. Ye can, too."

"In that case, I'd like to thank you and your friends for your help, Jock."

The man's smile lacked a couple of front teeth. The Mackinnon—an odd title, she couldn't help thinking—had excellent teeth. Strong and straight and white. She wondered what he looked like when he smiled. Despite her discomfiting suspicion that he found her amusing, he hadn't smiled properly once.

Stop it, Marina.

Jock had called him the laird. She wasn't familiar with the word, but it must mean something like lord. And he owned a castle.

Madonna mia, he must be a great power in this wilderness. Perhaps his arrogance had some basis. No wonder he hadn't liked her addressing him as an underling when he'd arrived to help them. She supposed she should have been a little more polite. But years of travel had taught her that a commanding attitude was the best way to produce the results she wanted.

Part of her wasn't sorry that she'd pricked his self-satisfaction. She had an inkling that the man received far too much wide-eyed admiration and unquestioning obedience.

"Don't worry." She took her father's gloved hand. The ride was as smooth as human endeavor could make it, but she could tell that even gentle movement pained him. His brief burst of vitality faded fast. "The Mackinnon said it was only a mile. We'll get you inside soon."

She hoped this castle wasn't a ruin, like so many she'd seen on her way north from the border. She hoped it had a fire and a hot meal and some dry clothes she could change into. All her beautiful dresses had gone into the river—the burn as Mackinnon called it—with the carriage. She was grateful she and her father were alive, and she'd retrieved the one really irreplaceable thing, but that didn't reconcile her to the loss.

Blasted fool of a coachman.

"What I'd give for a plate of *ossobuco* and a good chianti," her father said in a dreamy voice.

She smiled. "More like we're getting half-raw mutton, and some more of that unpronounceable spirit." The cooking during their week in Scotland had failed to impress her.

"Right now, even that would be welcome."

Inevitably, her eyes found the tall man on the gray horse. The Mackinnon. An unusual name for an unusual man. An annoying man. But without doubt, a capable one. And breathtakingly handsome.

Whatever she thought of his managing ways, no woman in creation would argue with the conclusion that he was very pleasant indeed to look at.

CHAPTER THREE

For what felt like a long time, although Marina knew it couldn't be, they plodded along in the dark. Papa became quieter with every yard, which was a troubling sign. He was usually the most voluble of men.

She stared out at the dark hills crowding close around the frail brightness of the lanterns. Then a massive shape took form against the starless sky. Towers and turrets, and a blessed light shining through the gates.

Dio, a castle indeed.

The cart rattled across cobblestones and under a raised portcullis. Her father groaned at the sudden bumping, and she tightened her grip on his hand. "Almost there, Papa."

As they rolled into a courtyard lit with flaming torches, Marina had the bizarre sensation that she retreated several centuries to an earlier, less civilized time. A time when rough Highlanders seized the women they wanted and bundled them away to a mountain fastness to provide strong sons for the clan.

Something primitive and powerful stirred inside her. Something that felt almost like excitement. It was clear she'd been reading too much of Sir Walter Scott's poetry on this journey into the north.

"I promised ye a castle," a soft, faintly mocking voice said at her side. The Mackinnon now rode beside the cart. The sight of her home for the night was so overwhelming, it had diverted Marina's attention from her host.

"And you're a man of your word," she said, cursing the betraying rasp in her reply.

"I'll show ye over the place in the morning, if you like."

"Thank you, but as soon as Papa is splinted up and able to travel, we'll be on our way."

He laughed, still with that mocking note. "Will ye indeed?"

"Although I appreciate you coming to our aid and offering to put us up." She paused and frowned. "That is, if you are offering."

"No, lassie, I've brought ye here, just so you can sit outside on the brae in the rain, shivering and wondering what's going on inside beside the fire."

She studied his face, through long habit breaking it up into patterns of planes and colors. His bone structure was extraordinarily pure. For a dazed interval, she became lost in that perfect symmetry. Then she blinked as what he'd said registered. "I beg your pardon?"

"If I'm feeling generous, I might send ye out a bowl of cold porridge. Then again, I might not."

The remarkable face was expressionless. She blinked again. "You're joking."

His lips twitched. "Aye, I am at that. Let's get your father inside and onto a bed. He must be ready to rest somewhere comfortable."

"*Si, si, pronto,*" her father said weakly.

More impressive efficiency and people scurrying in every direction to do the Mackinnon's bidding. Marina saw her father ensconced in a cozy chamber and watched as an elderly woman with greater skills than hers replaced the makeshift splint with a more substantial support. An ingenious wicker cage raised the blankets over the broken leg and kept the weight off the injured limb.

"Aye, it's a bad break, but it could be worse," the woman said in a singsong voice." Aye, it could, it could. Rest and quiet will fix this."

His face a worrying shade of white, Papa slumped back against the heaped pillows. Changing the splint had been a painful process.

"Should we get a doctor?" Marina asked.

"The nearest doctor is thirty miles away, lassie. Dinna fash yeself. I've been caring for Achnasheen's bumps and scrapes for the last fifty years. Ye'll no' do better with the quack at Strathcarron."

"I'm sorry if I offended you."

The old lady shook her head. "No reason ye should ken our ways. The Mackinnon has entrusted your father to me. I willnae let him—or you—down."

More homage to the omnipotent Mackinnon. *Santo cielo*, no wonder the man was insufferable.

"Now I'll show ye to your chamber, and ye can get out of that gown and get ready to have supper with the laird. I dinna want another patient on my hands, and it's no' the night to be standing around in wet clothes."

Marina had remained close to the roaring fire to keep from shivering. When they'd reached the castle, the Mackinnon had ordered her to her room so she could change, but she'd insisted that first she'd see her father settled. Her host hadn't appreciated her defiance, even on such a minor matter.

"I'll come back and sit with Papa, once I've put on something dry," Marina said quickly.

"Och, I'll see your da eats his dinner, then I'll give him a wee sleeping draft. There's nothing for ye to do here, lassie."

With reluctance, she complied, not least because the old lady was almost as authoritative as her master. And good manners insisted Marina offer some polite return for the laird's hospitality and for putting his household out to care for two strangers in trouble.

It seemed dinner with the Mackinnon was inescapable. If only the laird didn't send her composure whirling into the wind. She felt much more like her capable, assured self when glittering gray eyes didn't observe her every move.

Her room was next door to her father's and quite as well appointed, with another blazing fire, and a shy young girl of about sixteen who prepared a hot bath for her. When Marina caught the scent of lavender rising from the steaming water, she almost groaned with longing. The hard day's travel, the effects of being flung around the carriage, and a wait in the cold had left her tired and stiff and aching.

More thoughtfulness from the laird? If he meant to give her a good meal as well, she could almost forgive him for being such an imperious devil.

By the time she ventured downstairs an hour later, she felt considerably more human. And her native cynicism had set in. The Mackinnon had impressed her, hard as she'd fought to resist his rugged appeal. But she'd been far from her best after the accident, and frantic about her father, too. Now that she met the laird in more prosaic circumstances—if this gothic setting could be described as prosaic—she was sure he'd shrink to mundane proportions.

The maid had given her directions to the drawing room. Marina had stayed in several large country houses south of the border and was used to having footmen on hand to guide a confused guest, but this house wasn't so conventionally staffed. From what she'd seen thus far, the Mackinnon had retainers rather than servants.

She descended the wide stone staircase, decorated with heraldic beasts—the Mackinnon family crest appeared to feature a griffin—and crossed a cavernous hall lit with more burning torches. The walls were decorated with weapons arranged in concentric circles, and ghostly figures loomed out of ancient tapestries hanging from coffered ceiling to flagstoned floor. Marina shivered, not because of the cold this time, but with a return of that sensation that she ventured back into the distant past.

If a man in surcoat and hose, or even a suit of armor, had greeted her when she stepped into the elegant drawing room, she wouldn't have been surprised. Instead, the gentleman who turned away from the crackling fire at her arrival wouldn't be out of place in one of those elegant English mansions she'd visited over recent weeks.

Marina was almost sorry to find the Mackinnon wearing a beautifully tailored black coat and trousers, snowy neck cloth, and elegant silvery silk waistcoat. That austere face belonged to an earlier age, one of chivalry and faith and danger, not the modern world with all its comforts and compromises.

He bowed like a civilized man. As his head inclined in her direction, firelight sheened across his thick auburn hair. What an intense red it was, like flame. The extraordinary color held her transfixed, and her fingers curled at her sides as if she held a paintbrush.

When she didn't curtsy straightaway, familiar ironic amusement lit the gray eyes. In a way, they were as remarkable a color as his hair. Oh, dear, any hopes that less dramatic circumstances might banish his larger-than-life air faded fast.

"Good evening, *signorina*. You found me withnae difficulty?"

"I'm sorry." She performed a wobbly curtsy. "You must think I'm utterly rag-mannered."

His lips quirked. "I think ye held your nerve with stalwart courage through some difficult hours, and now you're tired."

All that was true, but she had a horrible suspicion that weariness wasn't what made her pulses flutter and her breath catch in her chest.

She couldn't mistake the admiration in his eyes as he surveyed her. Peggy, her maid upstairs, had made the best of the ill-fitting dress and had done a good job with Marina's mass of slippery black hair, weaving it into an elegant chignon and decorating it with some pearl pins.

As Marina rose from her curtsy, the Mackinnon took her hand. Heat rushed up her arm and set her heart skipping and racing like a spring lamb. She might be tired and sore after her ordeal, but right now the world appeared brighter and more vivid than it had this afternoon. Life just seemed more...lively in the Mackinnon's presence.

Maledizione, this really wasn't good.

At twenty-eight, she was old enough to guess what lay behind this wealth of uncontrollable physical reactions. Her brain might tell her that this man was far too used to getting his own way for her ever to become his friend. While her unruly female body wanted to spread itself before him and invite him to do whatever wicked things he wanted.

She was used to discouraging predatory men. A woman who dealt with gentlemen through business as often as she did met flirtation, and sometimes propositions that went way beyond flirtation.

What was exceptional—and worrying—about her encounter with this forthright Scotsman was that her first reaction wasn't the usual vexation, but anticipation and a slow, swirling heat in the pit of her stomach.

"I see my sister's dress fits you, although it's a trifle short."

"I owe your sister a debt."

She tried not to notice how his glance flickered down to the ankles on display beneath the pretty yellow gown with its delicate lace trim. His sister also owned the stockings and filmy undergarments. Marina hid a shiver as she imagined this man choosing her intimate clothing, although more likely he'd set a servant to the task.

There had been a selection of shoes of various sizes waiting in her room, too. "You even found slippers to fit me."

"Aye. We raided every wardrobe in the house to find those. They're my Great-Aunt Frances's. My sister is small and blonde."

And Marina was tall and dark. She blushed— and she never blushed—to realize that her hand remained in his. "Well, they've both come to my rescue," she stammered like some fool of a debutante attending her first assembly.

"Come and sit beside me and have a glass of wine. Dinner willnae be long."

Sitting next to him seemed unwise, but making a fuss would only draw attention to her prickling awareness of his proximity. She drew a shaky breath and decided to pretend that she was used to evenings alone with dashing gentlemen.

Keeping hold of her hand, the Mackinnon led Marina across to a velvet-covered chaise longue and waited for her to sit before he took his place beside her. More fluttery feelings in her stomach, and she hardly noticed her aches and pains anymore.

Perhaps, she thought without much conviction, she was just hungry. It was a long time since she'd eaten. She tried to muster a bit of backbone by telling herself the Mackinnon was pushing her around again. But after the day she'd had, it was marvelously soothing to accept his care and admiration, even if it came with a side dish of command.

Marina cast around for some subject to distract him from watching her with such unabashed masculine interest. "No dogs?"

His gaze didn't waver. "They're down in the kitchen, cadging for scraps."

She pretended interest in a gloomy landscape hung over the mantel, although if anyone had asked her, she couldn't have named a single object in the painting. She had a sinking feeling that if she met the Mackinnon's eyes, he'd guess her unwilling fascination with him. She developed an inkling that this was a man who understood a woman's weaknesses—and how to take advantage of them. "What are their names?"

"Macushla and Brecon. They're brother and sister. Their father Bailey was the best dog in Scotland. He died of old age last year."

The sadness in his voice made her stop avoiding his eyes. "I'm sorry."

"Aye, so am I. He was the companion of my youth. I still feel like his ghost is running at Banshee's heels when we're galloping over the hills."

"Perhaps it is," she said softly. She fought a crazy urge to take the elegant hand that rested on his thigh and offer comfort. They were chance-met strangers. There was no reason for her heart to melt at the love in his voice when he spoke of his old dog. "I like dogs."

"Do ye have one?"

"No, I'm away from home too often to have a pet."

"And am I permitted to ken the name of the bonny lassie who likes dogs and who owes such a debt of gratitude to my sister Clarissa?"

Shocked, Marina straightened. She struggled to ignore that sneaky "bonny" in his question. "*Cielo*, we never did introduce ourselves, did we?"

His long, expressive mouth twisted with the mocking humor she now knew was characteristic. "For most of our acquaintance, we had other things on our minds. I'm Fergus Mackinnon."

"*The* Mackinnon."

"Aye. I'm chief of the clan, and Laird of Achnasheen."

That smooth baritone turned the three outlandish syllables of the place name into music. "What a lovely name for an estate."

"It means 'field of rain.' Which as you've discovered today is regrettably accurate."

"At least it stopped after a little while."

"Still, you didn't get the best introduction to my home, Signorina...?"

"My name is Marina Lucchetti."

"And you're Italian?"

"Half. Mamma was a wellborn English lady. She met Papa in Florence when she was eighteen and eloped with him."

"So that explains why ye speak like a Sassenach."

"Sassenach?"

"Aye, the English."

Her mother had tutored her in British history. She could well imagine her accent wasn't a welcome sound in this corner of the world.

"I hope you'll overlook my unfortunate antecedents," she said with a smile that came far too easily. "Perhaps it will help if I tell you Mamma's family disowned her after her marriage, and I've never met them."

"In the circumstances, I'll forgive the connection, then."

She gave a gurgle of laughter and didn't miss the interest brightening his eyes. "*Grazie*."

He rose and crossed to lift a decanter from the sideboard. "I hope you dinnae mind dining with me. I realize it's not strictly proper for us to be alone, but we're no' so finicky about the rules of society here in the Highlands as they are down in London. If you'd rather, I can have a tray sent to your room. Or I could ask one of the maids to sit with us if you'd like a chaperone. But it's a pity to waste the chance for some interesting conversation, when I get so few visitors at Achnasheen."

Another compliment, and one for her mind, not for her looks. Accompanied by something that could almost be an apology for assuming she'd join him for dinner without checking with her first.

It became more and more difficult to recall how he'd barked orders to her down by the bridge. *Diavolo*, this charm was dangerous.

Already she knew she'd be sensible to avoid his company. He wasn't at all her sort of gentleman. And he'd given her a perfect excuse to say her goodnights.

Marina stayed exactly where she was. "We're not so careful in Italy either, especially as I'm neither an aristocrat nor just out of the schoolroom. I think my reputation will survive a meal with you."

"I'm delighted to hear that." The warmth in his eyes lit an answering warmth in her blood. "Would ye like a wee glass of wine?"

"Yes, please."

He poured two glasses of claret. "So what is a pretty half-Italian lady doing in wildest Scotland?"

"Shivering," she said, accepting her wine. She really must tell him not to waste any more time on compliments. They never worked with her. Well, they usually never worked. "I'd lay good money our coachman was lost when we crashed. We're supposed to be on our way to the Isle of Skye."

The Mackinnon sat down beside her again, stretching his long legs out toward the fire. Marina was painfully conscious that mere inches of blue velvet separated them. One subtle shift, and she'd bump into his hip.

The thought tightened her throat. Down by the bridge, he'd touched her, slinging her around like a piece of furniture, and she'd wanted to slap him. When had that changed?

He raised his glass. "*Slàinte mhath.*"

"*Salute.*" She returned his toast, then sipped the wine, which turned out to be excellent. What else did she expect? She had a feeling the Mackinnon arranged everything here to suit himself.

"You're undertaking a tour?"

"In a way." She swallowed some more wine and strove to keep her mind on the conversation and not on her stirring attraction to her host. "I'm an artist. The Duke of Portofino has commissioned some Highland scenes. On the Continent right now, Scotland is all the rage."

Interest sharpened his gaze. "Ye work for a living?"

"I do." His skepticism, the standard reaction she received from the male half of humanity, reminded her that she was too old and pragmatic to throw her bonnet over a windmill for the sake of a pair of bright gray eyes. Even if the eyes were *bellissimi* indeed. "I told you I don't come from society's exalted ranks."

He ignored the unspoken dig at his background. "And you've had some success as a painter?"

"I've been lucky," she said.

He paused as if he was considering her reply, then his frown melted away. "By God, I think I've seen your work. M.R. Lucchetti? Is that you?"

She shouldn't be so pleased. "It is."

More admiration sparked in his eyes, and she resisted the urge to bask. Marina was much more comfortable with praise for her work than for her feminine appeal. She was proud of what she'd achieved in her career. In the early days, many people had dismissed her as yet another woman who dabbled in watercolor, the medium every genteel lady learned from her governess.

The Mackinnon went on. "Clarissa's husband did the Grand Tour as a young man, and he bought a set of your pictures when he was in Italy. Views of Naples. They're exquisite. Forgive me, I assumed they were done by a man."

Her lips firmed, although she, more than anyone, knew the prejudice against female painters. It was why she used her initials and not her Christian name when she signed her work. "Many people believe women have no real talent with a brush."

"Well, ye disprove that," he said shortly. "What does the R stand for?"

She'd been geared up to defend herself. When she didn't need to, she felt winded, as though he'd punched her in the belly.

"Repton. Mamma's maiden name." Because his partisanship disarmed her, she said more than she usually did when she described her beginnings as an artist. "Mamma was the one who fostered my talent and fought tooth and nail until the best drawing master in Florence took me as a pupil."

Even then, Marina hadn't been allowed to attend the school's life classes along with the male students. A reason she confined herself to landscapes, now she earned her living as a watercolorist.

"And is there a Signor Lucchetti?"

Did she imagine that the question held a particular intensity? Up until now, she could almost dismiss the conversation as an exchange of harmless pleasantries, if her heart wasn't lodged high up under her ribs and her blood wasn't fizzing like champagne. "*Si*, there is."

Was that disappointment in the silver eyes, or was she reading too much into his expression? Did the Mackinnon find her as intriguing as she found him? Did she want him to?

Common sense and self-preservation said no, she didn't. She had her life arranged as she wanted it, and an inconvenient liaison was the last thing she needed. Yet some hitherto unsuspected female impulse wanted to see where this unprecedented reaction to a man would take her.

"And where is he?"

"Upstairs in bed. Papa will be horrified when he realizes you've given us shelter without a proper introduction."

Definite relief. "You're no' married?"

"No, I'm my own woman." Marina spoke the words deliberately, because she guessed the concept wouldn't please him. She needed to remember how patronizing he could be before she melted into a puddle of longing at his feet.

He frowned. "I'm no' sure the world recognizes such a creature."

Marina shrugged. "Then it should. I live off my talent. As long as people are willing to buy my pictures, I'm independent."

Those expressive brows rose in inquiry. "Yet ye travel with your father as chaperone?"

Diavolo, she should have known he'd pick up on that point. "I must bow that far to social convention. There are some battles I can't win. If I traveled alone, I'd be called a—"

He broke in before she could pronounce the unflattering word. Loose woman. Meaning "whore." "So ye do need a man for some things."

"For the sake of appearances." She met burning silver eyes. She'd been wrong. This conversation extended past polite platitudes after all, and they both knew it. "But Papa works for me. He travels at my direction. I pay the bills. I make the decisions. I'm in charge."

The Mackinnon set his glass on a side table with a distinct click. "It's unnatural."

"No." His reaction shouldn't disappoint her. It wasn't as if he sought to hide what an autocrat he was. And it was clear from everyone else she'd spoken to at the castle that his word was law. "What's unnatural is one half of the population believing it has an inalienable right to control the other half."

"Signorina Lucchetti, you're dangerous. Ye preach revolution." His gaze uncompromising, he rose and stood in front of the hearth. "Men have always been in charge."

"That doesn't make it right." She spoke with some heat.

All her life she'd fought against the uncritical acceptance of masculine superiority. She'd seen male painters with half her talent end up twice as successful, in a world that believed no woman could compete with a man when it came to art.

"Ye needed my help tonight," the Mackinnon pointed out in an odiously superior manner.

She should be grateful that he'd started to act like a blockhead. His attitude might serve to shred the net of attraction strangling her common sense. If only his sheer physical magnificence didn't draw her. It was so difficult to dismiss him as an ignorant brute, when every turn of his head had her itching to capture that male beauty on paper.

But his jibe reminded Marina that she enjoyed this man's hospitality, and she owed him her courtesy, if not her respect.

Oh, who was she trying to fool? He'd rescued her father from deadly danger. How could she fail to respect him?

Beyond her gratitude, she admired his competence and his power. His was a penetrating intelligence, even if she ignored his beauty, which for an artist was impossible. Much as she'd like to condemn him as nothing more than a bigoted bully, he was more complex than that.

She sucked in a breath and told herself to settle down. "Yes, I did, and I appreciated it," she said quietly.

He arched one russet eyebrow, and she might almost say he looked piqued at her quick capitulation. "Giving up the argument?"

"Staging a strategic retreat."

"Good Lord, ye must forgive me." His mouth turned down in self-reproach. "I havenae asked after your welfare."

He wasn't touching her—of course he wasn't, they were strangers—but the genuine concern in that deep voice wrapped around her the way her ruined crimson velvet cape used to.

That was the problem with masterful men. The other side of all that pushiness was the urge to protect. She loved her papa dearly but was under no illusions about who was the stronger personality in the partnership. Nobody had offered up their strength as her shield since her mamma died.

Sitting on the wet hillside with her father, she'd felt shaky and vulnerable and alone. That must explain her sudden urge to nestle against the Mackinnon's powerful chest and rest in the knowledge of perfect safety.

If only for a moment.

"I'm fine," she said stiffly.

"I cannae believe that." He shook his head. "You must have suffered a few knocks, when the carriage crashed. Here I am, getting ye to sit up and make polite conversation."

"Hardly polite," she muttered.

His lips twitched, although his eyes remained concerned. "At least I can blame your mad ideas on concussion."

"Mackinnon..."

He raised his hands in a gesture of conciliation. "Tell me, would ye rather eat upstairs?"

She shook her head and summoned a smile. "I've got a few bruises, but the worst of it was waiting in the cold. A bath helped. Anyway, if I go upstairs, you'll dismiss me as a frail woman, and think you've won the point."

"Och, you've worked out my evil scheme."

Despite everything, his humor disarmed her, and she laughed. "Just one thing—were we on the way to Skye when we crashed?"

"Aye, in a way, if all ye want is a view. You can see Skye across the channel. You were miles off track if you want the ferry."

"That idiot driver." She took another sip of wine, hoping it might soothe her turmoil. "When we hired him in Glasgow, he swore he knew this part of the world like the back of his hand. Once we were on the road, though, he never listened to orders, and he always drove too fast. That's what happened today, when he lost control of the carriage."

"I should have tossed him in the burn."

"Instead, I'm sure you've taken him in, as you've taken in Papa and his outspoken daughter."

The Mackinnon was too wise to rise to that. "I believe we might have found him a bowl of soup and a bed. I can send word to have him pitched out into the rain if ye like."

He wasn't smiling. He didn't seem to be a man who smiled much, she'd noticed. But he did like to tease.

"Maybe tomorrow." She sighed. "At least he doesn't drink."

"Given what happened today, he might as well. How is your father? I should have asked that, too, when ye came in."

"He's under expert care."

"Old Maggie? Aye, she's better than any doctor I ken."

Marina set down her glass and met her host's enigmatic gray gaze. "After a night's rest, Papa should be well enough to travel on. We won't inconvenience you for long."

The Mackinnon responded with one of those already familiar huffs of sardonic laughter. "My bonny *signorina*, do ye have much experience of broken bones?"

"I'm sure if you'll lend us a carriage..."

"And I'm sure that your father is stuck here for several weeks. Perhaps longer."

Marina couldn't conceal her horror. "Several weeks?"

Per l'amor di dio, several weeks of this man telling her what to do? Several weeks of fighting this roiling sexual attraction? Several weeks of reminding herself that she wasn't a woman who crumpled into a man's arms, just because he was bold and strong and he had a spark in his eye that told her he wanted her?

This time he did smile, and how she wished he hadn't. He was a handsome man anyway. The smile made him more approachable, irresistibly charming. Within reach, when she knew the danger of reaching out to take him.

The inchoate, unwelcome impulses that had tormented her from her first meeting with the Mackinnon solidified into desire.

A hint of wolfishness entered that smile. "Aye, Signorina Lucchetti, you'd better face the fact that you'll be my guest for at least the next month."

CHAPTER FOUR

Fergus leaned his elbow on the mantelpiece and watched her reaction. His unexpected house guest wasn't at all the sort of woman who met with his approval. But by God, Marina Lucchetti was the most interesting thing that had happened to Achnasheen since...

Well, since forever.

And she was stuck here in his power until her father could walk again. Who knew what mischief a man could get up to, when he had a reckless lassie to pursue?

Beneath their odd, rather spiky conversation, a growing attraction bubbled. He nursed a suspicion that he wasn't any more her preferred type of gentleman than she was his type of lady. He also had a feeling that their preferences would soon matter less than the passion flaring between them.

Did her claims of independence mean she'd come to a lover's bed without promises of marriage? He didn't know enough about this exotic creature, a woman outside a man's control, to be sure.

The signs were good. She seemed to take his company in her stride, and she hadn't accepted his offer to provide a chaperone tonight. In Scotland, that indicated a woman of some experience, and perhaps an eye to an affair. Was it the same in Italy?

He'd never traveled further than London, and that was five years ago. What the devil did he know about society in lands across the seas?

But a laddie could hope, couldn't he?

What he did know was that he'd never experienced such a swift and powerful yen to have a lassie. The moment he'd met those snapping black eyes staring him down from the window of the wrecked carriage, he'd wanted her. His hunger had only grown since. He couldn't be happier she was staying.

But the dismay with which she greeted his announcement of an extended visit indicated that he was getting ahead of himself. "We can't put you out so long," she said.

"You're going to argue with me again," he said in a long-suffering tone, as he stepped away from the hearth and extended his hand. "I feel it in my bones."

She had the grace to smile. "Probably."

When she took his hand and rose, heat sizzled up his arm like raging flame. His heart crashed into his ribs with the sort of force that had brought her carriage to grief at the bridge.

All from merely holding her hand. If she ever kissed him, he'd explode like a keg of gunpowder.

"Then come through to supper." It was an effort to hide the titanic effect she had on him, but at this early stage, he didn't want to make her skittish about his intentions. He tucked her hand into his arm. "You'll need your strength, if ye plan to take up your cudgels again."

"My goodness, this really is a castle," she said in awe, as they entered the vaulted dining room, with its tall lancet windows and tapestries. "No wonder your ideas are so out of date."

The prospect of her company put him in such a good humor, her jibe made him laugh. "After you've been here a month, I'll wager ye'll agree that what's tried and true works at Achnasheen."

Fergus pulled out a heavy chair for her. The massive oak table was designed for clan gatherings, but he'd asked for Signorina Lucchetti's place to be set beside him at the head. Heavy silver candelabra extended down the length of the table, but only the two nearest ones were lit, lending an air of intimacy.

Kirsty and Jenny brought in the food, and Jock took charge of the wine. Then they left Fergus alone with his intriguing guest.

Signorina Lucchetti tasted her soup, then set down her spoon and sent him one of those uncompromising looks that rapidly became familiar. He was used to lassies who sidled around telling a man what they thought and were quick to bend to a stronger opinion. He had a feeling this lady's opinions were as strong as his own, and she wasn't at all shy about expressing them.

A novelty in a woman. A disaster in a wife.

But perhaps lending an extra touch of spice to a mistress?

"It will be a vast inconvenience to you, if we stay until my father's leg is mended."

Fergus tried his soup before he answered calmly and with authority, because he knew he was in the right. He always was. "In the Highlands, we have a strong tradition of hospitality. I'd be delighted to have you and your father as my guests as long as ye wish to stay."

"That can't be true." He rather liked the wry amusement that curved her lips.

In fact, apart from her outlandish ideas of female equality and her tendency to flout his will, there was quite a lot he liked about her. Not least how she wore his sister's dress. The frothy yellow concoction should look absurd on tall, dark Marina Lucchetti, but it only emphasized the elegant sparseness of that long body. Not to mention he approved of its pleasing tendency to droop over her bosom. He'd already noted that although her breasts mightn't be abundant, they offered plenty of scope for a man's entertainment.

While she wasn't a conventional beauty or the sweet-faced blonde he usually favored, her features were interesting and vivid. Nobody looking at her would expect a biddable woman. But he'd had plenty of biddable women, and they'd failed to hold his attention once the initial heat faded.

Perhaps it was time to seek a challenge. At least for a while. This woman mightn't be the oasis of calm he preferred in a lover, but in recompense, he sensed she contained oceans of passion inside that slender body. Perhaps he ought to set sail on the open sea, and discover what excitement the world held, once he left his safe harbor.

"As ye can see, *signorina*, I have plenty of room, and the prospect of some fresh company at dinner is welcome."

"That's so kind," she said in a firm tone. When was the last time a woman had spoken to him with that peremptory note? "But I can't possibly accept. I need at least six weeks to complete my work, and I've been told September is the last month when I can rely on the weather. Not that the weather here *ever* seems reliable."

He ignored her disrespect for the mercurial Scottish weather. "That's all very well, lassie, but your father has a broken leg. It would be dangerous to move him. Ye willnae want to risk permanent damage."

"Of course not, but Maggie said it was a clean break."

"Aye. But he'll only heal if he stays in one place and lets the bone knit."

Displeasure tightened that luscious mouth to a pout and made Fergus think of kisses. Fearing that his lustful thoughts must show in his eyes, he devoted his attention to his soup.

"Poor Papa." She paused. "Could I take advantage of your kindness and ask you to keep him here, while I hire someone from the estate to take me on to Skye?"

Let her go when he'd only just found her? Not while he still drew breath. "Ye wouldnae rather stay and see how he recovers?"

The gesture she made was strangely helpless. It was clear that she was a woman who didn't like to give up her plans. Fergus understood. He didn't like it either.

"You know I would, but I've accepted a substantial sum of money to deliver a dozen Highland scenes to His Grace by next Easter, and I can't break my contract."

"Highland scenes or scenes of Skye?"

She paused in eating her soup. "I beg your pardon?"

"Did the duke specify that he wants pictures of Skye, or did he ask for views of Scotland?"

"Highland scenes are what he ordered, but everyone I spoke to said that Skye offers the best variety and the most typical landscapes."

He spread his hands. "Then why not paint the scenery at Achnasheen? You'll find as many lochs and mountains and eccentric rustics on my estate as ye will on Skye. Not only that, but from the hills behind the castle, you can see across the sea to Skye, so you can include a few views of the isle if you're so determined. This way, you can stay with your father. You can recover from the accident—I daresay ye were being brave when I asked how you feel. And you can complete your assignment. Even better, ye can give the duke views that have never been painted before."

She still looked doubtful. He waited while Jenny appeared to remove their soup bowls and bring around the platter of roast mutton and vegetables.

Once they were alone again, he refilled the wineglasses and leaned back in his chair, watching her. "I cannae see how—or why—you'd say no."

"You're being extraordinarily generous." She began to eat, but her expression said she was turning his offer over in her mind. "You must think I'm both foolish and ungracious to object."

Actually he thought she was a smart woman who suspected her host's invitation might conceal another agenda.

She'd be right, the canny lassie. He was determined to have her in his bed. He couldn't manage that if he was at Achnasheen, and she was painting somewhere between Armadale and Portree.

He didn't underestimate the challenges of an affair with his attractive guest. Even if he convinced Signorina Lucchetti to take him as her lover, the people on the estate wouldn't much like him flaunting a mistress. His clan subscribed to a strong moral code, so he'd have to be discreet.

"I'll be disappointed if ye say no," he said calmly. "I can arrange a guide to take you out, someone who knows every rock on these hills. You'll be safe and comfortable and productive, and on hand to observe your father's recovery. No need to travel any further on our atrocious Highland roads."

As she lifted her wine, her rich red lips curved. Signorina Lucchetti looked good in his dining room, as if she fitted. "There's that."

"So will ye agree?"

A frown creased her brow. In the flickering light, the olive tinge to her skin was more marked than it had been outside in the rain. She looked very exotic to him. How he hungered to explore that mystery before she returned to Italy.

When had he found a woman this interesting? He wasn't likely to encounter anyone like her again.

"I'll be taking advantage of you." Candlelight turned her eyes to dark pools.

They'd be taking advantage of each other, if he had any say in it. Hell, this was Achnasheen. He had a say in everything. "I'd enjoy your company."

"I can't feel it's quite proper for me to stay. After all, you're a single man and I'm a single woman."

He cut into his meat and shrugged. "We have your father and a house full of servants to chaperone us."

"A man who can't leave his bed and people bound to you in clan loyalty."

He drank more of his wine, letting the smooth claret tease his senses, although nothing could compare with his pleasure in watching the lovely woman sitting at his elbow. "Why not stay for a couple of days, then make up your mind? Ye can see the country and decide whether it meets your requirements."

She stared down at her half-empty plate and pushed a piece of potato around as she considered his suggestion. "You must think I'm hypocritical to worry about my good name, when I proclaim my independence with such fervor."

"Och, you're just being practical."

"I told you it's difficult for a woman to make a career as an artist." She raised those remarkable eyes, and desire hit him so hard, he wondered why he couldn't smell the sizzle of lightning striking. "I've worked too long and hard to let scandal destroy everything I've built."

"I understand," he said.

He did. Which didn't stop him from scheming to bring them together.

Fergus wanted her now, but it was too early to invite her into his bed. He hadn't yet convinced her to stay past tonight. He couldn't risk his sinful intentions frightening her off.

Somewhere in the back of his mind, he wondered why he was so determined to have her. He'd always liked compliant women. Compliant was the last adjective he'd apply to Signorina Lucchetti.

But while his common sense warned him she was likely to be nothing but trouble, he couldn't deny the heat swirling like a whirlpool in his blood. Whatever the future held, he'd made his decision. He wanted her, and it was too late to turn away.

She set down her cutlery and nodded, as if she reached a conclusion after a long argument. "Very well, Mackinnon. Thank you. I will accept your offer to stay, at least for the next few days."

For an overbearing male, the Mackinnon proved surprisingly good company. Marina enjoyed hearing about the clan's long history. It sounded like something out of a romantic novel, full of feuds and battles, forbidden love and revenge.

Every word he spoke conveyed his love for this wild and dramatic landscape. Over the last days as she and her father had wended their way further into the Highlands, she'd been impressed with the magnificent scenery. Yet only as she listened to tales spun over a candlelit dinner table did she at last feel the powerful lure of this land.

Her artist's soul burned to capture something of that untamed spirit. She was far from convinced that staying at Achnasheen was wise, but wisdom lost its battle against increasing fascination. A fascination not with the turbulent history alone, but with the man weaving the magic.

She realized that despite its beauty, this was a harsh country and only the strongest survived. Perhaps the Mackinnon had reason for being such an autocrat. It became clear that the fortunes of the entire clan had always hinged on the chief's strength.

When he caught Marina stifling a yawn, he interrupted a story of a beautiful girl kidnapped from a nearby glen. "Och, lassie, I've kept ye up too long, maundering on about long ago."

"It's still early." As if to confirm that, the clock on the mantel struck half past nine.

"Time for all good lasses to seek their beds."

"I must check on Papa. He was sleeping when I left him."

"If Maggie's given him one of her potions, he'll sleep until morning."

"That will do him good. But I'd still like to look in on him." She lifted her hand in appeal. "At least finish the story. Did the Drummonds besiege your castle and demand their kinswoman back?"

Humor lifted the corners of his lips. So far tonight, he'd smiled fully just once, when he'd told her she had to stay at Achnasheen. For the sake of her heart rate, she was grateful for that. These half-smiles were appealing enough. "They did, but too late, I fear."

Marina's eyes opened wide in horror, and her hands curled into the arms of her chair. "The Mackinnons murdered her?"

He shook his head in mock disapproval. "You're a bloodthirsty wench."

"Given some of the stories you've told me this evening, it's a possibility," she retorted.

One tale had the Drummonds trapping a band of Mackinnon raiders in a cave and setting a fire at the entrance, resulting in mass suffocation. That would probably give her nightmares tonight.

"Aye, I suppose so."

"So what happened to Bonny Mhairi?"

That smile still flirted with his lips. "By the time her kinsmen organized themselves to mount a raid, she'd fallen in love with the Mackinnon. We're such braw laddies, ye ken."

"Is that so?" Marina said, unable to deny the statement, although she knew he teased her.

"The bonny wee lass stood on the battlements and told her family to take themselves away home, as she was quite happy where she was and intended to stay. She's my great-great grandmother."

"What a nice story." Relief flooded Marina, although these people were strangers and meant nothing to her. "I think that might be my favorite."

He came around to pull her chair out as she rose. "Aye, a wee romance for ye to dream about." He crooked his arm in her direction. "Let me escort you to your room."

She wanted to accept the gesture as simple good manners, but when she curled her fingers around his elbow, a wash of sensual heat enveloped her head to toe. Astonishment stopped her from moving straightaway. Her attention usually focused on her work, on pigments and outlines and perspective. Until now, no mere male could compete with her devotion to her art.

Yet all night, awareness of the Mackinnon had kept her on edge. Now his touch ignited that stirring attraction to wildfire. His command to go to bed took on suggestive overtones.

"Thank you for a delightful evening," she said, meaning it.

She'd imagined he'd have her hackles raised all night, while the discussion had been—mostly— harmonious. And her fears of a dreadful dinner to match the other dreadful dinners she'd had in the Highlands hadn't come to pass. The fish soup had been delicious, and the mutton had been cooked to perfection.

"Better than ye expected?" he asked in a wry tone.

She narrowed her eyes at him. "Yes, especially once you controlled your impulse to tell me what to do."

"I made sure I approached ye with due care."

With an unpleasant shock, Marina realized that over the course of the evening, she'd yielded to everything he asked of her. She'd had dinner with him. She'd agreed to stay at the castle. She was even, blast him, going to bed on his orders. "Very clever, Mackinnon."

He drew her into his side. "Do ye mind?"

More of that cursed heat radiated through her as their hips brushed. She'd never in her twenty-eight years been so conscious of her body.

"I might, once I've had a chance to think about it." When she shifted, she felt stiff after sitting for so long, but her legs soon started to work properly. They strolled toward the great hall and its staircase up to her room. She wondered where the Mackinnon slept, then told herself to behave.

"Och, you're no' the sort to bear a grudge."

She was tall enough that she had no trouble matching her steps to his. "Tomorrow I'll be too busy climbing around the hills on your estate to worry about anything else."

"Not tomorrow, lassie."

She told herself "lassie" wasn't a term of endearment, despite it sounding like one. Now. It hadn't when he'd called her lassie down by the bridge. "Mackinnon, I have work to do and—"

"Dinna get your feathers all puffed up. I'm not laying down the law. There's more rain on the way. No weather for hill walking. So stay in. Talk to your father. Talk to me. Rest. Maybe do a few sketches inside the castle. Or if ye like, we can do our tour of the house."

"You've got it all sorted out," she said with a touch of resentment, although after her wait in the cold with her father this afternoon, she had no wish to be out in the weather again.

"Aye, I'm the Mackinnon." They started to climb that impossibly impressive staircase. "Sorting out is what I do."

Her laugh was soft. "I'm not one of your clansmen. I can sort myself out."

The glance he cast her was disconcertingly penetrating. "Isn't it nice when ye don't have to?"

A weak, feminine part of her agreed. It had been a difficult day. Cold, wet weather and long hours of travel over appalling roads, culminating in that terrifying crash when she'd been so certain she and her father were doomed. Then on top of that, her fears about Papa's injury. Not to mention the tumult of finding herself so suddenly, so completely in thrall to an arrogant stranger.

The stalwart part of her that had carved out her career fought back. If she ceded her will to this man, it might be easy in the short term, but afterward her lonely path would only prove more difficult.

Lonely path? What was this? She loved her life. She loved that she was in charge of where she went and what she did. If after mere hours, the Mackinnon had her questioning such a fundamental truth about her existence, he was even more dangerous than she thought.

"I'm fine." Perhaps because the idea of leaning on him remained so appealing, her answer held a touch of tartness.

"You're a prickly lassie," he said easily. "I don't know why I put up with ye."

He sounded as if he was fond of her. Which was ridiculous, when they'd known one another for a single evening.

She summoned a light response, although the warmth in his tone made her wayward heart wobble. "And to think you've invited me to stay as long as I wish."

They'd reached her father's door. Flickering light from the candle the Mackinnon carried cast shadows across that striking bone structure. Her fingers itched to draw him like this, a man half lost in the world of the past.

"Aye, well, madness runs in the family."

She shook her head. "Not madness. Vengeance. Passion. Power. Violence. All those. None of the stories you told me tonight indicated anyone on the family tree was out of his mind."

When he moved closer, she gave a start. On unsteady legs, she faltered back until she bumped into the door behind her. Although she generally wasn't nervous around men.

"Perhaps I've saved the stories about the mad Mackinnons for next time." That deep voice with its alluring lilt played glissandos up and down her backbone. "Or perhaps the first mad Mackinnon is going to be me."

The words echoed between them with the force of thunder, although they weren't precisely a threat, and he'd spoken in a murmur, as if he didn't want the shadows hearing.

He leaned in closer and every tiny hair on her skin stood up in expectation. *Per l'amor di dio*, was he going to kiss her? If he did, did she mean to kiss him back? Or send him away with a flea in his ear?

And if he did kiss her, did that change her decision to remain at this isolated castle?

Hurriedly she turned and pushed open the door with a shaking hand. Candles lit the room to gold. Her father snored softly. Maggie lifted her head from where she sat knitting beside the bed. She smiled as Marina stepped inside and ventured close enough to see that some color returned to Papa's cheeks. Sleep smoothed away the deep lines of pain that had marked his face since the accident.

"He's peaceful as a Sabbath morning, lassie," Maggie whispered.

Marina stared into her father's relaxed features and said a silent prayer of gratitude that they'd both come through the accident. Hiding a wince, she leaned in and pressed a kiss to his forehead. Bending over reminded her yet again of her bone-jarring arrival in the glen. "*Buona notte*, Papa."

He didn't stir. She glanced up at Maggie with a smile. "Thank you for looking after him."

"Och, it's nae trouble," the old woman said. "Nae trouble at all. Now away with ye to bed, my bonny."

Marina said goodnight and crept out of the room, although Papa was so deeply asleep, she doubted a brass band could wake him. The Mackinnon was waiting in the corridor.

"Oh, I didn't think you'd stay."

"I said I'd walk ye to your door, *signorina*."

Those warm fingers closed around her arm once more, and the blast of heat made her stumble. He regarded her in concern as they walked the short distance. "I really have kept ye up too late. How are you feeling?"

"Like I've been in a carriage accident," she said drily. "But it's nothing a good night's sleep won't cure."

"I hope so." The breath caught in her throat when he leaned in again, but he merely stretched past to release the latch so her door opened behind her. He frowned when he glanced into the dark room. "Didnae Peggy wait up?"

"I told her not to. I'm used to looking after myself."

Her eyes clung to the derisive quirk of that expressive mouth. "More of your blasted independence?"

"Probably," she said, telling herself it was silly and dangerous to be disappointed at the lack of a kiss. If he kissed her, her situation at Achnasheen would become impossible.

The Mackinnon stepped into her room. "Let me light a candle."

It shouldn't feel like he intruded on her intimate space. After all, before she came downstairs, she'd only been in the bedroom for an hour, and he owned the whole deuced castle. But there was something powerfully evocative about watching a long, lean Scot prowl around a room where in a few minutes she'd undress and lie down to sleep.

Marina stayed in the doorway as he lit the candle on her dressing table from his. When he stood in front of the mirror, there were two Mackinnons. She was so tired, she started to lose her hold on what was real and what wasn't.

He came toward her, bearing both candles. For one lunatic second, she thought of asking him to stay, to answer the physical attraction blazing beneath their interactions with a resounding yes.

"You're dead on your feet," he said softly, passing her the light. "Ye should have stopped me from talking so long."

"I liked it," she said.

A faint smile touched his lips, and she felt an almost painful hunger to see him smile properly again. She blinked and swayed on her feet. Tiredness, or the yen to step into his arms?

"I told ye we're starved for company here at Achnasheen. You'll be lucky if I ever let you go."

"Lucky..." she said, not sure if it was a question or not.

He lifted his candle, and she flinched from those searching eyes. Heaven help her if he guessed what she was thinking right now.

"Goodnight, Signorina Marina."

"Goodnight, Mackinnon," she whispered in return and stood to watch him stride away down the corridor on those long, powerful legs.

Fergus Mackinnon mightn't be her sort of man. But, *diavolo*, what a man he was.

CHAPTER FIVE

arina didn't see the Mackinnon again until late the next morning. She'd slept like the dead and late—which she never did, as she liked to catch the early light for her work. After Peggy brought her breakfast in her room, she'd changed into the yellow dress she'd worn last night. Her blue traveling ensemble was drying in the kitchen after its soaking yesterday.

If she was to stay here, she'd have to do something about clothes, although goodness knew what. It wasn't as if there was a street of shops outside where she could order a new wardrobe.

How annoying that the Mackinnon had been right about the weather. If Achnasheen meant field of rain, it lived up to its name this morning. If she'd decided to travel on without Papa, she wouldn't get far today.

Marina went in to sit with her father, who was more comfortable than she'd expected and as a consequence, bored and starved of company. Luckily the castle turned out to have a large library. She was reading to him from a recent Blackwood's Magazine when the Mackinnon appeared in the doorway.

In the clear, gray light of day, Marina had hoped good sense would conquer her inconvenient yen for this Scotsman. But when she looked up from the page to find him watching her, her heart resumed its acrobatics and heat rushed through her blood.

It didn't help that this morning he could have modeled for an illustration in a Highland romance. Last night, he'd worn conventional clothes, like the men she met in Italy and London and Edinburgh. He'd been devastating enough then. Now when he appeared in a loose white linen shirt and a kilt in a pattern of red and black, he was breathtaking.

To avoid those knowing gray eyes, she glanced down, only to find herself staring at powerful bare legs. She blushed as she caught her father's curious stare and returned her attention to the magazine. Except the words blurred into nonsense. All she could see was a tall, red-haired man in a costume that should strike her as hopelessly theatrical. Instead, the sight of the Mackinnon in his native dress stirred something wild and free inside her.

"Good morning, Signor Lucchetti, Signorina Lucchetti." The Mackinnon came in and with every step he took closer, her heart slammed in time against her ribs.

"Good morning, sir," her father said.

Marina remained tongue-tied, which was a new experience. *Porca miseria*, she acted like a foolish girl in the grip of her first puppy love.

"How are you feeling this morning, sir?"

"Much better, *grazie*." Her father smiled. "Thank you for taking us in. After yesterday's rescue, we already owe you such a debt of gratitude. I fear we can never repay you."

The Mackinnon lifted a chair from under the window and brought it forward. When he sat beside

Marina, the gap between them was more than proper. It was considerably wider than the space had been last night on the chaise longue. She had no reason to feel that he staked a claim on her.

"There's nae need. Here in the Highlands, we're used to helping each other, as there's nobody else to rely on. And I'll appreciate the company. New faces are rare in this part of the world."

"You never go to Edinburgh or Inverness?"

"A few times a year. When I have to. This is wild, isolated country, but a man grows to love it."

"I also must introduce myself. I am Ugolino Lucchetti of Firenze. My daughter is the esteemed painter Marina Lucchetti. It's her work that brings us to your land so *bellissimo*."

Marina cast Papa an incredulous look. Given that all he'd done since they arrived in Scotland was complain, this laid it on a little thick. Her father was a creature of the sun, and even in late summer, Scotland was too cold for him.

"I'm delighted to make your acquaintance, *signore*. I'm Fergus Mackinnon. I found out all about your famous daughter when we dined last night."

"Hardly famous," she said, setting aside the Blackwood's Magazine and picking up the pencil and small sketchbook that never lay far from her hand.

The Mackinnon turned to her with a polite interest that made her want to scoff. She'd seen the possessive glitter in his eyes when he'd caught sight of her. "Signorina Lucchetti, I hope you're well this morning."

"*Si, grazie*." She avoided his stare and began to trace a few lines on the paper.

This was a lovely room, a pleasing mixture of old and new. So far, every part of the castle she'd seen was like that. It was a change from the grand formality she was accustomed to in noble Italian houses, but there was something vastly appealing about the lack of pretension.

"I have good news for both of you."

This made her raise her head from a drawing that suddenly included a long-boned Scotsman at the center of the scene. She tipped her sketchbook away from him to hide what she was doing. "You've worked out how Papa and I can travel on to Skye?"

He shook his head with mock disappointment. "Here I thought you'd reconciled yourself to staying in my humble abode."

The abode wasn't humble, and neither was its master. She flashed him a repressive glance. "I don't want to burden you past our welcome. What do the French say? Fish and visitors start to stink after three days?"

"Marina, *figlia,* I'm sure a little gratitude is called for," her father said.

But the Mackinnon gave one of his brief laughs and wasn't at all put out. As she'd expected. She wondered why she felt like she knew him so well, when they'd only just met.

"Och, your daughter and I have reached an understanding, *signore*. Has she told ye that I've offered you both a place here for as long as you need, while you return to health? And if the scenery on my estate meets with her approval, paintings of my home will one day adorn the Duke of Portofino's palazzo."

Marina stifled a wry laugh. From the Mackinnon's tone, it was clear that he thought the duke should consider himself lucky to enjoy views of Achnasheen.

"She said you'd suggested a brief stay before she goes on to Skye with a hired guide. In the meantime, I'll remain behind."

"*Signore*, I protest. I'd never entrust your daughter's safety to a stranger."

Marina bristled. Despite her vow to treat the Mackinnon as just one more obnoxious man to be ignored or outmaneuvered, she couldn't let that pass unchallenged. "It's not for you to make such decisions for me, Mackinnon," she retorted, as half-unconsciously, her pencil outlined the impressive arms and shoulders.

His rich auburn hair was damp and clung to the strong lines of his skull. He must have been out in the weather already. This was a man who belonged in the open air, free and strong. Even in the castle's generous rooms, he seemed too vital to have all that energy confined within four walls.

"She doesnae like to be guided, does she?"

Her father gave a shout of laughter. "She's a headstrong *ragazza*, but a good one. From the first, you could persuade Marina, but you could not command. I see you've already noticed that, my lord."

The Mackinnon shook his head, ignoring the murderous glare Marina directed at his handsome hide. "Not a lord, *signore*. I'm laird here, but have no other title. You may call me Mackinnon—or Fergus, if ye feel we'll be friends."

"That's very kind of you. You must call me Ugolino. We don't stand on such ceremony at home as they do in England."

"That's the Sassenachs for ye," the Mackinnon said.

"Remember, too, that we're not from the highest levels of society, Papa," Marina said, as her pencil began to tackle the fascinating lines of her host's face. Since she first saw him, the artist in her had hankered to draw him. "We work for our living."

"At least you do, *carissima*."

She wondered if the Mackinnon noticed that she, unlike her father, hadn't offered him the use of her Christian name. It seemed absurd to deny him, and formality provided no brake to blossoming attraction, but still she resisted the intimacy that first names would encourage.

"You handle most of my business affairs." Largely because the rich and powerful men who bought her art preferred to deal with a man when it came to money.

"I do what you tell me, Marina," her father said without resentment. He'd never argued with her role as the captain of their particular ship.

She smiled, partly because she could imagine how the Mackinnon would react to a daughter making decisions and not the parent. But when she checked him for disapproval, he just looked interested. In the conversation—and in her, blast him.

"I still appreciate it," she said. "While you're charming my customers, I have more time to paint."

"You said you had news for us, Fergus." Papa's Italian accent turned the Scottish name into "fair goose" and made Marina smile again, as her busy pencil shaded in a hollow beneath a high Celtic cheekbone.

"Aye, I think you'll both be pleased." The Mackinnon leaned back in his chair. "We've managed to rescue your luggage. It's no' even waterlogged. The fine Florentine leather of your trunks looks to have kept everything inside clean and dry."

Amazement froze Marina's pencil. "I thought my dresses must be floating around in the Atlantic by now."

The familiar faint smile lengthened the Mackinnon's lips. "The coach is still stuck on *Eilean*

Mhairi. We managed to swim out this morning to retrieve its contents."

Wet hair. Now she understood. She frowned as she recalled the torrent of gray water rushing down the mountainside and under the bridge. "You swam out," she said sharply.

He shrugged. "Well, someone had to."

"It's only luggage." When she recalled how she'd regretted the loss of her belongings, she felt almost guilty. She should have been thankful that she'd managed to save her sketchbook and that she and Papa carried their money and letters of credit on them. "It's not worth risking your life over."

The Mackinnon's brilliant silvery eyes pierced her to her soul. "I appreciate your concern, lassie, but once I made it out and fastened a rope to a tree on the island, it was straightforward. Becoming as my sister's wee dress is on ye, I have a feeling you'll tire of it before your father's leg heals."

He seemed to take it for granted that she was staying for the duration, whereas she was far from reconciled to the idea.

"I say you're very gallant to retrieve our belongings." Papa sent his daughter a critical glance. "Marina, you should thank our host."

She hated to think of the Mackinnon taking such risks over something as frivolous as a pretty dress for her to wear. However, as her father said, she should say thank you. "It was thoughtful of you."

Another twitch of the lips, but the Mackinnon's tone remained urbane. "I want ye to be comfortable here. I've got the castle's lassies checking that everything's dry. They'll bring your luggage up, once they're sure no water got in. We couldn't do anything to salvage the carriage. It's fit for nothing but firewood."

"You've done more than enough," she said, sounding less grudging.

The deed was done, he'd survived, and having her own clothes would be welcome. Although she'd miss the luxurious coach. Over the years, it had become something of an old friend.

"His lordship, the Conte Rossini, won't be pleased," her father said.

The Mackinnon didn't look pleased either. "Why is that?"

"The carriage was a gift from Marina's first patron, one of the greatest nobles in Firenze."

"That is an extravagant present." The Mackinnon's tone was flat.

By "extravagant," the Mackinnon meant "unsuitable," Marina could tell. Temper prickled as she recognized the signs of a man who learned of a possible rival. Her host had no right to proprietary feelings.

She decided to torment him a little to put him in his place. "His lordship has always been most...generous."

The Mackinnon's eyes narrowed on her. "Has he indeed?"

"*Si, certo.* The *signore* is a great lover..." Enjoying herself more than she ought, she raised her hand to touch her lips, as if she recalled passionate kisses. "...of the arts."

"Aye, a man of exquisite taste," the Mackinnon said with a hint of grimness.

Before Marina could spin more of a tale, Papa spoiled her fun. "*Sua signoria, il conte* has been so kind, like a grandfather. He noticed my daughter's talent from the first day he visited the school where she studied. He takes a great interest in Firenze's unrivaled artistic heritage and wants to make sure it continues into the future. Many artists in our beautiful city owe him their gratitude. When he commissioned Marina's first landscapes, he gave her the carriage so she could visit the places he wanted her to paint. He said that since he's too old to travel, her paintings brought the world to him."

"A gift from an ageing admirer." Wry amusement deepened the attractive creases around the Mackinnon's eyes. *Maledizione*, he was onto her game now. Pity. She'd rather relished her power to make him grumpy. "What a charming picture ye paint, *signore*."

It was her turn to narrow her eyes on the Mackinnon. "The *conte* has a very handsome son."

"I hope he's married with a dozen bairns."

"Five." Although Marina was familiar enough with high society to know that a wife and children presented no barrier to dalliance.

She grew to enjoy the Mackinnon's brief grunts of laughter. Deciding she'd made enough of her aristocratic Florentine connections, she turned to a more neutral topic. "How long do you think this rain will last? I need to get out onto the hills."

"My daughter likes to work," her father said with a note of pride. "Always painting, painting, painting."

The Mackinnon lifted his gaze to the soggy scene outside the window. "It should clear overnight. You'll be able to go out tomorrow, *signorina*."

"And have you found me a guide?"

"Indeed. I've put our best laddie on the job."

"Excellent," she said and went back to her drawing, as the Mackinnon and her father began to speak of the journey north and where the idiot coachman had gone wrong.

"I've arranged for Coker to sail down to Oban with some sheep I'm sending to market," the

Mackinnon said after about ten minutes. "He can make his own way back to Glasgow from there."

Yet again, the Mackinnon imposed his will where he had no right. Marina glanced up from her finished sketch. It wasn't bad, but it failed to capture the man's crackling energy. She'd have to try again. "I might need him to drive me to Skye."

She said it more for form's sake, than because she meant it. After yesterday's debacle, she felt nothing but contempt for the useless fellow.

The Mackinnon tilted his proud head in her direction. "*Signorina*, I hope you'll trust me to see ye safely to wherever you need to go."

"Of course she does," her father rushed to say.

He was capable of acting in his own interests rather than hers, when he thought it necessary. Right now, he wouldn't want to risk losing the comfortable berth he'd found for his convalescence.

"Do ye really want to keep him on?" the Mackinnon asked.

She sighed. The strange thing was that she did trust the Mackinnon as far as practical arrangements went. Nothing she'd seen indicated he was anything other than a man of his word. He was acting for her benefit, even if he didn't ask her permission first. "I suppose not."

"Anyway, what is he to drive, *sciocchina*?" Papa asked. "Unless our host lends us a carriage. If you fear we already ask too much of Fergus, well, that's yet another obligation."

Her father was right. But Marina couldn't help but feel that every time she gave in to the Mackinnon, even about an issue as minor as her coachman's fate, he eroded a little more of her independence.

If she lost her independence, how could she survive in the world she'd chosen to inhabit?

"Very well, Papa, you've made your point," she said with a hint of impatience and turned to her host. "It seems I owe you more thanks. You'll soon tire of my conversation, sir, as it will be nothing but an endless stream of gratitude."

A faint smile. "I cannae imagine ever tiring of your conversation, *signorina*."

She cursed the heat that rose in her cheeks. "Wait until you know me better before you make such rash assertions."

"I look forward to it."

The smile hovered. Without thinking, she lifted her sketchpad and quickly turned to a clean page. To her irritation, the fleeting expression vanished before she caught it.

"Are ye thinking of painting my portrait?" the Mackinnon asked.

The heat in her cheeks, barely conquered, rose again. "I'm just passing the time."

"She draws the way you and I breathe, Fergus," Papa said. "Although most of the time, she finds landscapes of more interest than people."

She shot her father a repressive glance. "I'm stuck inside today."

Her parent responded with a speculative look that shifted from her to her host.

The Mackinnon gave another of his grunts of amusement. "So in the absence of a hill or a river, I'll do?"

"Precisely," she said, although the unwelcome truth was that she found his features irresistibly compelling.

"I cannae imagine your noble patron will want a picture of me among his Scottish scenes."

"I don't know." She arched an eyebrow. "You have the untamed quality he asked for."

Wicked humor sparkled in the silvery eyes. "I'm glad ye think so, lassie."

The fleeting expression she'd sought to depict was nowhere to be seen. Right now, he looked predatory and far too interested in her. With sudden violence, she scribbled over the few lines marking the page.

The Mackinnon laughed again. "Och, that puts me in my place."

"I have no skill in portraits," she said, closing the book even as her eye fell on her first sketch of her host.

The Mackinnon stood. "Anyway, you need to excuse me. *Signorina,* would you like me to show ye around the castle this afternoon? It may inspire your artistic impulses, despite the weather."

She was sure it would. It was her other, more carnal impulses she was worried about. On the other hand, how often did she have the chance to tour a genuine Highland castle?

"Thank you," she said with a docility that provoked another mocking arch of a russet eyebrow.

The Mackinnon turned to Papa. "If you'd like it, *signore,* I thought perhaps your daughter and I could dine with ye in here tonight to keep you company. I imagine time will hang heavy while your leg heals."

"*Grazie,* that's so kind," her father said. "I'd like that beyond measure."

Marina cast the Mackinnon a curious glance. She'd imagined that he'd try to get her to himself again. What was his game?

The silvery eyes were enigmatic. *Diavolo,* she was completely out of her depth. Which was absurd when she'd been fending off amorous overtures from ardent gentlemen since she set up as an artist. She knew the danger signals, and she knew how to defuse masculine interest. Or at least she thought she did.

"Then I'll leave ye to rest." He bowed to Marina. "*Signorina.*"

Once the Mackinnon had gone, a charged silence fell. Marina pretended an interest in a sketch of a crofter's cottage she'd done on the way north.

"Daughter, look at me," her father said in soft Italian.

Unwillingly, Marina obeyed. "*Si,* Papa?"

"He has his eye on you, that one. Be careful."

She gave a derisive snort and answered in the same language. "If you're worried about the Mackinnon, why on earth are you doing your best to push us together?"

"I'm not," her father said. If he'd met her eyes when he spoke, she might almost believe him.

"Anyway, even if he is interested in me, men have been interested in me before. I've always been able to handle them."

"Yes, but this time I fear you're interested in him in return." Her father frowned. "And we're under his roof."

"He's a fascinating man, but too much the master," she said with utterly spurious self-confidence.

Her father didn't smile or make his usual teasing remarks about her going her own way. "But you always like a challenge."

"I know the price of a scandal, Papa." Her hand clenched on the pencil. "Don't worry about me."

"But I do worry. Listening to the two of you talk is like being caught between lightning strikes. I don't want you to get burnt, *cara.*"

"He said if I want to go on to Skye, he'll give me a guide. But it means leaving you behind. You can't travel as you are." Reluctantly this morning, she'd admitted that the Mackinnon hadn't exaggerated her father's immobility over the next few weeks.

"That fool of a coachman."

"Yes, well, there's no point crying over spilt milk." When she spoke the proverb in English, her father chuckled.

"You and your mother, such strange things you say in your barbarous tongue. Only a fool would waste tears on a drop of lost milk." His expression turned somber. "I always miss her, but right now, I miss her more than ever. I have a feeling you might need her guidance in time to come."

"I miss her, too." Marina rose and kissed her father on the cheek. "Now stop fretting. I promise I'm in no danger. All I want you to do is lie back and get better, and all I need to do is finish my paintings for His Grace. Then we can go back to Italy and forget this country where the sun never shines. You're getting into a state over nothing, Papa."

"Am I?" He didn't smile. "I'm more worried now. When I accused you of an interest in Fergus, you failed to deny it."

What would be the point? "*Basta*, he's handsome enough, but too inclined to order me around. I'm sure I can keep my girlish passions in check."

She wanted her father to smile, to treat this issue as the unimportant matter she desperately hoped it was. But he remained troubled. "Perhaps you should accept Fergus's offer of a guide to Skye. If he lets you take a maid as well, I'm sure it will all be respectable."

"I don't want to leave you, Papa, at least at this early stage. Let me see what the country is like tomorrow when I go out. If there isn't sufficient material for my commission, I promise I'll move on.

Or I will, once I'm convinced you're on the road to recovery."

But as she left the room, her father's misgivings only added to hers. Was she a fool to stay even one more night at Achnasheen?

CHAPTER SIX

Signorina Lucchetti—Fergus noticed that unlike her father, she hadn't been quick to offer the privilege of using her Christian name—swept down the main staircase to the great hall. Macushla and Brecon both barked in welcome, leaped to their feet, and loped toward her.

"*Buongiorno, amici,*" she said with a smile less constrained than the ones she usually bestowed on Fergus. She paused on the landing at the turn of the stairs to give the dogs an enthusiastic greeting. She'd been at ease with them yesterday in the rain, too, he remembered.

She liked his dogs. That was a point in her favor, as if he needed anything else to make him appreciate her.

When she straightened and descended to the flagstoned floor, the dogs trotted at her side. She'd changed into one of her own gowns, now her luggage was out of the burn. It was another fiendishly stylish frock in a rich purple that added an ivory tinge to that smooth olive skin.

He had to give her dressmaker credit. The gown was as modest as a nun's habit, yet it skimmed that tall, slender body in a way that left a laddie aware of every alluring curve and line it covered.

This laddie, anyway.

As she came forward, her smile took on that familiar hint of a challenge. Fergus wasn't sure she knew she did it. It always made him want to either kiss the insolence out of her, or fling her across his shoulder and carry her up to his tower.

Why choose? He wanted to do both.

She gestured toward the pikes, halberds and muskets arrayed in orderly patterns on the stone walls. "This house is an armory."

He gave an amused grunt. "Aye, we're always ready to fight, if the Macgillivrays or the Drummonds take a fancy to land or livestock that by rights belongs to the Mackinnons."

She stopped a few feet away. The gloomy day turned the great hall into a realm of shadows and mystery. The greatest mystery of all was this intriguing woman. "Even now?"

"Aye, even now." Although these days, the Highlands were a mostly law-abiding part of the kingdom.

"How exciting."

Aye, this lassie would have fitted right in, back in the wild old days. He pictured Marina Lucchetti standing on the battlements at Achnasheen and defying an invading army. Last night at dinner, he hadn't missed her interest in his dramatic stories about the clan.

"Come away, and I'll show ye the rest of the castle."

It was a struggle not to touch her as they wandered in and out of the ground floor rooms. When he took her down to the vast, vaulted kitchens, designed for the era when the entire clan dined with the laird every day, his guest's curiosity about his home matched his servants' interest in her. As he climbed behind Signorina Lucchetti up the stairs from the kitchen, his shoulder blades tingled with the knowledge that Jenny and Kirsty watched avidly from below.

He had enough distractions, without worrying about what his kinfolk were saying about his beautiful guest. Under the purple dress, the *signorina's* slim hips swayed with each step. How could a man look anywhere else when, as she mounted the stairs, the material slid to outline the luscious roundness of her buttocks. His hands curled at his sides as he fought the impulse to haul those curves hard into his body.

Self-derisive amusement quirked his lips as he imagined her reaction if he did that. She'd likely punch him in the nose. Or lower.

Which didn't stop a man from wanting her.

This was an odd attraction, unprecedented in his experience. It was a wee bit like holding a lit firecracker in his hand and waiting for the explosion. Not peaceful, but without doubt, exciting.

She turned her head and caught his expression. "What are you thinking, Mackinnon?" she asked in a dark tone. "And whatever it is, stop."

This was also the one lassie in creation who gave him orders. He had no intention of obeying, but the novelty had its charms.

"Och, you're no fun, Marina Lucchetti," he said with a tragic air, following her back into the great hall.

"I'm pleased to hear it." Her eyes narrowed on him as the dogs settled contentedly at her feet. Traitors. "Girls who are no fun live long and respectable lives and die in their beds."

"Aye, that's true. But perhaps when they die, they wish they'd visited a few other beds in the meantime."

"Mackinnon…" she said in warning.

He widened his eyes in mock innocence. "I'm only trying to entertain ye with a wee bit of flirtation."

She wasn't impressed, he could see. "The tour is entertainment enough. May we go upstairs?"

His heart crashed against his ribs, although he knew the question was innocent. Och, what he'd give to carry her up to his tower room and keep her there. By God, she'd find entertainment aplenty, if he had any say in it.

Behave yourself, Fergus.

She wasn't ready to fall into his arms. Although if he wasn't mistaken—and he rarely was—she was interested. She mightn't want to find him attractive, but he hadn't missed the sparkle in her eyes or the color on those haughty cheekbones when she bandied words with him.

Aye, she was interested, all right, if far from reconciled to the idea.

"It's a pity it's such dreich weather. You'll love the view from the battlements."

"Perhaps you can show me when the weather improves."

That cheered him up. Despite her concession last night, he feared she still might move on to Skye at the first chance. "That's a promise."

"Do you have a portrait of Bonny Mhairi?"

"Aye."

While it was too soon to ask his visitor to share his bed—hell, she hadn't agreed to stay past the next few days—he'd be damned if he put off touching her any longer. He stepped forward and took her arm.

By now, after touching her so many times, he should be used to the immediate shock of heat. A blast of desire tightened his gut and set his heart galloping. The force of his need seared away good sense and left yearning in its place.

The *signorina* started at the contact. Surprise, or did she share the same powerful reaction?

Too soon. Too soon. But by the devil, before long, he'd sweep her into his arms and kiss her until she couldn't see straight.

Fergus swallowed and battled to sound like a civilized man. No lassie had ever had him in such a lather, and he hadn't even kissed her yet. God help him when he did. "Let's go and visit my great-great grandmother."

As they climbed the wide staircase, the Mackinnon told her more about the castle's history. Marina didn't hear a word. She was too conscious of that strong, capable hand curled around her arm above her elbow. The rainy day was cold, once they moved away from the fires blazing in the castle's hearths. Marina hardly noticed the chill. Instead, with her host so close, Marina felt like she was burning up.

She'd been a fool to think that a tour of the castle was an innocuous way to pass the afternoon. It turned out that any time she spent with this handsome Scot threatened her defenses.

Nor did it help that whenever she looked into that striking face, she saw sexual interest mirrored back. The flaring attraction was reluctant on her part, but she couldn't seem to do anything to stifle it.

She resented her agitation. Not just because she'd never imagined any man could rival her obsession with her art, but also because her focus on the Mackinnon stopped her appreciating her surroundings as they deserved. The castle was fascinating, or at least it should be, like something out of a legend.

Her attention only really became engaged—inevitably, she supposed—when they entered a long corridor leading between the north and east towers.

"You have a gallery," she said in pleasure.

"Aye. This is where we keep the family portraits. Ye want to see Bonny Mhairi."

"I do," she said, although she stopped in front of a pair of primitive panels from the sixteenth century that were much too early to feature the kidnapped heroine.

A man wearing black velvet and fur stood beside a desk that held a thick leather-bound bible. A woman in a black silk farthingale and a white ruff clutched a baby wrapped in swaddling clothes. The baby's face looked shriveled and ancient as it stared out of the painting.

"Those two always look like dolls to me," the Mackinnon said from far too close. "So stiff and formal."

The portraits were of no great quality, although the artist had done a fair job depicting the luxurious clothing. The sitters' features, however, conveyed little animation. As the Mackinnon said, they looked like wooden mannequins, particularly that grotesque baby.

"It was the fashion to paint them like that," she said, wandering down the wall and noting the way fashions changed through the ages. She paused in front of a painting of a woman wearing a dark blue gown with an elaborate lace collar. If she'd added up the generations right, this was the picture she was looking for. "Is this Mhairi?"

"Aye, that's her. She doesnae look like she led such an adventurous life, does she?"

This artist had been even more ham-fisted than the earlier one. The woman's features showed no personality at all. Generic Scots redhead was the best description Marina could come up with. "What a pity."

"You cannae tell she was as beautiful as her reputation says, although the family legend is that my great-great grandfather fell in love with her the moment he saw her."

"I wonder how much actual kidnapping was involved."

The Mackinnon gave a grunt of laughter. "For the sake of Drummond pride, we've always agreed that she was stolen away." He gestured to the next painting, depicting a tall, lean man with marked brows and a mane of gray-streaked ebony hair. "This is her husband, Black Callum Mackinnon."

Black Callum's portrait had a little more life than Bonny Mhairi's. Not much.

"He was a handsome man, although he doesn't look much like you." Except perhaps for the commanding nose and haughty expression.

"Most Mackinnons have red hair and gray eyes. He was one of the few exceptions."

The varied quality of the portraits couldn't hide the way good looks ran through the line. Good looks, and a certain arrogance of bearing that she knew too well from her dealings with the current laird.

Marina paused in front of a pair of paintings that, in terms of artistic merit, were by far the best in the collection. The man was another long, lean Mackinnon and had a look of the laird she knew. His hair was powdered to a soft gray and tied back with a black silk ribbon in the mode of last century. The woman was soft and blonde and looked like she'd never had an opinion to call her own. Wearing a loose white gown that emphasized her voluptuous bosom, she reclined in a brocade chair.

"Your parents?"

"Aye."

"Is your mother alive?" She'd been a pretty woman.

"No, she passed away five years ago. She and my father met in Edinburgh, and he paid Allan Ramsay to commemorate their betrothal with these portraits. They were among the last paintings the artist finished."

"I've never heard of him, but he has marvelous skill. See how he's captured their personalities with a few brushstrokes. Is this what they were like?"

"He's caught my father's devil-may-care attitude. My father died in an accident at a race in Inverness. He was riding a horse that was reputed to be unbreakable."

Shocked, she met the Mackinnon's gaze. "You take your role as laird so seriously, I'd imagined your father must have been a stern taskmaster, all duty and hard work."

He released a dismissive huff of breath. "Anything but, lassie."

When she returned her attention to that handsome, painted face, she looked more closely. At first, she'd only noticed the resemblance to the man beside her. The imperial nose and clever gray eyes were familiar, but the mouth hinted at self-indulgence. The current Mackinnon's mouth was all firm self-confidence. She should know; she'd spent enough time staring at it and wondering how it would feel if he kissed her.

Marina turned to study the Mackinnon the way she'd studied the beautiful portrait. "So where did you get your sense of responsibility? It's obvious that your people love and admire you, so you must be a good master."

What a revelation it had been, walking around the castle in the laird's company. She'd wondered if Jock had exaggerated the level of fealty the Mackinnon inspired. She'd soon realized the brawny retainer had, if anything, played down the respect the people here gave their chieftain. She'd started to feel like she was on a tour of heaven, with the Almighty as her personal escort.

No wonder Fergus Mackinnon believed he was omnipotent.

"I try to be." He regarded his father's picture with a faintly troubled expression. "When I grew up, the estate wasnae well managed, and everyone here suffered as a consequence. My father was more interested in his own pleasures than in seeing his clansmen prosperous and settled. I swore that when I was in charge, things at Achnasheen would be different."

She couldn't criticize his intentions, but that air of omniscience niggled. "And does nobody ever offer a contrary opinion, a better way to go on?"

With a shrug, he returned his gaze to her. "An army marches best when there's one general in command."

"And you're that general?"

"Aye. Who else?"

It was her turn to frown. "But you're running an estate, not a war."

Wry humor creased his eyes. "Och, what's the difference?"

She'd realized last night, when she'd listened to his tales, that in past centuries, this part of the Highlands had been lawless and dangerous. But it was 1817. The kingdom, even its wild northern reaches, was at peace. "These days, there's nothing to defeat. The battle's over."

"You wouldnae say that if you'd lived here in my father's day."

"So you have subordinates, but no equals."

"I'm no raging tyrant, lassie." Those expressive brows drew together in displeasure. "If you don't believe me, ask the people who live here."

She didn't need to. It was apparent that everyone at Achnasheen was more than satisfied to have Fergus Mackinnon in charge.

The Mackinnon directed her attention to a portrait of his grandfather wearing the familiar red and black plaid, but her mind, for once, couldn't focus on art. Instead, she kept stewing on the laird and the military terms he'd used to describe himself.

There was no doubting his power within this glen. Or his capacity to fulfill his role as protector and custodian. Yet, despite the adulation he received from his followers, she couldn't help thinking that the master of this estate sounded as if he was heartbreakingly alone.

CHAPTER SEVEN

Fergus stood in the shadowy courtyard, holding two stocky ponies. Macushla and Brecon waited at his side. The sun peeped over the hills, and as he'd predicted, the day was fine.

His intriguing guest breezed through the castle's doors and paused on the top step to survey her surroundings. Then her gaze fell on him, and she smiled with an openness he'd rarely seen in her. Her long, graceful body bristled with energy, and her pleasure in the forthcoming excursion made her black eyes shine.

With the exception of his friend Hamish's formidable mother and her interest in politics, he wasn't used to women dedicated to anything outside home and family. Signorina Lucchetti's ideas went against everything he believed about the ordained way of things, but he couldn't deny that he found this unusual lassie appealing.

She wore a rather masculine ensemble in dark green merino, designed for a day in the outdoors. The elegant, unadorned lines revealed the feminine charms of the body beneath. The portfolio she'd saved from the wreck hung from one shoulder, and she carried a wide-brimmed dark green straw hat in her hand.

"Good morning, Mackinnon," she said, crouching to pat the dogs who trotted up to meet her. "You didn't have to get up to wish me well."

"You said ye wanted to leave early to catch the light."

She descended the steps with that long-legged, loose-hipped prowl that always set his heart racing. No other woman he knew walked like that either, as if she required nobody's permission to go where she wished.

"I did, but there was no need to crawl out of bed at dawn to see me off." She glanced around curiously. "You said my guide would be waiting."

Ah, they reached the point where there might be trouble. "He is."

Fergus gave her credit for being quick on the uptake. A few feet away from him, she went completely still. "I...see."

He wasn't in the habit of explaining himself, but nor did he want her storming back inside. "Nobody knows these hills better than I do. I wouldnae entrust ye to anyone else."

"I appreciate your kindness—" she began hotly.

"No, you don't," he said with a huff of amusement. "You're wishing me to Hades right now."

"*Certo.* Yes, I am." To his relief, laughter brightened her black eyes. "I also recognize an argument I'm not going to win. You'll soon regret your chivalry, Mackinnon. Be warned. A day with an artist is extremely dull. Papa always brings a book when we go out. So if you find yourself wishing you hadn't come, remember this moment. I suspect tomorrow you'll be more than happy to hand me over to Jock or one of his friends."

As if he'd consign her to another man's care.

"You shouldn't challenge me, you know," he said in a neutral tone, leading the black pony up to her. He released the bridle and took her portfolio, tying it to the saddle. "It just makes me more determined to prove ye wrong."

"We really aren't designed to get along, are we?" she said easily. "We're too alike. Too accustomed to getting our own way."

"The weaker will must yield in time." When he caught her by the waist, he let his hands linger.

Every time he touched her, it was like holding high summer in his grasp. Only a Highlander could appreciate how appealing that was. Winters at Achnasheen were long and dark and cold. When Marina Lucchetti gave herself to him, she'd flood his world with Mediterranean sunlight.

Her sleek dark eyebrows rose and to his pleasure, she didn't try to break his grip. "Of course, you assume the weaker will must be mine."

"Of course," he said, appreciating her spirit. It was inevitable that he'd win the battle between them, but by heaven, he'd have fun along the way before he did.

"Pride goeth before a fall," she said, then gasped as he hoisted her onto the pony's broad back. She settled her delectable rump into the sidesaddle and took up the reins.

"In that case, you'd better do your best to hold on, *signorina*." He caught the dun pony's rein and rose into the saddle. He noted her sardonic expression. "What is it?"

"I'm not sure the pony fits the lord and master image as well as that spectacular gray mare did."

Fergus brought his pony up beside hers. "There's no mount more surefooted and hardy in the hills than these wee beasties. They're very strong, too – they'll easily carry a full-grown stag of over 500 pounds." He paused. "I forgot to ask if you ride."

"I'm no great horsewoman, but I can just about manage something this size." They headed out of the castle under the archway, the two shaggy black dogs trotting at the ponies' heels. "At the English houses I stayed in, my reluctance to join in the fox hunt provided great amusement."

This lady was sophisticated, accustomed to dealing with society's upper echelons. He needed to remember that. Had any of those fine English gentlemen been her lover? No doubt they'd desired her. Any laddie would.

He'd recognized straightaway that she was temperamental and stubborn and headstrong, and not at all the kind of lassie he usually took on. Now that he'd known her a day and a half, those qualities made her the most exciting woman he'd ever met.

Their affair wouldn't be a simple matter, but it seemed Fergus was in the mood for fireworks.

Marina should have expected Fergus to offer himself as her escort. She'd read the usual masculine signals that he considered her his exclusive concern.

She should be annoyed at yet more high-handedness from her host. Part of her was. Yet part of her was flattered and...thrilled.

As they wended their way into the hills behind the castle, she jogged along behind him. The track wasn't wide enough to accommodate their ponies side by side.

"I suppose if I insist on going to Skye, you'll come along as my guide there, too."

Those wide, straight shoulders moved in a dismissive shrug. "A good friend told me that once someone saves your life, the two of you are linked forever more."

"That's an alarming thought," she said, her tone dry.

An amused grunt greeted her comment, although she hadn't been entirely joking. "Aye, it is at that."

"So if you're to dog my footsteps, what is the point of my leaving Achnasheen?"

She felt the Mackinnon's brief backward glance like a knife. "Is it so bad here?"

He didn't look where he was going. She wasn't exactly steering her pony either. With its broad back and swaying gait, the pony made her feel like she was in a boat, rocking on a gentle swell.

"I don't like being a prisoner."

"Is that really how ye feel?"

"If I'm trapped and can't leave by my own free will, how else would you describe it?"

Taking her pony by surprise, he pulled up. There was almost a nose-to-tail collision.

He turned in the saddle to face her. "Marina, I'm hellishly sorry if ye believe that's the truth."

The bristling silence extended. After a few seconds, she sighed.

"Oh, it's not the truth, and you know it," she admitted grudgingly. "And given your kindness to my father and me, that was an ungracious thing to say. I don't understand why I have to assert myself against you all the time. I've met overbearing men before and handled them with a modicum of tact, while still managing to get my own way."

"Overbearing, am I? Ye don't pull your punches, do you?" Humor lit his eyes to bright silver. "I've never met a lassie who wants to fight me the way you do."

She looked at him curiously. "In your whole life, no woman has ever stood up to you? What about your mother?"

"My mother was a sweet wee thing, absolutely helpless once my father passed away, and no' that effective when he was alive, if truth be told."

The reasons Allan Ramsay had chosen to paint the pretty blonde in that languorous pose became clearer. "And your sister?"

"Sisters. There's two of them." He shrugged. "Much the same. After my father's death, I became head of the family, so both of them grew up obeying me." His lips twitched. "It helps that I'm always right."

Marina rolled her eyes. "Don't make me hit you."

"I might enjoy that."

Startled, she looked at him. "What?"

The gray gaze remained unwavering. "Ye heard me."

Unwise to pursue the subject, when she had a whole day of his company ahead. "How long have you been laird?"

He clicked his tongue at his pony. It ambled on, and hers followed, the horses as obedient to his will as everything else in the glen was. Damn them, and damn him.

"About twenty years."

She frowned. She'd assumed he was about her age, but this put the lie to that idea. "You must have been little more than a boy when you inherited."

"We grow up fast in the Highlands."

He avoided her question, which was interesting. "How old were you, Mackinnon?"

"Nine."

Shock silenced her. Nine years old? He'd been a mere child. How had a child shouldered all this responsibility? His father had left things in a mess, she gathered, and his mother didn't sound like she'd been any help at all. In fact, she sounded like just one more duty. He hadn't told her his sisters were younger than he was, but something made her think they were. More duty.

He glanced back with the familiar sardonic expression. *Maledizione*, even on the stubby little pony, he looked like a prince. "Nothing to say?"

"I'm trying to imagine being a child and having so much care thrust upon me." No wonder he'd grown up arrogant and sure of his abilities. She couldn't approve of his attitudes, but she came to understand the reasons behind them.

"Och, it wasnae so bad as all that. I had trustees, and there was plenty of experience and goodwill among the local folk."

"But you were still the Mackinnon, head of the clan."

"Aye. It's a privilege."

"And an obligation."

"That, too."

Marina chewed over what she'd heard. "All right, I can see that the estate isn't overrun with women ready to put you in your place." She frowned in thought. "You said you go to Inverness and Edinburgh. Somewhere away from Achnasheen, you must have run into an outspoken woman."

The sardonic light deepened. "I've even been to London."

"London?"

"I went to a few balls and the opera, and a place called Almack's that was heaving with giggly debutantes. Dreadful crush, hot as Hades, and the waiters only served lukewarm lemonade. What sort of drink is that for a red-blooded laddie, I ask ye? No wonder the Sassenachs are all so lily-livered."

"Does that include the ladies?"

He made a dismissive gesture and faced the front again so she couldn't see his expression. "All the lassies I danced with seemed to have a proper understanding of a lady's role in life. None of them tried to take the lead when I waltzed with them, anyway."

She narrowed her eyes at that long, straight back in its loose white shirt, wishing she could find some physical imperfection to mar the magnificent sight. "You're just saying that so I'll bite back."

He cast an amused look over one broad shoulder. "When ye puff up your feathers like an angry hen, you're awfully bonny, Marina."

With a start, she realized that this wasn't the first time he'd called her Marina. "I didn't give you permission to use my Christian name," she said stiffly, knowing she sounded like a fool.

"Och, Signorina Lucchetti is such a mouthful for a poor, ignorant Highlander."

"He'll get used to it," she said, still grappling with what she'd learned about him this morning. "At least one of your friends must have married a girl with something to say for herself. Not every woman in Scotland is a doormat. I refuse to believe it."

He shook his head. "My neighbors' wives all ken their place. My two closest friends are yet to marry. One's Laird of Glen Lyon down on the coast near Oban, and the other's Laird of Invertavey a little north of here."

"And do they also resist the concept of a woman who can think for herself?"

"Perhaps they're not quite as convinced as I am. Actually I can bring an exception to mind, now you mention it. Hamish at Glen Lyon has a dragon of a mamma, who writes books and sets the wee Sassenach gentlemen in Parliament jumping. She's a terrifying monster. Ye wouldnae want to be like her, Marina. She's unnatural."

Marina choked back a laugh at the theatrical dread he injected into his description. "And what about the Laird of Inver…"

"Tavey."

"Yes. Him. What about his mother?"

"Och, she was a wild one. I never met her. She ran away with a soldier when Diarmid was sixteen. She died of a fever in Jamaica a year later."

"Oh, how sad."

"Aye. And an example of what happens when a man's no' master in his own house."

She supposed the Mackinnon would look at it that way. "I like the sound of Hamish's mother."

He sighed. "Aye, I thought you might. You're sisters under the skin."

"Do I terrify you, too, Mackinnon?" She rather liked the idea.

"Aye, you're the stuff of nightmares."

She laughed. "In that case, are you sure you don't want to send me on my way?"

He turned his pony up the hill, following a track she couldn't see. "Och, a man has to face his fears if he wants to prove his courage."

"Very commendable," she said drily.

They climbed higher. She'd been so fascinated—and horrified—by the conversation, she'd hardly paid attention to her surroundings.

Which was absurd, given her sole reason for being in Scotland was to find suitable scenes to paint.

The hills rose ahead of them, stretching into the blue sky. A pretty haze of purplish pink covered them. Heather, she knew. And a brown and green patchwork of bracken. After yesterday's rain, the colors were sharp and clear.

A waterfall tumbled over the escarpment above. She glanced back, surprised to see how far they'd ascended. Below, the castle looked like an illustration from a fairy story. In the distance, islands floated in the sparkling blue sea.

Coming north, she'd seen many pretty scenes, but this was the loveliest yet. Perhaps painting here rather than on Skye might prove a smart move.

At least for her art.

Her fingers weren't tingling to paint yet, although the shapes of the landscape sank into her mind and started to create patterns. Instead, she couldn't help going over her discussion with the Mackinnon.

What must it have been like to take over as master of Achnasheen at such an absurdly young age? At nine, she'd been playing with dolls, although her lifelong obsession with painting was already stirring. The Mackinnon had not only been master of the estate, but a pillar of strength for his mother and sisters, who sounded like a spineless trio.

Marina was so lost in her brown study, she didn't realize the Mackinnon had reined in on a wide ledge to let her catch up to him. "I'm worried. You're not usually so quiet."

"You haven't seen me at work yet," she retorted.

"Do ye truly feel I've tricked you into staying, and you can't get away? I'd hate that to be the case."

She'd almost forgotten their earlier conversation. Still, it was a troubling issue. "If I insisted I wanted to leave on my own today, you'd arrange it?"

"I wouldnae let you go on your own. Remember, I saved your life. You belong to me now."

Something about those words set up a traitorous quiver in her stomach. "Be serious, Mackinnon."

"I am." He frowned. "But aye, if you must go, I'll see you to somewhere safe, and you can plan the rest of your tour from there. I'll stay around long enough to make sure ye hire a coachman who knows where he's going. I'll also give you introductions to people who can help along your way."

She hid a smile. This was outside his remit—despite his absurd claim to be responsible for her, they remained strangers. She'd already noticed that a strong streak of protectiveness ran alongside his penchant for dishing out orders.

"So I'm free to go?"

"Do ye want to leave your father?"

"You didn't answer my question."

"Aye," he said with audible reluctance. "You're a foolish and headstrong lassie to want to travel on by yourself, given everything ye need is here already. It's unfortunate we turned the dungeons into wine cellars a hundred years ago, so I cannae chain you to the wall until you see sense."

"You could lock me in my room."

He shot her a disgruntled glance. "Don't give me ideas."

"Very well," she said.

Dark red brows lowered toward that regal nose. "What does that mean?" he said with a bite of annoyance. "That it's time to go back to the castle and order up the traveling chaise?"

She smiled slowly, loving that for once she had the upper hand. "No, Mackinnon, it means I'm pleased to accept your hospitality, now I know it's not in the nature of a prison sentence. I look forward to giving my father some company as he recovers."

It was childish, but delicious to relish the Mackinnon's growl of frustration. "You're bonny, Marina Lucchetti, but you're a wee besom, too."

He didn't need to translate the word. She got the gist. At least he called her pretty as well as troublesome. "I don't like people trying to compel me."

"So I gather," he said, the line of his mouth unhappy. "Now if Her Majesty will deign to agree, there's a hillock over the next rise that's a braw spot to stop for breakfast."

"I bow to your local knowledge," she said sweetly.

"At least ye bow to something," he muttered. He coaxed his pony forward, and Marina's followed without her bidding.

After a pause, she asked the question that had been worrying her more than her right to leave—although she appreciated having her freedom confirmed. "Don't you get bored with all these women who agree with everything you say?"

He looked back. "Not really."

Marina supposed that talk was the last thing this virile man wanted from a woman. The thought was strangely stirring, although she was sure it had to be too early in the morning to fall victim to sensual yearnings.

"Well, you should," she said, annoyed with him, annoyed with herself.

He gave a short laugh. "I'll say one thing—I havenae been bored with ye yet, lassie."

"Could you be any more patronizing?" she snapped. "And, no, you don't have to answer that."

Feeling cross, she urged her pony to trot past Fergus's horse. Suddenly, it seemed too humiliating to trail after the Mackinnon, like a dinghy bobbing in a yacht's wake.

CHAPTER EIGHT

Fergus glanced over to where Marina perched on a tussock, painting the view. Her traveling set of watercolors lay open on the grass beside her, and Macushla and Brecon stretched at her feet, snoozing in the afternoon sun. The laird wasn't this lassie's only admirer at Achnasheen.

She'd unbuttoned that fearsomely masculine jacket to reveal a plain white shirt beneath. Her hair was a silky black tangle on the back of her neck, half undone from this morning's tidy chignon. When she was concentrating, she tugged at it, he'd noticed.

He'd soon realized that she hadn't exaggerated her devotion to capturing the landscape on paper. During their frequent stops for her to make quick sketches, he watched her disappear into a world of her own. Over the short time he'd known her, he'd become used to the crackle of attraction, sparking away beneath their every interaction. When she vanished into her art, he might as well be a tree or a rock.

In fact, he felt like he added up to less than a tree or rock. At least they contributed something to her finished painting.

He wasn't used to women ignoring him. He didn't much like it, especially when Marina was the focus of all his attention. Perhaps she might be right to accuse him of conceit.

Fergus had to give her points for being a gallant companion on a vigorous Highland outing. They'd been up and down some steep slopes today. Now and again, she'd had to get off her pony and lead it. She'd coped with bogs and thistles and freezing burns. When they'd stopped for breakfast, she'd sat on the ground, and she'd leaned against a rock to eat when they'd had lunch.

He knew this first day was just a chance for her to look for scenes she could paint to fulfill her commission to the Duke of Portofino. She spoke of her noble patron, as she spoke of the aristocratic families in England, with a casualness that indicated her ease in society's highest levels. Yet she made no claim to being anything more than a woman who worked for her living. He loved that her talent provided its own badge of honor, even if her confidence in that talent made her far too contrary.

By now, he was almost accustomed to Marina taking the opposite view to his about everything he'd grown up to accept. He hadn't missed her shock at how young he'd been when he became laird, nor her appalled reaction when he struggled to name a woman who set her will against his.

Good God, damn few men did. Diarmid and Hamish were both laddies of decided opinions, but most of the time, they took the same sensible, masculine perspective on things that Fergus did, so there was little conflict.

Life must have been saving all its opposition for the moment this unusual woman stumbled across his path.

He turned his attention from his exasperating lassie to the magnificent view across the Hebrides. This was one of his favorite spots on the estate. From the high ledge, the ground fell away steeply to the sea. A pattern of islands spread across the blue, and the sun shone bright on Skye's strange, bare Cuillins across the water. If Marina looked north, she'd see the hills of Harris. If she looked south, she'd see Rum and the other Small Isles, with a glimpse of Mull further south again.

She must like it, too. She'd lingered to complete several sketches. He should be bored, but the day was so fine and warm, and the chance to observe his fascinating guest without her prickling up was such a gift, that he didn't mind the lack of activity.

And much as he hated to admit it, she'd given him a lot to think about. Not least what he'd like to do to her before she went back to Italy and her retinue of dukes and counts.

Fergus lounged back in the thick grass and watched a pair of golden eagles perform lazy circles in the sky above him. As his eyes closed, for some odd reason, he remembered that eagles mated for life.

When Fergus opened his eyes, the sun had moved toward the west. He was warm, and drowsiness weighted his limbs. Sitting on the grass facing him was a lovely woman with a touch of sunburn across her slanted cheekbones and on the bridge of her straight nose. She'd brought a hat, but he noticed that most of the time, she forgot to wear it. Her sketchbook lay open on her lap, and she was watching him with curious eyes.

A tender smile curved his lips, and he brushed his hand across the hint of color. "The sun has caught ye, lassie," he murmured.

As if it was the most natural thing in the world, he slid his fingers behind her neck and drew her down until her lips met his.

Her mouth was soft, and he tasted her gasp of surprise. Sweet warmth flooded him as her lips fluttered against his.

The muscles beneath his hand tensed, and he waited for her to pull away. Then in a movement so subtle, if he hadn't been touching her, he would never have recognized it, she shifted to a more comfortable angle and leaned closer. Her mouth turned even softer, as she joined in the kiss.

Satisfaction filled him. His hold on her nape firmed, and he swept his tongue along the seam of her lips in a request to enter the honeyed interior.

For a long moment, her lips remained closed. The delay before she yielded gave him a chance to drink in a wealth of splendid details. The heat of the afternoon sun on this sheltered dip in the hillside. The loose strands of silky hair tickling his fingers. The scents of dusty heather in the air, and floral soap rising from her skin. The lush cushion of her lips.

With a muffled sound of pleasure, that sumptuous mouth opened, and her tongue flickered out to meet his. The contact was almost shy, but it made his heart expand with longing for more. Growling deep in his chest, he caught her waist with his free hand. He rolled over until she lay beneath him.

Now he'd captured her ready for ravishing, the kiss caught fire and he tasted her fully. She was luscious as toffee. More sweetness flared into passion when her tongue danced with his, and her arms slid around his back to hold him closer.

She gave herself up with a wholehearted voluptuousness that beggared his experience. He'd kissed plenty of lassies, even bedded a few. Never had he lost himself in a sensual mist, the way he did kissing Marina.

It was inevitable that he should start to want more. Wondered if perhaps he didn't need to negotiate too hard to find his way into her bed after all. Would this glorious kiss in the open air lead without hindrance to possessing her long, lissome body?

He sucked the tip of her tongue between his lips and placed his hand on the delicious rise of her breast. Under the fine lawn of shirt and shift, he traced the wanton peak of her nipple. He scraped her gently with his fingernail, and anticipation rose as she jerked in response. He did it again, then caught the beaded tip between thumb and index finger and rolled and squeezed.

She moaned into his mouth and arched up. He settled between her thighs, cursing the hampering skirts between him and where he wanted to be.

When he raised his head to look down into her face, her eyes were heavy with passion. Her mouth was red and swollen from his kisses, and parted to give him a glimpse of small white teeth. Her skin glowed with awakening desire. She was the most gorgeous sight Fergus had ever beheld.

He gave her another quick kiss, although he could already see the dreamy pleasure draining away, replaced by a troubled expression.

"*Basta*," she said unsteadily. "*Basta*."

He frowned. "Are you calling me a..."

As he'd hoped, the frown dissolved in humor. "No. Enough. *Basta* means 'enough.'"

In his opinion, he'd achieved anything but enough. He should have guessed he was too optimistic when he imagined this would be simple.

He shifted to the side to rest on one elbow and stare down at her. Her thick black hair was ruffled, and her tight nipples pressed against her shirt. The memory of touching her there pounded through him like thunder.

By God, he was ready for her. Hard as a bloody caber at the Portree Highland Games.

"That was foolhardy." Her gaze swept down his body. She'd see how excited he was, too. Under his kilt, he might have a chance of concealing his arousal. Trousers weren't so forgiving.

"Perhaps." He dug up a smile and smoothed the strands of midnight hair clinging to her wide forehead. "But I've wanted to do that since I first saw ye."

The pleasure that brightened her face at his admission made him kiss her again. This time her push on his shoulders was more emphatic. "This won't do, Mackinnon."

"Fergus," he said softly.

She pursed her lips in frustration. It made him want to kiss her again. "Safer to call you Mackinnon."

"Who cares about safety?"

"I do."

He traced a line down her cheek. Her skin was soft and smooth. He couldn't wait to see the rest of it. Surely soon he would.

"Are you saying ye didn't think about kissing me, too?" He'd thought about more than kissing, but didn't want to push his luck.

She lifted a hand to bat his caressing fingers away. "You jolly well know I have. That doesn't mean we should give into temptation."

Lord above, she was pretty. Even when she was cross, she was pretty. Particularly then, because the heat sparking in those lustrous dark eyes made him think of a different heat that he and she could conjure together. "Why not? Do ye have a lover who owns your loyalty? You haven't said so."

"Why on earth would I say anything?"

Displeasure pricked at his arrogance. "Because ye know I'm interested." He paused and stared at her, surprised at how important her answer was. He'd wanted her before, but since kissing her, he was in a fever to have her. "Is there a lover, Marina?"

Her eyes flickered down. She had such lush eyelashes.

"No," she mumbled.

"Not for me either. And ye have no husband."

"No."

"And I have no wife. If we want one another, why should we resist?"

Her eyes opened and settled on him with a cynical light that placed another puncture in his satisfaction. Why didn't Fergus remember that talking to this perverse creature was sure to tie him into knots? He should have kept kissing her until she gave in.

"I'm available. You're available. The nights are getting cold. We may as well start going at each other like rabbits?"

Hell, now he was annoyed, and he'd been in such a good mood after his nap and kissing her. He sat up and scowled. "You're twisting my words."

She sat up, too, and he regretted the foot of space stretching between them. She'd been so lovely and loose-limbed in his arms. Now as she pulled her knees up to her chest and curled her arms around them, she was closed up like a barricaded door. "Tell me what you want."

You.

His exasperation couldn't change that. In fact, every word she spoke stirred the urge to kiss that insolent mouth over and over until she gave up the fight.

"I want ye to be my mistress," he said baldly.

As he should have expected, the declaration sparked no excitement in that midnight gaze. She wasn't the sort of lassie to swoon at hearing a man express his preference. "Because I'm an independent woman with no husband to control me, and therefore I share my favors with all and sundry?"

"Damn it, Marina, why do ye want to fight with me?" He ran an impatient hand through his hair. "You asked me a question, and I answered you. There's no need to attack me. I'm not your enemy."

Actually he had a suspicion she was crabby because she suffered the same sexual frustration he did. It didn't contribute to an equable temper.

"I apologize, Mackinnon." She sighed, and he saw the tension ease from those tight shoulders. "I've had to discourage overenthusiastic suitors before."

Real anger, as different from his huff with her as a candle from a forest fire, stabbed his belly. "I'd like to beat the presumptuous bastards to a pulp."

She gave a shaky laugh. "Oh, dear, I'm glad you weren't there, then. A lot of them ended up becoming my patrons."

"I hope they kept their hands to themselves once ye said no."

"Mostly," she said, and raised her hand to stop him snarling. "I've learned how to deflect unwelcome advances."

What about welcome ones? It was absurd to resent her sophistication, when that very sophistication meant there was a chance she might become his mistress. He couldn't make this offer to a well-bred virgin. The only way he'd get an ingénue, like those girls at Almack's, into his bed was via marriage.

"Is that what you're doing now?"

"*Porca miseria*, stop fishing for compliments." She sighed again, with exasperation this time. "You know quite well I liked kissing you."

"But you're not happy I want ye in my bed?"

"I wouldn't even say that." She lifted her hand again, before he could reach for her and take up where he'd left off.

Fergus spread his hands in a helpless gesture, which was something he didn't make a habit of doing. For once in his life, he felt completely at sea. "Dinna imagine I jump on every woman who falls into my clutches either. I'm discreet with my liaisons—and selective."

Marina arched an ironic brow. So far, his wooing wasn't overwhelming her, devil take her. "I should be flattered?"

"No. Aye. No." He growled. "I dinna bring women to Achnasheen."

"It's beneath the chieftain to play the rake?"

"Aye, something like that."

"But you must have had affairs."

He shifted uncomfortably. The women he pursued never put him through an inquisition. About anything, let alone his conquests. They'd been a complacent lot. Until now.

"I'm a red-blooded man. I willnae pretend I come to you a novice, Marina." He paused. "I've a friendly widow in Inverness who's been kind enough to favor me. She's getting married again, so our affair has ended, although we parted as friends. Over the years, there have been a couple of lassies in Edinburgh. I'm not a rakehell."

"*Dio*, so you're at a loose end, and I'll do?"

He launched into an angry denial, before he caught the provocative glint in her gypsy eyes. "Ye wee besom, you're teasing me."

"It's not hard."

Something else was, but he refrained from pointing that out. "What I'm trying to say is I'm offering ye an arrangement I've never offered another woman. And you're not the only one with a care for reputation. If we come together while you're here, we'll need to be careful, for the sake of both our good names."

"You've thought about this." She didn't sound as if she liked the idea.

"Aye, every minute since I first saw you." He paused and spoke the stark truth. "I have a powerful hunger for ye, lassie. Give me a chance to feed that appetite while you're here. A month. Two. Otherwise I'll go mad, if you mean to stay within reach but won't let me touch you. Say you'll agree. Say yes, Marina."

"Fergus..."

At last she spoke his name. Nor did he miss the longing his passionate words lit in her expression. Anticipation began to pulse in his gut. Had he convinced her to take him as her lover?

CHAPTER NINE

Marina drew a shaky breath and strove for calmness. It was difficult when Fergus's kisses—and the lure of more—left her giddy. During those heady minutes in his arms, he'd swept her up into the whirlwind. After an experience like that, it was difficult for a girl to find her feet once she landed back on solid ground.

She made herself meet his gaze. Never had she imagined gray eyes could burn like that. As he stared at her, the heat seared her skin. Tightening her grip on her knees, she told herself that taking this attraction any further was impossible.

"This is lunacy. We don't get along. There's nothing in the world we agree on."

Another half-smile. "We agree on one thing— we want one another."

Marina didn't bother denying it. The lie would be too coy for words. The temptation of being close to him without touching him became too much. She stumbled to her feet and stepped toward the rim of the escarpment. Her eyes registered nothing of the breathtaking view. All she saw was the ferocious intensity of Fergus's expression, as he proclaimed his desire with a fearlessness that threatened to melt her very bones to syrup.

"What are ye thinking, lassie?" he asked behind her. She hadn't heard him rise and approach her. *Diavolo*, he could move like a ghost when he wanted to.

She turned to face him, feeling less vulnerable now she was standing. "There was another girl at the art school in Florence. Her name was Rosa Sabattini."

Marina waited for him to ask why she told him this, but he folded his arms over that impressive chest and gave her his complete attention. He was the wrong man for her in every way that mattered, but she also liked so much about him. Not least the way he listened to her, despite his conviction that he was always right. And his patience. He was willing to wait for what he wanted.

Although given she was what he wanted, perhaps that wasn't an altogether reassuring quality.

"She was talented. And pretty. A year younger than me." She swallowed to ease her tight throat. Even after a dozen years, this was hard to talk about. "Then one day, she wasn't there anymore."

Fergus didn't interrupt, and his eyes were somber as they settled on her. She saw he already guessed where this story ended.

"They pulled her body out of the Arno." Her voice lowered to a whisper. "She was going to have a baby and couldn't bear the shame."

"What a tragic story," Fergus said, russet brows lowering over his gray eyes as he assessed what she'd told him. After a pause, he went on. "I'm sorry about your friend, but you're stronger than that."

Although the afternoon wasn't cold, she wrapped her arms around herself. "Am I?"

"You don't want to conceive my bairn. There are ways of making that unlikely."

"I don't want to lose the career I've taken years to build."

A crease marked his forehead. "Surely with your other lovers…"

A painful blush flooded her cheeks. He hadn't understood as well as she thought he had. "You're not listening."

Shock descended over his features, and he faltered back as if she'd struck him. "You're saying…"

Marina licked dry lips and lowered her arms to her sides, clenching her fists. She'd never had such a discussion in her life. *Cavolo*, she hoped never to have another. "No other lovers."

His frown deepened. "When ye kissed me…"

Embarrassment had her shifting from one foot to the other. She almost began to wish she'd let his kisses find their inevitable conclusion, to save her from having to talk about this.

Dio l'aiuti, did that mean she was on the verge of taking this man as her lover?

She spoke in a rush, wanting to get it over and done with. "I had an adolescent romance with one of the other students at the school. A very nice boy called Paolo Martini. We used to kiss in the Boboli Gardens and talk about what life would be like when we were both famous."

"But nothing more." It wasn't a question, and she realized Fergus at last pieced together what she'd told him. He didn't look shocked anymore. Instead he looked thoughtful, almost…calculating. "So all those gentlemen who approached ye…"

"I remained dedicated to my art." She flinched when she realized she used the past tense.

"I misunderstood. I assumed you were experienced."

"I know." She cast him a quick glance, then looked away. "Does this change your mind about wanting me as your mistress?"

When she looked at him again, that half-smile was back. "Dinna be daft, lassie."

Was that relief loosening her limbs? It would be easier, *safer*, if her confidences gave him a distaste for her.

"When I started gaining a reputation as an artist, there was too much at stake for me to gamble it all on a love affair. It isn't just Rosa, although she's example enough of what happens to girls who risk everything for a man's sake. I need to keep my good name, if only to stop my patrons from becoming my pursuers."

"If nobody has ye, you remain out of reach as a woman, while you can reign as an artist."

He did understand. "I told you, one breath of scandal, and everything I've worked for disappears. The world won't see me as a talented painter, fit to vie with the men. Instead, they'll dismiss me as one more silly, fallible woman who didn't know what was good for her."

Fergus moved closer and took her hand. Warmth surged up her arm and settled around her heart in a way that warned her how perilously close she was to giving in.

"So you're telling me that while you're tempted, you mean to say no because the dangers are too great."

She stared up into his face. She'd never met anyone like him. "We'd be impossible together."

"We'd be exciting."

"We'd end up wanting to kill one another."

"Or each time we tumbled into bed, we'd die of pleasure."

Probably both. She didn't underestimate the physical attraction raging between them. Even now, when he wasn't doing anything overtly seductive, she wanted to press herself against that tall, lean body and run her hands over his skin. She wanted to kiss him and suck his tongue into her mouth. She wanted to shove him back onto the grass and beg him to show her everything that her nun-like devotion to art had so far denied her.

The flaring heat in his eyes told her he guessed the trend of her thoughts. And he approved.

She broke their gaze to stare down to where her hand lay in his. The choice should be clear. Compared to everything she had at stake, what did it matter that the merest sight of Fergus Mackinnon set her heart dancing?

"Are ye still in love with Paolo?"

The question was so surprising, her attention jerked back to his face. "Paolo?"

"The other art student."

"Of course not. I was only sixteen." Was Fergus jealous? How delicious. "He's married with six children now, anyway."

"Good." Fergus's grip on her hand tightened. "I don't want you thinking of any man but me."

Frowning, Marina tried without success to withdraw. "Fergus, I've told you why I must say no."

His expression remained serious. "You've told me why you're careful, and why I must be careful with ye."

He lifted her fingers to his lips and kissed them. Heat engulfed her. Another warning of the power he'd wield if she broke the rules of a lifetime.

"*Per carità*, stop it," she said, as he kissed her fingers again.

She couldn't blame him for ignoring her command. Her protest sounded like a breathy invitation for more.

"You've said you don't want to risk a bairn. I'll do my best to see that doesn't happen." He lowered her hand but kept hold of it. "You've said ye don't want gossip to stain your name. Here at Achnasheen, we're a world away from fashionable society. Who's going to spread tales to your patrons? You have my vow I'll never tell another soul that we came together, and I'm credited as a man of my word."

Marina knew he was. She mightn't agree with him about much, but she respected his integrity. "We've only known one another three days," she said almost despairingly.

"So ye want time to think?"

"I've told you..." She cringed at her voice's continuing lack of conviction.

He raised his free hand to cradle the side of her face. Straight after he kissed her, he'd touched her like this. Glancing little contacts that spoke of affection and tenderness rather than seduction.

Although they were powerfully seductive, too. As he was well aware.

"Haven't ye been lonely, Marina? It's all well and good, living for your art, but brushes and paints and canvas willnae keep you warm at night."

She had been lonely. Since meeting Fergus, she'd realized how much. She suspected he'd been lonely, too. There was only room for one at the top of his mountain. She couldn't dismiss the picture of a brave nine-year-old boy setting aside his grief for his dead father and taking charge of his family and estate.

"It's dangerous to listen to you," she whispered, as the warmth of his palm on her face curled through her like a drift of scented smoke. "It's dangerous to kiss you."

He stepped closer, changing his hold as he angled her up for another kiss. This was gentle, persuasion rather than insistence. Yet the same magic transported her to paradise. His kisses claimed her very essence. It was many years since those adolescent experiments with Paolo, but she didn't remember such a profound reaction.

She did however remember the way a passionate kiss made her stomach twist and ache with desire. She remembered how frustrated her sixteen-year-old self had been when Paolo got her all stirred up, and they'd both been too frightened to take the next step.

That hadn't changed. In fact, it was worse.

She leaned into Fergus, seeking more heat, more pressure. But he, *il cattivo*, kept the contact essentially innocent. She was mad to resent his restraint, given she was the one who placed limits on what they did.

"Aye, it is dangerous." Like her, he whispered, although she doubted if there was another person between here and Iceland. "But it's delightful, too."

This time when she tried to break away, Fergus let her go. Perhaps because he knew that, despite her misgivings, she wasn't ready to forsake this perilous enchantment.

She raised trembling hands to burning cheeks. "*Madonna*, my head is spinning."

Then came the fatal moment. He smiled at her as he'd smiled just once before. As though she was a treasure he'd unexpectedly found in a field and that he meant to cherish forever.

For more smiles like that, any risk might be worth it. Perhaps denying herself the chance to know him as only a lover could was the sin, not yielding a chastity that in Fergus's presence seemed more burden than blessing.

"I'll no' trouble ye with more now." He paused and tilted an inquiring eyebrow in her direction. "Unless you've reached a decision, that is."

Marina should give him a categorical refusal. She should stick to the path that provided her with success and independence and a future. Especially as a love affair between two such disparate individuals as she and the Mackinnon was sure to be a catastrophe.

But, *cavolo*, he was handsome standing before her with that quizzical expression on his face. And he kissed like a dream. This was the first time she'd tasted adult passion, and its power left her astonished.

She should say no to Fergus's proposition, but by heaven, she was tempted to say yes.

With a quaking breath, she buried her trembling hands in her skirts. "No, no decision," she said in a faint voice, loathing her cowardice.

CHAPTER TEN

When Marina and Fergus joined her father for dinner in his room, she was sure Papa must guess something significant had happened to her today. It was lucky that he was used to her distraction when she was wrapped up in her work.

Whereas for once in her life, painting was the last thing on her mind.

Could she become a man's mistress? For all the reasons she'd given Fergus, she'd long recognized that a woman who wished to pursue a career as an artist must remain chaste.

Rosa's death retained its power to inspire nightmares. What Marina hadn't told him was that she was there when they pulled her friend's body from the Arno. Ever since, that pale, waterlogged corpse had served as a warning of the price a woman paid for passion.

But that was before Marina discovered how powerful passion could be. This afternoon's kisses had swept her into a new and fiery world, radiant with heat and excitement and pleasure.

And all Fergus had done so far was kiss her. Imagine what else she had to discover.

If he'd made demands, she'd have no difficulty refusing him. But devil take the Mackinnon, for once he didn't order her around. He left it to her to decide—and she was far from convinced she had the strength to walk away without sampling more.

Her mind recognized the wise choice. Her traitorous senses insisted that desire must rule.

The internal argument continued all evening, as she battled to pretend she was the same independent woman who had set out to paint this morning. The fine dinner stuck in her throat, and she heard hardly a word of the conversation between her father and the man who wanted to become her lover.

But she watched him. *Dio,* how she watched him. All her life, her soul had fed on beauty, and the Mackinnon was an extraordinarily beautiful man. On a physical level, she couldn't choose a more perfect specimen.

One strong, elegant hand made a slashing gesture, as he described a banquet he'd attended in Edinburgh Castle. Her gaze fastened on that spare, almost austere face with its subtle hints of humor and intelligence. That long, lean, efficient body...

A shudder ran through her as she imagined lying beneath that body while he pushed inside her. A heavy pulse set up in the secret hollow between her legs, and she gave a surreptitious wiggle in search of relief.

Most of the night, Fergus had treated her as a casual acquaintance. He seemed happy to talk to her father about places they'd traveled, and the great families in Italy who had opened their homes to Marina in recognition of her talent. Warning enough of how much she risked, if she trusted herself to this man's honor.

But while she'd made no sound and the chairs at Achnasheen were far too sturdy to creak, Fergus must have sensed some change in her. When he raised his gray gaze, she had to bite back a gasp.

At times tonight, his ease had made her wonder if she'd imagined that sizzling encounter on the hillside. But one flickering, incendiary glance told her that he burned, too.

Every drop of moisture dried from her mouth, and she had to look away or betray herself. To hide her trembling hands, she made a great show of picking up her sketchbook and choosing a pencil.

But art couldn't distract her from this dilemma.

She'd sworn she'd be no man's mistress. Yet with every breath she took, she wanted Fergus Mackinnon more.

The mullioned windows behind her opened on hills shrouded in purple twilight. A gentle breeze brushed over the bare skin of her arms and shoulders like a lover's touch.

Would she soon know a real lover?

Fergus watched Marina struggle against the impulse to stare at him. He fought the same battle. He knew if he gave in, he'd look too much like a starving dog slavering over a steak.

An hour ago, Kirsty had come in to light the candles. He was almost sorry to see the maid. He'd loved watching the soft light of the gloaming on Marina's face. Although it turned out that candlelight was just as fascinating. He was bristlingly aware of Marina's every movement, although for discretion's sake, he'd chosen a chair on the opposite side of the bed from where she sat under the window.

Ugolino seemed oblivious to the charged atmosphere, but the canny daughter had a canny father. Fergus wouldn't be at all surprised if Marina's father was awake to the unspoken tension in the room.

He was damned glad he'd braved the icy water to get her luggage. The sight of her in the pink silk gown cut low across that enticing bosom made every second in the raging burn worthwhile. A cream lace shawl draped around her bare arms, and she'd twisted her heavy weight of hair into an elaborate arrangement. The style emphasized the noble lines of her jaw and her long neck. She might belong to the middle ranks of society, but right now, concentrating on her drawing, she looked like a queen.

As deft fingers guided the pencil, light flickered gold on her shining black hair and found fascinating hollows under a cheekbone and in the dip of her collarbone. He itched to free her hair, so it fell like a cape around her naked shoulders. His hands would smooth that silky mass, slide through to explore the thrust of a pale breast...

Her eyelashes fluttered up, as if she guessed his thoughts. Hell, she probably did. Large black eyes met his for a breathtaking second, and he could swear he saw a longing to match his own.

Before he could be sure, she snapped her sketchbook shut. "Papa, I'm going to bed. If the weather holds, I've got another day of work in the hills tomorrow."

Fergus stood and crossed to the window to look out on the stars, bright as fire. The starlit skies above Achnasheen put him in mind of Marina's eyes. That same air of eternal mystery.

"Aye, I think we're in for a spell of sunshine," he said, although he'd known that before he shifted. He didn't have to check the sky to predict the weather in this glen.

But keeping his distance over these last hours had been torture. Now he dared a surreptitious caress down Marina's neck as he turned back into the room. Craving blasted him, and he was close enough to hear a shaken gasp as she exhaled. She didn't look at him, but her hand clenched on the sketchbook.

"Were you happy with your work today?" her father asked.

"I think it has...potential," she said, and Fergus bit back a groan as the corner of her lush mouth curled. "I can't be sure yet."

Teasing wench. Fergus liked her father, but right now he wished that good gentleman to Hades. Then he could seize the lassie in his arms and kiss all the nonsense out of her. At the thought, his hands closed into fists.

"That's good," Ugolino said.

"Isn't it?" she said, and Fergus caught the hint of irony in her answer.

"We'll leave ye to rest, then, *signore*," Fergus said.

"*Buona notte*, Fergus. It's been a delightful evening."

It had. And it had also been the vilest torment.

Marina gathered her shawl about her and rose to kiss her father's cheek. "*Buona notte,* Papa. We're making another early start, but I'll see you tomorrow night. Kirsty said the Reverend Angus is coming to play chess with you, so you'll have some company."

"*Si*, and I'm sure Maggie will be on hand to nag at me."

"There's nothing she likes better than a new patient," Fergus said.

Surely it wouldn't be too outrageous to take Marina's arm, as she turned to leave the room. Yet the result was anything but innocent when he curved his fingers around her warm flesh.

How he loved to touch her. With even this constrained contact, he felt the energy pulsing inside her. How she'd blaze when she gave herself to him.

He closed her father's door behind them and walked the few steps down the corridor toward her room. He lasted about three seconds, before he let go of her arm and pushed her back against the heavy oak door.

She raised her head, and he waited for her to object. After all, he'd promised to save her from scandal, and the servants were due to prepare Ugolino's chamber for the night and clear away the last of the dinner.

But she threaded her hands through Fergus's hair, and after a charged second of studying him with those fathomless black eyes, she drew his head down.

All night he'd simmered, half-afraid to look at her, in case he revealed the volcano of desire threatening to erupt inside him. He'd wanted to seize her in his arms and devour her in one bite.

But at the seeking touch of her lips, sweetness tempered his urgency, and he sipped from her as if tasting honey. Tiny kisses that teased her, until she slumped against the door.

He wasn't feeling too steady himself. One hand settled on her slender waist, the other cupped her jaw, holding her still for more kisses.

She made a smothered sound of encouragement. He lifted away just far enough to speak. "Whisht," he whispered. "They'll hear us."

He nipped at her lower lip. This time, when he kissed her, passion flared and threatened to snap the bonds of discretion. He pressed into that slender body and felt her tremble against him.

Hot darkness rose to overwhelm him, and he struggled to summon the strength to pull away. He closed his eyes and buried his face in the curve of her neck. She smelled like lilies. She smelled like a woman on the verge of surrender.

With a stifled groan, he released her and placed his hands flat against the wall on either side of her head. He gasped for breath and stared down into her unforgettable face.

Marina looked dazed and needy. She leaned against the door, as if she didn't trust her knees to support her. Desire jolted him as he took in her boneless abandon. She didn't look at all like the defiant woman he'd met on the road a few days ago. Heavy eyelids drooped over eyes alight with frustrated longing.

"Let me into your room, lassie," he groaned under his breath.

The pause before she spoke made him hope. Then she gave a small shake of her dark head. "My father is in the next bedroom. I can't. You know I can't."

He bit back another groan. Aye, he knew, but that didn't make the denial any easier to bear. "Let me in for five minutes, so I can kiss ye properly."

"You're a wicked man, Fergus Mackinnon."

"I'd like the chance to be."

"You know what will happen if I let you inside my bedroom."

Aye, he did. She'd end up taking him inside her body. He could hardly wait. He jutted forward until his cock pressed into her belly. It was a blatant demand. He watched her eyes turn glassy and her lips part. He couldn't resist kissing her again, although every second in this corridor heightened the chance of discovery.

The kiss lasted a mere second, then she pulled free. "Stop it," she said, although she softened her rebuke with a breathtaking caress along his jaw.

With a quick twist of his head, he kissed her fingers before she lifted them away. "Let me in, Marina."

When she shook her head, he strove to find comfort in her unconcealed regret.

"No." As he tilted in again, her hand covered his lips. "Don't kiss me again. It just gets me all stirred up for nothing."

"It doesn't have to be for nothing," he whispered against her fingers.

She sent him an unimpressed look, as she lowered her hand. With every moment, the melting creature with the sultry eyes was less in evidence. "I'm not giving myself to you when my father is sleeping a few feet away."

That sounded encouraging. "So when will ye give yourself to me?"

"I'm not sure I will yet."

This time he couldn't stifle his groan. She giggled, then pressed her hand to her lips and looked horrified. "Papa will hear us."

"Then come to my rooms."

"Where do you sleep?"

She hadn't said no. Did he have a chance? He knew it was reckless to seduce her in the castle. But he'd never been so mad for a woman. "In the south tower. Nobody will disturb us there."

"Fergus, you know it's impossible."

He shook his head. "I know I starve for you."

Her smile conveyed a great dollop of self-satisfaction. "That's good."

He nipped the side of her neck. "You're enjoying this, you witch."

She shivered under his teeth. "It's rather nice to see you toppled off your high and mighty perch."

He stared at her in frustration, starving for more kisses.

Fear sparked in her eyes. "Stand back," she hissed, straightening.

It was pure luck that as Kirsty and Jenny approached the turn of the corridor, they were bickering. Hell. That was close. Fergus had been deaf to everything but his desire.

Before the maids came into sight, he stepped away from Marina with a bow. "Goodnight, *signorina*. I'll see ye early tomorrow."

She performed a shaky curtsy. "Thank you for a delightful evening, Mackinnon."

The girls passed with a couple of quick bobs and barely hidden curiosity. Their interest reminded him that much as he'd sell his soul for the chance to share Marina's bed tonight, he owed her better than to sully her name. More, he'd given his word he wouldn't.

"We'll have privacy up on the hills," he said, once he and Marina were alone again.

Another unimpressed glance. "I'm working tomorrow. I'll thank you to resist any impulse toward flirtation."

He almost kissed her for that piece of nonsense, but the girls had sharp ears, and they were only a closed door away. "We'll see."

"*Certo*, we will." With that enigmatic statement, she slipped into her room and closed the door on him, leaving Fergus to his suffering.

CHAPTER ELEVEN

Marina spent a restless night. What little sleep she managed was disturbed by hot, wicked dreams of Fergus stripping her naked, setting her on a bed, and kissing her into a fever. Each time, though, she woke before consummation. Her sexual frustration followed her into her dreams, and the torment didn't ease when she was awake.

Her eyes scratchy with tiredness, she now sat at her bedroom window watching the dawn rise over the hills behind the castle. Another fine day, when some craven part of her wouldn't mind an excuse to stay with her father. If only to put off her decision about becoming Fergus's lover.

She supposed she could cancel the day's painting, but Fergus would know why. Somehow admitting her weakness was worse than facing him.

Did she want a lover with whom she waged a continual battle for supremacy? Surely not.

Then she recalled the way she'd melted under those sweet kisses on the hillside. And the delicious conspiracy of kisses last night in the corridor, when discovery had come so close.

She loved her life, she loved her work. Nothing compared with the excitement she found in the Mackinnon's arms.

Prudence insisted she leave Achnasheen. But could she relinquish this promise of passion?

Once more, when she went downstairs, Fergus waited in the courtyard. Those silvery eyes conducted a thorough inspection, and she was sure he noted the signs of sleeplessness and worry. "Are you ready for another day on the estate, lassie?"

She was ready for Achnasheen. She was far from ready for its master. Still, she nodded and summoned a smile. "I look forward to it."

His hands didn't linger at her waist as they had yesterday, but even the fleeting contact as he tossed her onto her pony turned her blood thick and sluggish with yearning. Nor did she mistake the heat in his eyes as he stared at her. Words jammed in her throat. This powerful reaction left her feeling raw and horrifyingly vulnerable. She wasn't used to it, and she hated it.

Needing to get away, if only for a second, she clicked her tongue at the pony and headed out of the castle before Fergus mounted.

"You're in a braw rush this morning," he said, catching up and snatching her pony's bridle to bring her to a stop. As light spread across the hillside, they sat facing one another like adversaries.

Marina bit her lip and tightened her grip on the reins, not that Fergus was going to let her go anywhere. And wasn't that a large part of the problem? "I don't think I can do this."

A thorny silence descended, before he spoke slowly. "You're no' talking about the paintings."

"No, I'm talking about...us."

He looked stern, and a muscle flickered in his cheek. "You've spent all night fretting, haven't ye?"

"Yes," she admitted in a low voice, staring blindly at her pony's stubby black mane. "It's best if I leave tomorrow. I'm sure given the situation, you won't mind lending me a coach and driver as far as Skye."

When she glanced up, that formidable jaw had set like granite. "No, lassie, if you're going, I'll take ye."

She made a sound humiliatingly like a whimper. "I'd rather you didn't."

He frowned. "You're no' frightened of me, are you, Marina? I couldn't bear to think that's true. If ye don't want to share my bed, I'll accept your choice."

"Don't be a fool, Mackinnon." She blinked away stinging tears. "You know I'm tempted. If I wasn't so tempted, I could stay. I want to stay."

His frown darkened. "Then stay, for God's sake." He reached for her hand where it held the reins, but she jerked back.

"That only means torture for both of us."

His lips turned down. "The torture will be worse if ye leave me."

Marina knew what it cost him to make that admission. She shook her head, more in perplexity than denial. "How on earth have we come to this pass? A couple of days ago, I didn't even like you."

"I liked you."

Despite her wretchedness, her lips twitched with reluctant amusement. "No, you didn't. I offended every ounce of your masculine pride."

He gave her one of those half-smiles that became so dear. "Ye still do, but that doesn't mean I don't like you."

She raised one shaking hand to keep him at bay, although he made no attempt to come closer. "Please don't be charming. I can't bear it if you're charming."

Her voice cracked. "Order me around. Tell me you're always right. Trample my feelings."

He looked troubled, although she'd hoped to lighten the heavy atmosphere. "Aye, well, here's a command for ye."

"I'm listening."

Marina braced for him to declare he meant to have her in his bed and after the way she'd encouraged him, she owed him her consent. Shame tasted like acid on her tongue. Her hungry kisses yesterday must convince any man that she was ready to yield.

But when he spoke, he surprised her. "Don't decide yet. Let's spend the day as planned."

Fergus still respected her autonomy. He still respected her. Relief made her sag in the saddle. "Then what happens tomorrow?" she asked in a muffled voice.

He shrugged, although she could see this wasn't a subject he took lightly. "Tomorrow ye may change your mind about becoming my mistress."

Her lips flattened. "I can be quite as stubborn as you."

"I'm sure ye can." His voice deepened into alluring sincerity, and she had to fight against edging closer to that rich baritone. "I've only just found you, Marina. Give me more."

Her hands clenched on the reins, until her placid pony shifted in protest. She'd never found it so difficult to discourage an unwanted suitor. Perhaps because, in this case, the suitor was very much wanted. "I've said I won't give you anything."

"I'll take your company."

"While doing your best to change my mind."

He frowned. "While showing you that ye can trust me to look after you."

The awful fact was that she did trust him to care for her, at least on a physical level. What she didn't trust was her ability to leave Achnasheen as the same heart-whole woman who had arrived. When she saw Fergus in the courtyard this morning, she'd faced the terrifying revelation that much more was at stake here than her chastity. She didn't trust herself not to fall in love with this impossible man.

Per pietà, she was already half in love with him. Anyone who flicked through the pages of sketches she'd made of him yesterday would see that at a glance.

Fergus Mackinnon wasn't the man for her. Yet he was the one man who made her burn.

Madonna, even if the impossible happened and he offered marriage, she'd have to refuse. They'd never be able to live together in amity.

"If I stay, you must act only as my host. No wooing. No kissing. No touching."

He sat in the saddle, straight as a ship's mast. "Ye ask too much."

"I know." Sadness roughened her voice. "Which is why I must go."

"No." Those formidable shoulders tightened, as if he were indeed a general facing an implacable enemy. "I can abide by your rules."

"Can you?" Marina subjected him to a searching stare. "You don't like playing by anyone's rules but your own."

"Neither do you," he said, his expression grim. "And in this particular game, you hold the winning hand."

His bitterness shocked her, scraped a wound across her heart. He sounded as if she did him great injury, whereas she'd assumed that after a bit of grumbling, he'd take her decision in his stride.

She made a helpless gesture. "You said the choice was mine."

His head tilted in a strangely courtly gesture. "It is at that. But I dinna have to like it."

Neither did she, curse her level head and her need to protect herself. "I still think I should go ahead to Skye."

He shook his head, and she waited for a stinging response, but when he spoke, his voice was heavy with regret. "No. Give me your company, even if you'll give me nothing else."

She'd imagined his considerable pride would revolt at begging for such a small concession. *Cielo,* no doubt it did. When she'd met him, he'd struck her as a man above human frailties like doubts and longings. She'd been wrong.

Guilt at how she hurt him sliced at her. She wasn't proof against the fierce misery she read in his eyes. And he hadn't tried to take advantage of her susceptibility for him to change her mind, when they both knew he could.

Fergus was indeed a man of honor. She felt sick at what she did, but if she gave in, the risks were far too great.

Marina looked away across the heather-covered hills and fought against the hot tears rising to sting her eyes. "Very well, Mackinnon. I'll stay. For now."

CHAPTER TWELVE

*M*arina was right about one thing, even if Fergus was convinced she was wrong about everything else. That day on the hills proved to be the vilest torture, and so did the next three.

In a torment of suspense, he waited for her to declare that the tension spinning tighter and tighter between them became unbearable, and she intended to leave. He should want her to go. Having her within reach but forbidden drove him to the edge. His joke about being the first mad Mackinnon came back to bite him with sharp teeth.

Surely if she left, he had a chance of finding some peace. It made no sense that the prospect of never seeing her again made him want to rampage around like a wounded lion.

More than once, he regretted that the world had moved on from ages past. Present mores forbade him from seizing Marina, the way Callum had seized Bonny Mhairi, and holding her captive until she saw sense.

Perhaps the misery might be easier to bear, if he thought Marina was any more content than he was. But with each day, she became more subdued. He missed the vital, scintillating creature who had so fascinated and appalled him on their first meeting. What he'd give to hear just one claim to female independence.

The irony was that this new, dispirited Marina was much closer to the kind of woman Fergus used to admire. Somewhere during this last week, he'd learned to appreciate a challenge.

Tonight they'd dined with Ugolino. Fergus supposed that now the meal was over, he should go downstairs and catch up with the estate work that piled up while he moped after his guest.

Except that soon she'd decide to go—she must. Be damned if he'd waste what time he had left with her, even if her nearness was sheer purgatory.

Fergus glanced across to where Marina sat beside the bed, sketchbook in hand, although she hadn't opened it. That was something else that had changed. She didn't draw anymore, or at least not just for the pure joy of it.

Her father was talking about a book he'd read. Over the last few evenings, the burden of conversation had fallen on Ugolino. Whether he noticed the strain between Fergus and Marina or not, he seemed content to fill the lengthening silences.

Fergus remained at the small table where he and Marina ate each night. Over the rim of his wineglass, he observed the woman he wanted. Wanted more with every day. Gloom hung about her the way a rainy day hung about the glen.

"How is your work going, Marina?" Ugolino cut off his critique of the novel, as if realizing he was talking to himself. "You never say."

The question made the lassie start. Fergus had a suspicion that her thoughts weren't much different to his own—and no jollier. After all, she'd admitted she wanted him, despite having no intention of yielding. "I'm making progress, Papa."

"That's good. Are you finding plenty of scenes to please His Grace?"

When Marina looked shifty, Fergus was surprised. While they were out on the hills, she kept her head down and sketched diligently. "*Certo*. I'm making the preparatory drawings. Once I've decided on my final subjects, I'll do the color studies."

Ugolino turned to Fergus. "This is how she works, painting a draft from life, then finishing the picture in her studio in Firenze."

"How interesting." Though he was sincere, Fergus's flat response sounded like sarcasm. A couple of days ago, Marina would have called him on that. Now she didn't seem to notice.

"Can I see what you've done so far?" her father asked. "Perhaps I can help you choose."

Her hands tightened on the sketchbook, as though she feared Ugolino might rip it away. "There's plenty of time yet, Papa."

Her father looked puzzled. "You always show me your work."

"Not this time," she said with a hint of sharpness, rising to her feet. She wore the pink dress again, the one that showed her bosom. All night, the display of satiny olive skin had taunted Fergus.

Now that bosom was heaving with disquiet. He wondered why.

Preparing to escort her as he did every night, he stood, too. More torture. Saying a polite goodnight on the threshold of her room highlighted the futility of all his hopes.

He crossed the room to take her arm, waiting for her to stiffen under his touch. To the devil with her, he refused to give up what few miserly contacts propriety allowed him. The chance to hold her arm, to lift her onto a pony, to pass her a glass of wine when, with luck, fingers might brush.

Hell, it was like a slow death by starvation.

He and Marina said their goodnights to Ugolino, then they were outside in the corridor.

"You don't have to walk me to my door." She pulled away, clutching her sketchbook to her chest like a shield.

Fergus stepped back, because the temptation to grab her became too powerful. "It's all ye permit me."

She looked stricken, and her knuckles whitened. "Oh, Fergus, I hate how things are between us."

He braced to hear her say she wanted to leave. In truth, he was surprised she'd stayed this long. His heart felt like a stone.

"Is your work really going well?" he asked, when she didn't fill the pause with a request for his traveling coach.

"*Dio*, you know it's not." Her eyes were dark with suffering.

For God's sake, if resisting him made her so distressed, she knew how to cheer herself up. He was keen to cooperate.

Fergus waited again for her to announce her departure. After all, painting was her reason for living.

"You havenae looked happy with what you've done since that first day." When her pencil had flown so fast across the page, it was like she raced time to get the details down. Afterwards she'd glowed with satisfaction.

Over the last days, the glow had gone. He wished he could take her in his arms to soothe her roiling unhappiness.

Except they both knew that if he started with comfort, that wasn't where he'd finish.

"I haven't been." Another reason for her to move on. The smile she summoned was a mere shadow of what it used to be. "Perhaps tomorrow will be better."

"Perhaps." He sounded as convinced as she did, which wasn't very. Then he realized what she'd said. So he faced another day of this hell. He was in such a confused state, he was delighted to hear it.

"I'll see you in the morning."

"Aye." He stared at her, willing her to betray the smallest sign that she wanted his touch. The heat rising in his blood threatened to incinerate him.

This was always the worst part of the day. The time where he left her without a caress, and she retired behind a stout oak door to sleep alone. When in any correctly ordered universe, she'd lie in his arms until dawn.

Those fathomless black eyes met his, and he wondered for a flaring instant if this might be the night she relented.

The blazing second disintegrated into ashes. She turned and lifted the latch. "Goodnight, Fergus."

He didn't answer. Sour disappointment crammed every unspoken word in his throat. Not sparing him a backward glance, she disappeared into her room.

With aching tenderness, Fergus leaned in and pressed one hand against the closed door, spreading his fingers as if he reached through the wood. Then with a heavy sigh, he trudged away.

CHAPTER THIRTEEN

Marina sat on a green hillside overlooking a pattern of sunlit islands in a silver sea. She'd never seen a finer view, yet her pencil lay motionless in her fingers and her heart failed to lift as it always did in the presence of beauty.

Since Fergus had kissed her, every day had been like this. She frittered away her time, while aware that this could be the last spell of good weather before she went home to Florence. It was both urgent and imperative that she finish her sketches, then return to make detailed studies of the dozen scenes she chose for the duke's pictures.

The Duke of Portofino was paying her a fat fee, and more important, he was a noted art collector, an influential voice in Italian cultural circles. When he'd offered her this commission, she thought that at last she broke through to a career at the highest level. She'd been overjoyed and flattered to say yes.

Now her pencil felt as dead and unwieldy as a brick, and the magnificence around her wouldn't transfer to the page. She wished she'd said no to artistically minded noblemen and stayed in Florence where she made a good living, selling her work to local aristocratic families and rich travelers.

Except in her heart, she didn't wish that at all. Because if she'd never come to Scotland, she'd never have encountered Fergus Mackinnon. He was unlike any man she'd ever met, and he became the measure by which she'd judge all men in the future.

The wisest thing would be to leave, even if that meant bearing with Fergus's company as far as one of the houses on Skye where the duke had arranged an introduction. But as with her art, so with her ability to make decisions. She couldn't summon the will to go.

Right now, she was alone. Her host wasn't in sight, although given how he occupied her thoughts, he might as well be. Fergus never hovered by her side, but took the chance with all this hill walking to consult with his crofters and shepherds. As someone who also had a purpose—before she came to Achnasheen anyway—Marina admired his diligence. Macushla and Brecon had come out with them, but had soon disappeared across the hills to pursue mysterious canine affairs.

With a sigh, she considered the few uninspired lines she'd set on the page. Perhaps the problem with this sketch was the angle of the view. She rose, dusted off her skirts and climbed the slope.

When she'd been sitting, she'd heard running water. Now she saw a stream tumbling toward a cliff, then over. Perhaps a dramatic waterfall might awaken her dormant urge to draw. She forded the water and edged around for a better look. This had definite possibilities. She ventured closer to the edge.

Marina was so busy studying the landscape for artistic potential, that she forgot to look where she was going. The heel of her half boot, wet after wading the burn, skidded across a bare patch of rock. With a scream, she plunged over the escarpment.

Fergus was checking recent repairs to a small stone bridge when he heard Marina's shrill cry. Immediate fear froze him on the spot. These braes were steep and dangerous, and even folk who knew them came to grief.

He shook himself out of immobility. His heart racing faster than the water rushing down the mountainside, he dashed back to where he'd left Marina. When the dip in the ground proved empty, terror like he'd never known turned his guts to water.

"Marina!" he shouted. "Marina, for God's sake, lassie, answer!"

The breeze whipped his words away, and for the first time in his life, he felt small and powerless in this rugged landscape he'd always loved. The burns were swollen, and the towering Mare's Tail waterfall had turned into a torrent. If Marina had slipped into that, they'd be bringing her broken body up from the stony riverbed at the base of the cliff.

Why in Hades had he left her alone? It was agony to be near her, but he'd promised to keep her safe. *If he lost her...*

"Marina! Answer me!"

In a black fog of fear, he stumbled up the brae. He was the Mackinnon. These glens and hills were his domain. He wouldn't permit them to steal his woman away.

"Marina!"

Was that a reply? Between the rushing water and the strengthening breeze, he couldn't be sure.

He ran to the brink of the waterfall, his belly clenching at the thought of seeing a crumpled figure hundreds of feet below.

Nothing.

"Marina, darling, talk to me."

"Fergus, help me. I'm stuck."

Gratitude made him stagger. She was alive. Hope more intoxicating than Bruce Mackenzie's best whisky pulsed through him. But when he scanned the bare hillsides in a frantic search, he couldn't see her.

Puzzled, he struggled to work out where her voice came from. "Where are you?"

"I'm caught on a ledge, but I can't get up without help."

He already moved toward the sound. "Are you hurt?"

"Only a few scrapes and bruises."

He whispered a prayer of gratitude. "Keep talking so I can find ye."

"I was trying to see the waterfall, and I fell."

"You're no' safe out on your own," he said, although he was too relieved to be angry. That moment when he'd peered over the cliff would live in his nightmares. He'd been convinced she'd left him at last, and in the most permanent way imaginable.

Compared to the fact that she was alive, nothing else mattered, not even the purgatory she'd put him through these last days.

"Right now, I might agree with you."

"Did I hear right?" Fergus was too worried to appreciate that this wry banter echoed the way things used to be between them. "Signorina Marina Lucchetti agrees with one of my conclusions?"

"Yes, it's a miracle."

He followed the sound of her voice and realized it rose over the lip of the cliff. Now he was near the place where she'd lost her footing, he saw broken bracken and torn grass that bore witness to how she'd scrabbled to stop her fall.

"I'll raise a flag to mark the occasion when we get back to the castle." He dropped to his stomach, not trusting the edge to hold his weight.

"If you get me out of this, I'll help you."

As he looked down, any urge to smile forsook him. Instead, icy fear dug its claws into his flesh.

"Good God, lassie, what have ye got yourself into?" He struggled to sound as if terror didn't tangle his intestines into knots.

Marina turned her dirty face upward and managed a smile. By heaven, she was gallant. She put the men he knew to shame.

Her back pressed into the side of the hill. Her feet balanced precariously on a narrow ledge that looked none too secure. On either side, she spread her arms against the rock wall. One hand curled around a protruding boulder. The other maintained a white-knuckled grip on a spindly sapling growing over the void. Below her, the hill fell away in a series of jagged ledges.

"A mess." He was close enough to hear the panic beneath her jauntiness. "I need a big, strong brute of a Scotsman to save me. Fate has a sense of humor, it seems, and mocks my claims to self-sufficiency."

"Aye, that's fate for ye," he said, assessing her plight with sharp eyes. What he saw made his chest constrict with dread.

He could rush back to fetch one of the ponies and a rope, but he doubted he had time. As if to confirm his decision, Marina shifted an inch, and a shower of gravel rattled down the cliff.

"Will you trust me, Marina?" he asked as calmly as he could manage.

"Yes."

This was no time to appreciate her swift confirmation. "I can pull ye up, but you'll have to turn around and climb toward me."

God above, let his plan work. He could try to tug her to safety as she was, but she'd be dead weight on his arms, and he couldn't risk the ground beneath him crumbling away.

"I can do that." He hated to hear the quaver in her voice.

"Be careful, *mo chridhe*."

"I promise that, at least."

"Don't wait." This time, his voice held no false bravado at all.

Despite his command, she didn't move straightaway. To Fergus watching from above, the few seconds' delay lasted forever. Then gingerly she released her grip on the rock and started to shuffle mere inches at a time on the same spot as she tried to turn. More gravel came loose and bounced down the rock face. With every second of waiting, Fergus felt like he aged a millennium.

"Please talk to me, Mackinnon," she muttered.

With his heart in his mouth, he wasn't sure he could muster a single word. But her courage deserved any tribute he could pay. He struggled to swallow the terror blocking his throat and defied heaven to snatch her away before he had the chance to kiss her again. "Do you ken what I thought the first time I saw ye?"

Her fingers dug into the rock behind her as she shifted with infinitesimal movements. "That somebody needed to take me in hand and show me who's in charge."

He made himself laugh, because he knew she wanted him to. It was even less convincing than her attempt at a smile. "Och, I did think that within five minutes, but that wasnae my first reaction."

"What was?"

Fergus cursed that she remained out of reach. Holding her while she moved would do wonders for his peace of mind. "I thought a woman with such flashing eyes belonged in my bed."

"Eyes?"

"Aye." He paused. "Although I have a recollection that I might have given your bosom a wee bit of attention, too."

A choked laugh escaped her. "You're such a man, Mackinnon."

"Aye, well, a man is just what ye want right now."

"I have a horrible fancy that's what I want anyway," she muttered.

Before he could question that astonishing admission, one of her feet slipped. She gave a broken cry as he surged down in a futile attempt to catch her, barely saving himself from falling, too.

With half-disbelieving horror, he saw her fumble at the sapling. The frail tree bent to an impossible angle. Surely, surely it must break.

By a miracle, it held, and Marina's other hand scrabbled then found purchase on the rock face. Each second stretched into an eon, as she flung herself face-forward into the cliff.

It took him a few seconds to realize that she was safe. At least for the moment.

The breath he sucked in felt like broken glass. "Don't...don't scare me like that again, lassie," he said, unable to stop his voice cracking.

Her brief laugh sounded more like a sob. "I wanted to check you were watching."

"I was watching, all right." His voice deepened. "You say ye trust me."

"Yes, I do."

If he got her out of this, he'd remember that. "Then lift your arm as high as ye can, and I'll take your hand."

Without hesitation, she did. By God, she was a woman in a thousand. He dug the toes of his leather boots into the ground behind him and prayed to heaven with a fervor he'd never demonstrated before, that he was strong enough to hold her.

Because the possibility of losing her was anathema. He'd known her little more than a week, but in that time, she'd marked him indelibly. He refused to relinquish her to death's greedy clutches, when he needed her to stay this side of heaven.

Fergus reached over the lip of the cliff and grabbed her wrist in a hold so tight, it must hurt. He wasn't taking any risks of his grip slipping. "You have to let go of the tree."

This time, Marina did falter. She lifted her disheveled dark head, and he met dark eyes burning with fear and defiance. Right now, fear was paramount. "If you drop me, I'll never forgive you."

He prayed she'd live. He prayed his strength would prevail. He prayed that she wouldn't discern how close failure loomed.

"As if I'll let ye fall," he scoffed. "Then I'd miss out on your humble thanks for saving your life."

"Saving me for the second time," she said in a thick voice. "That must count as showing off."

"My granny always said things come in threes. I hope you dinna mean to prove her right."

"I'll do my best."

"Take my hand, Marina," he said. "I willnae let you fall." Let that be the truth.

"*Per l'amor di dio,* don't let me go."

"Never," he said, as if he made a sacred vow.

Something in his tone must have convinced her to take the risk, because with a jerky movement, she released the sapling. For a sickening moment, she clawed upward before he caught her other wrist in his hand.

Fergus took a massive breath and summoned every ounce of strength he could muster. "I'm going to pull ye up, but if you can use your feet as well, it will be grand."

"Now?"

He noticed she'd given up pretending this was a great adventure. Retreating from the edge, he dug his toes in deeper. "Now."

In excruciating increments, he began to heave her up. Every muscle in his body strained to support her. He felt brief resistance, then she began to rise with him. She was panting audibly. Her arms must be aching worse than his.

"You're a braw lassie," he said with what breath he could spare.

Her dangling weight shot agony through his sinews. He dug his hips, legs and feet harder into the ground, but still her weight pulled him forward toward the edge. He braced against the momentum.

"*Cielo*," she cried, as one foot slipped. The sound of her boot scraping over rock would enter his nightmares, joining the moment he'd looked over the waterfall.

"I've got ye." He ground his teeth and clung tighter as she dipped lower. His shoulders felt like they were on fire.

After a horrid second, she found her footing again, this time with more certainty.

When Fergus first found her on the ledge, he'd hardly dared to believe that he might save her. With each inch higher she came, his hope lifted, too. He backed away and hooked his feet into a rut that offered a little extra purchase.

The top of Marina's head appeared above the ledge. He wriggled back further, hauling her toward him with every ounce of strength. Her pale face gradually rose into view. There was a graze across one slanted cheekbone and dirt streaked her cheek.

She was the most beautiful thing he'd ever seen.

"Can ye pull yourself up now, using my arms?" he grated out.

"I think so," she gasped.

She must have found more secure footing, because after a few agonizing minutes, she managed to struggle onto the grass, with a mixture of treating him as a human rope and digging her feet into the cliff face.

It took an enormous act of will to release her wrist. With cramping hands, he lunged forward to grip her skirts and bring her legs up.

Panting, she collapsed on the rough grass beside him. Hardly able to believe he'd succeeded, he grabbed her in his aching arms and clutched her tight into his body. They were both shaking, as she burrowed into him with a broken sob. For a long time, they lay together in the sunlight as the horror slowly receded.

Once he'd caught his breath, Fergus released her and rolled onto his side. His heart galloped with exertion and remembered panic. And relief so overwhelming, it set his head spinning.

By all that was holy, he'd done it. He'd saved her. There had been stages when he'd feared he'd lost her forever. The world would turn into a grim, lightless place without Marina Lucchetti to tease and taunt him and make him glad he was alive.

"Are ye all right, Marina?" he asked in a raw voice, looking down into her ashen face. Her eyes were closed, tears stained her cheeks, and her chest heaved as she fought for breath.

When she didn't answer, he feared that she'd been injured after all. "Marina?"

After a fraught pause, she shifted gingerly on the grass and opened her eyes to stare back at him. "Kiss me, Mackinnon."

He frowned, ignoring the choked plea. Fear must have made her delirious. "Are ye hurt?"

She frowned back. "No."

"Are you able to stand?"

"I'm sure I will be." Her lips tightened in impatience. "*Cielo*, did you not hear me, you cloth-eared Scotsman?"

"A spoken thank you is enough, lassie."

"You'll get one of those, too." She flung out a trembling hand and clutched the front of his shirt, stained and torn after his efforts on the edge of the escarpment. "But if you don't kiss me this second, I swear that when I do stand up, I'll push you over that blasted cliff."

Fergus's heart slammed hard against his ribs and left him reeling with hope and disbelief. For pity's sake, he'd tried like a demon to do the right thing, but honor only extended so far. He surged forward and grabbed her in unsteady hands. His mouth crashed down on hers.

CHAPTER FOURTEEN

When Marina had been trapped on the ledge, fear turned her very blood to ice. Even after Fergus saved her with that prodigious demonstration of strength and determination, she still felt cold.

With the first touch of his lips, heat blasted her. Heat and relief and gratitude and blessed life.

Life, above all.

Because she'd come terrifyingly close to death when she fell down that mountain. And she didn't want to die. She wanted to seize life by the scruff of the neck and shake it until it gave her everything she asked for. She wanted to laugh and dance and learn and feel, and test her mettle against whatever the world could throw at her.

More than anything else, she wanted this man.

She curled her arms around him and gave herself up to his kiss. He shifted closer, moving over her body. But when his weight pressed into her, she heard a distinct crackle from the region of her chest.

Puzzled, Fergus raised his head. "What the devil..."

Lost in the hot ferocity of his kiss, she stared up at him in bewilderment. "What's the matter?"

He frowned and placed a hand over her torso. "Are ye wearing armor, lassie?"

After the storm of life and death she'd just passed through, the question made no sense. "Armor?"

With deft swiftness, he unbuttoned the jacket of her walking suit to reveal the sketchbook she'd tucked into the waistband of her skirt. He gave one of his short laughs. "I should have known."

To her regret—she'd waited days for him to kiss her, and what he'd done so far hadn't come near to answering her craving—he sat up and tugged the book free.

Abruptly Marina's haze of pleasure faded, and she remembered why she didn't want anyone snooping in her drawings. Her elation at surviving her ordeal evaporated, and all the old fears and complications came tumbling back in its place. "Put that down," she snapped.

He ignored her. "I cannae believe that in the midst of balancing on a cliff edge, you took the trouble to keep this safe."

She scowled at him and sat up, snatching after the book with an unsteady hand. "It's precious."

With little effort, he kept it out of reach. She cursed the long, powerful arms that had proven her lifeline on the cliff. "Obviously."

"There's nothing of significance to see."

He shot her a narrow-eyed look and rose to his feet. "Really?"

"Really." She stood, too, less smoothly. Now that the shock of her fall receded, her body became a mass of aches and pains. She was stiff and sore, and bruises began to blossom all over her.

"Give it back to me, Fergus." Stretching out her hand, she strove to sound casual. "You can have no interest in my scribblings."

He didn't comply, blast him. "On the contrary, I want to see what you've been up to, while I've been pining after ye."

Lunging for him, she slipped and nearly lost her balance. Her boots, still muddy from crossing the burn, lost traction against the thick grass. The sodden hem of her skirt slapped against her shins as she caught his arm. "Give it back to me."

"You're mighty keen to hide whatever is inside. Let me see why."

"No..." she cried, but he jerked the sketchbook further out of reach. The folio flipped open on a sketch of him standing on top of a mountain with the Cuillins of Skye rising in the background.

Bemused, he stared at the picture. "That's me."

She still hoped to escape the worst of the coming humiliation. "Just something I did in a spare moment."

His frown deepening, he stepped out of her hold and began to flick through the pages, quickly at first, then more slowly.

Miserable with embarrassment, Marina gave up trying to retrieve the book. What was the point? It was too late to save her pride. He now knew her shameful secret.

Fergus raised his head and shot her another puzzled look. "They're all of me."

"Not all of them," she said defensively.

The arch of his eyebrows said it all. "Everything close to finished is."

The mortifying fact was that he was right. Over the past week, she'd tried to concentrate on the landscape, she really had. Achnasheen was as dramatic and beautiful as any country she'd ever seen. But every line she put on paper to depict mountain or sea or tree lay lifeless against the white. While even the roughest sketch of Fergus Mackinnon conveyed a vigor and power that she'd never before achieved in a portrait.

Although she remained dissatisfied with her work. Some essence of the man continued to elude her. Which was why, or at least so she told herself, she kept trying to capture his image with her pencil.

Could her cheeks get any hotter? "It doesn't mean anything."

His glance was skeptical. "No?"

"No," she repeated with emphasis, feeling childish and flustered, and worst of all, as defenseless as a chick that had fallen out of its nest.

Because while many of Fergus's opinions might be misguided, he wasn't stupid. He'd know what these drawings meant—that Marina thought about him night and day. That she thought about him so often, she couldn't think of anything else.

"What about the duke's commission?"

"I need to go away to finish it. I'm not getting anywhere here." She raised her chin in a show of defiance. "In fact, I'll go tomorrow."

She waited for him to protest, as he had every previous time she'd told him she must go. Then struggled not to mind when no objection emerged. Instead he studied her with shrewd eyes that seemed to see right through her bravado to the confusion and longing that lurked in her traitorous heart.

"So that I stop haunting your imagination?"

Diavolo, she was right. He understood exactly what those sketches meant. "If I don't see you..."

"Maybe you'll miss me."

She shifted uncomfortably from foot to foot. The inescapable truth was that she would miss him.

This stubborn, confident, commanding man held her in thrall in a way that nobody else ever had.

"I doubt it," she lied, feeling even more like a gauche schoolgirl.

"Give it up, lassie. The evidence is all against ye." He stepped back and leafed through the sketchbook, taking his time to study each drawing. "You want me as much as I want you. The proof is here in black and white."

Her hands opened and closed at her sides, as she fought the urge to fly at him and grab the book away. "You're so smug," she said through her teeth.

He paused at a watercolor she'd completed last night. It showed him talking to her father. The candlelight fell across his hair and face, creating a striking study in shadow and light. "I like this one."

So did she, apart from what it revealed about her obsession with her dictatorial host. "It's not bad," she conceded grudgingly.

He closed the book and set it aside on a boulder. "You just kissed me as though ye were dying, and I was your last chance at a breath."

She'd thought her cheeks couldn't get any hotter. She'd been wrong. "You saved my life."

"So if Jock had pulled ye up that cliff, you'd kiss him, too?"

"Maybe," she said, knowing she fought a losing battle but too stubborn to give in. She was at least as stubborn as Fergus. That was one of the many reasons any affair was doomed before it began.

"Liar," he said without rancor. Before she could protest—even if he was right—he went on. "What I cannae understand is why you're putting both of us through this torment, when a simple yes opens the gates to heaven."

She wanted to accuse him of conceit, while the bitter truth was that she suspected he wasn't exaggerating. When he kissed her, the clouds parted in glory and she heard angels singing. Imagine what he could conjure up if they went beyond kissing.

"You know why," she muttered.

He shook his head in disbelief. "Because ye dedicate your chastity to your art like a bloody Vestal Virgin tending the temple flame. I want to know what good your chastity does you."

Right now, staring at this spectacular man and reading the desire in his eyes, she couldn't think of a single viable answer. "It keeps me safe," she said weakly.

He shook his head again, in denial this time. "Not good enough, Marina. You must ken that all the good stuff in life carries a hint of danger."

"I'm not feeling wise at all right now," she whispered and turned away as if the sight of all that male beauty scalded her. She knew she should say no, but she so wanted to say yes. This was like being ripped in two.

Giddiness made her head reel, and she fumbled for something to keep her upright. Her legs felt ready to crumple like paper.

"Marina, lass, I'm sorry. Forgive me for being a blockhead." Strong fingers wrapped around hers as he stepped in front of her. "I shouldn't harangue ye when you've just fallen off a mountain."

This precise moment felt like falling off a mountain. There was that same dizzy terror, that same sensation of losing her connection with solid ground.

Pride and common sense told her to reject Fergus's touch.

If she meant to leave Achnasheen tomorrow, what use was prolonging the agony with more physical contact? But both pride and common sense grew more tattered by the second. So she clung to his hand and didn't object when he caught her behind the legs and hoisted her high in his arms.

"Let's get ye back to the castle."

"My work?" she said, even as she rested her aching head on his shoulder.

She drew an unsteady breath. Fergus smelled so marvelous. Fresh air and leather and lemon soap, and something that was him alone, a scent that she'd remember for the rest of her life.

"You mean all those drawings of me?"

She didn't respond to the sardonic question. After all, what could she say?

He jiggled her as he picked up the sketchbook and passed it to her. Before she realized how revealing her actions were, she hugged it to her bosom like the most precious treasure in the world.

She waited for some mocking comment, but he merely settled her on her pony. "Let's call a truce, Marina," he murmured, staring up at her with a concerned expression. "You dinna have to be strong all the time."

How wrong he was. She did. Even if right now, her strength didn't strike her as an admirable quality, but the reason behind her excruciating loneliness.

When he whistled for the dogs, they came streaking over the hill, barking. He caught the rein and clicked his tongue to the pony. She should tell him she was perfectly capable of riding her horse back to the castle, but it was so nice to have someone taking care of her. Someone she lo...

She brought the traitorous thought to a shuddering halt. Blinking away futile tears, Marina stared straight ahead while the pony Fergus usually rode ambled after them. She'd developed a strong affection for these sturdy little horses with their stoic natures and broad backs. She'd developed a love for the wild landscape, too, however unsuccessful her attempts to paint it. She also liked the people who lived in this isolated valley. Jock and Maggie and Kirsty and Jenny, and the servants and crofters and shepherds she'd met.

She'd be sorry to leave Achnasheen.

The twist of her lips held scant amusement. Sorry? She'd be devastated. And not because she'd miss everything she'd listed, although she would. Her departure would leave her desolate, because she dreaded parting from the tall, red-haired man who led her pony along the rough track.

The man who made her want to hit him.

The man who made her want to kiss him.

As the castle came into view like something from a fairy story, Fergus's astringent question echoed in her mind. What use was her chastity to her? If she gave in now, what harm would ensue?

She recalled that instant of brilliant clarity when she'd thought she might die. Her greatest regret then had been that she'd let fear overrule her desire for Fergus. During these long days in the hills, she'd come to trust him. *Per l'amor di dio*, he'd saved her life twice. Wasn't it time to grant him the hero's traditional reward, the favors of the rescued lady?

To her relief, he didn't speak as they plodded across the hills. Only as he pulled the pony to a halt in the courtyard and lifted her from the saddle with more of that blasted consideration did he say anything. "You know, it's rather sad that when ye go, you'll have only the painted version of me to remember, when for the sake of one small word, you could have all you want of the real man."

The acerbic note to his words didn't hide the aching regret underlying them. She bit back a choked whimper and stumbled as she reached the ground. Fergus caught her up against him before, to her chagrin, he let her go.

"Be careful or you'll fall," he said in a low voice.

Marina had a grim feeling that was true. If she stayed any longer at Achnasheen, she would indeed fall.

CHAPTER FIFTEEN

Fergus approached dinner with the bleak certainty that this was the last night Marina would spend under his roof. He cursed himself as a numskull for taunting her to the point where she decided she must go. Especially as for one dazzling instant when she kissed him, he'd wondered if she meant to give him everything he asked for.

After he'd dragged her to safety, all he'd wanted to do was cherish her, and hold her tight, and give thanks for her survival. He was never going to let her do anything dangerous again as long as she lived.

But he soon admitted that was unfair. Daring and curiosity were part of who she was. No wonder he was at sea with his intriguing guest. He was used to women who sheltered in his strength. Marina met his strength with strength of her own.

Devil if he knew how to handle her. He made blunder after blunder. Orders only made her rebel. So far, while he'd been lucky enough to coax a couple of kisses out of her, his attempts at seduction had fallen flat.

Be damned if he'd let her go.

Be damned if he knew how to make her stay.

It was Ugolino's first night downstairs. Fergus's clansmen Jock and Ian had carried the older man down in a chair, and now he sat with his broken leg propped up on a stool. He was in good form, full of jokes, outlandish tales and bonhomie.

While the man's Italian-accented chatter flowed around him, Fergus couldn't take his eyes off Marina. Although the night wasn't cold, she wore the purple dress with the Elizabethan collar and long sleeves. He guessed she was trying to hide the evidence of her fall from her father. She hadn't mentioned her brush with death. In fact, she'd been quiet all evening.

For once, she hadn't brought her sketchbook. The sketchbook crammed with pictures of the man she meant to forsake.

Those drawings should give him hope. Not to mention the way she'd kissed him this afternoon. But she set her formidable will against him, and he didn't underestimate what that meant for his success. He feared his pursuit of her was doomed.

"Fergus?"

Fergus realized Ugolino must have asked him a question. Marina wasn't the only one distracted tonight. "I'm sorry. What did you say?"

"*Santa pazienza,* a man might as well talk to himself. I asked if today's good weather was going to last. My daughter says the views on the estate are magnificent."

Fergus couldn't refrain from casting Marina an incredulous glance. Unless she considered the sight of her host a magnificent view, she'd taken little advantage of the spectacular landscape.

A flush rose on those dramatic cheekbones, as she avoided his eyes and went back to pushing a piece of parsnip around with her fork. He hid a grim smile and answered Ugolino. "Weather here is unpredictable, but most years, winter starts to move in toward the end of October."

If Marina meant to travel to Skye, she needed to leave soon, so she had time to complete—start—her commission for the duke. The mere thought of her leaving made Fergus's gut twist into a painful knot of despair.

She gave up all pretense of eating and set down her cutlery. "I wasn't prepared for how beautiful the Highlands are."

"They're even beautiful in dreich weather, although I suspect only a Scotsman would say so." And tired of waiting for the ax to fall, Fergus went on. "If ye stay until next month, you'll see storms and rain, snow if you're unlucky."

He provided her with the perfect opportunity to announce her departure. Instead she went back to staring at her half-full plate, leaving her father to respond. "What inconvenient guests we are, arriving with no definite plans to leave."

Marina had plans to leave, but again, to Fergus's surprise, she didn't speak. "I told ye, you're welcome to stay as long as you like."

"If ever you're in Firenze, I hope you'll let us return your hospitality."

Should he pursue Marina back to Italy? Would she be any more receptive in Florence than she was at Achnasheen? Could some extravagant gesture tip her over from rejection to acceptance? He doubted it. She wasn't a woman who played flirtatious games.

Moodily, he studied her, and wished for the thousandth time that things had worked out differently between them. In the candlelight, she was all dark mystery. To a man denied her favors, that gown was a fiendish instrument of torture. It covered her so modestly, yet suggested so much.

Fergus struggled not to stare at the lush bosom filling out the deep purple silk. Once he'd been churlish enough to dismiss her curves as unimpressive. Now the thought of touching those elegant breasts made every drop of moisture evaporate from his mouth.

Not that she was ever likely to grant him that privilege. He could go to Florence. He could go to Timbuctoo. He could go to bloody Jupiter. Her answer would still be no.

What a tragic waste, that such a passionate creature should seal up her innate sensuality and devote herself to the altar of her art. When he'd accused her of being a Vestal Virgin, he hadn't been far wrong.

"Nae need to repay me." He paused. "Unless Signorina Marina would give me a picture. That would be a grand reminder of our time together. Apart from a few inept watercolors my sisters did in the schoolroom, I have no paintings of Achnasheen."

Marina's head jerked up, and she narrowed her eyes at him. "Why would you want the facsimile when you have the reality?"

Surprise struck him speechless, then his lips curved in a wolfish smile. Well, well. This was a direct challenge to what he'd said this afternoon, and her first sign of spirit tonight. "Sometimes in the winter, it's braw to have a reminder of summer," he said smoothly.

He knew she'd pick up on his meaning. He waited for her to retreat back into pensive silence, but she shot him a sly look that set his blood rushing. "Memories of summer aren't enough to keep you warm on a cold evening, Mackinnon."

"Without memories of summer, winter seems to last forever."

"Marina, after Fergus's kindness, giving him a painting is the least you can do," Ugolino said, taking the conversation on its literal terms.

"Perhaps one of the pictures you're working on now."

Fergus's silky suggestion earned him a glare. He shouldn't provoke her. It was as if he dared her to abandon him.

"None of those are worth keeping," she said with a hint of a snap.

His headstrong lassie wasn't short on effrontery. When Fergus couldn't contain an appreciative laugh, Ugolino shot him a curious glance.

Ugolino retired as soon as dinner was over. Fergus could see that despite the Italian's high spirits, the effort of sitting at a table tired him out. Marina rose when Jock and Ian arrived to carry her father upstairs.

"Don't let me spoil your evening," Ugolino said, unable to hide his disappointment at not making a better showing. "It's still early. Marina, perhaps you could play the piano for our host."

Fergus cast her a surprised glance. "You play?"

"And sing. She inherited her musical talent from her dear mother." Ugolino's smile was warm with nostalgic affection. "Do you have an instrument, Fergus?"

"Aye, my sisters learned. It hasnae been touched in years, though. It must be devilish out of tune."

"Like my singing," Marina said.

"I'm sure you're too modest."

Fergus wasn't just talking about her musical abilities. If she'd been a brazen wench, he wouldn't be suffering the torments of the damned. On the other hand, the merry chase she led him added to her fascination.

"If not music, perhaps cards?" Ugolino suggested. "*Dio*, there are a hundred things you could do."

There were indeed. Fergus had dreamed of every single one of them, before he woke up alone and empty-handed in his tower.

He waited for Marina to demur and say she had an early start. Or perhaps offer to go up and read to her father. She was a devoted daughter. Whenever he was inclined to condemn her as unwomanly—most of the time, because she wasn't womanly enough to tumble into his arms for the mere asking—he recalled her care for Ugolino.

She shot him an unreadable glance, then kissed her father's cheek. "Very well, Papa. To keep you happy, we'll stay down here, burning the midnight oil."

"*Eccellente!*"

Once Ugolino had gone, Fergus waited for Marina to tell him what she was up to. Perhaps she saved the news of her departure for when they were alone. He struggled to come up with some reason to keep her at Achnasheen, but he had nothing new to say.

I want you. I hunger for you. Please don't leave me.

None were likely to persuade her. What astonished him was how close he verged to kicking his pride aside and saying them anyway.

"Are ye going to play for me?" He struggled to pretend that having her near but forbidden didn't push him to the edge of madness.

"Would you like me to?"

With a sigh, he ran his hand through his hair. "Ye ken what I want."

He waited for some dismissive response, but the eyes she leveled on him seemed to weigh his soul in the balance. That was new, too. None of his earlier affairs had touched on anything more profound than carnal pleasure.

"I do."

"I suppose you're about to say you're leaving," he said flatly.

To his surprise, she laughed. "Chin up, Mackinnon. Faint heart never won fair lady."

Taken aback, he straightened and gave her a direct look. "What in Hades..."

"It's a lovely evening." Her smile broadened. "A thoughtful host might invite a guest for a walk."

"Marina?" he asked wonderingly, then to his utter astonishment, she stepped forward to curl her fingers around his arm. His heart performed a triple somersault, then crashed hard against his ribs.

"I'd like to see the loch by moonlight."

It was absurd, but Fergus had difficulty breathing. Some vestige of honor made him dredge up a warning. "If I get you alone in the moonlight, lassie, you willnae be wasting time admiring the view."

"That's a pity," she said with patent insincerity. "If the view doesn't hold my attention, how else can I pass the time?"

"You wee..." He bit off the rest of what he meant to say because Kirsty came in to clear the table.

Marina pulled away from him, leaving his skin tingling with the memory of her touch. "I have it on good authority that the fine weather won't last much longer," she said airily.

"Aye, winter can be cruel," he responded, paying little attention to what he said.

When Kirsty's surreptitious glance toward them held a hint of smug approval, an unwelcome insight hit Fergus. It was clear that he hadn't hidden his hankering after his lovely guest as well as he'd intended.

"Then a short stroll will be perfect." Marina paused. "One must seize happiness when one can."

Fergus hardly dared to hope that this meant what he thought it did. After all, Marina could just be talking about a walk in the night air. His heart thumping with anticipation—even as he told himself to calm down, he could be reading too much into this—he gestured toward the door. "*Signorina*?"

"With pleasure."

When he extended his arm, she slipped her fingers into the crook of his elbow. Was he a fool to find cause for optimism in this sudden willingness to touch him? She had him in such a spin, he hardly knew where to look. Was she merely thankful because he'd saved her life? Hell, he couldn't bear it if gratitude was the reason behind this thaw in her manner.

As they left the dining room and entered the hall, cavernous in the flickering candlelight, he could swear he heard muffled giggling behind him. The women in Achnasheen were getting above themselves. It was time he restored order. Marina Lucchetti was providing a bad example.

"You're smiling," Marina said curiously.

"Aye." Despite his confusion and turmoil, he was. "I'm thinking that the lassies here are losing all proper respect for masculine authority."

As they approached the castle doors, she cast him a taunting glance. "Well, one lassie is anyway."

Before he could contest that intriguing remark, Jock appeared out of the shadows to open the doors for them. Was a man never to find a minute's bloody privacy in this great barn of a house?

"Thank you, Jock," Marina said, as she and Fergus passed through into the courtyard.

Fergus placed his hand over hers, where it curved around his arm. "Are ye cold?"

"No," she murmured.

They went under the portcullis to emerge into a landscape touched with silvery magic. Or perhaps the magic stemmed from the woman beside him. A gasp of wonder escaped her. Her artist's soul would respond to this beauty.

In silence, Fergus and Marina strolled down to the loch, where the moon laid a shining path toward the black mountains rising in the distance. Apart from the soft lap of water on the bank and the hoot of an owl as it flew high above them, the night was quiet.

He wanted to badger Marina with questions and entreaties and demands, but something about the view's grandeur made his voice jam in his throat.

They paused on the grassy bank and looked up at the moon. Then Marina turned and smiled. The moonlight played games with his perception. He couldn't be sure that he read surrender in her eyes, or whether it was just more bloody wishful thinking.

"You saved my life today," she said, to his regret releasing his arm.

Fergus shuddered to think what might have happened on that hillside. His belly still constricted into a painful knot when he remembered seeing her teetering on the cliff face, inches from death.

Characteristically he sought refuge from turbulent emotion in humor. "You may drive me to distraction, lassie, but I'd rather have ye with me than lying at the bottom of a mountain."

Her expression turned serious. "When one balances on a few inches of crumbling ledge, one's mind becomes surprisingly clear."

It would be so easy to take this as an invitation and rush in. He'd learned over the last days to wait until he was certain. "Aye?"

"Thoughts of snatching opportunities, and how risks can lead to rewards."

Now, this sounded promising. Very promising indeed.

He spread his hands. "Marina, my darling, if you've changed your mind about an affair, ye need to tell me straight out. I can't risk any more mistakes with you. My heart won't bear it."

Impatience firmed her lips. "Must I say it?"

"For God's sake, if ye want me, say so." His voice roughened as agonizing hope lodged like a jagged rock in his throat.

Her dark eyes settled on his face. "I want you, Mackinnon."

He didn't take her in his arms, although the effort of holding back almost killed him. "And that means?"

Her lips curved in a beguiling smile. "It means you've won yourself a mistress, my braw Highland laddie."

"Marina..." he said, surging forward until to his astonishment, she placed a hand on his chest. "Not here."

"What the devil?"

Surely to God she wasn't still teasing him. Not now. Not after what she'd just said.

She tipped her head toward the castle gate. "We've got an audience."

Fergus glanced back and saw a huddle of figures in the shadows. Jock's bulk was unmistakable, and he guessed Kirsty and Jenny were there, too.

"Hell, you're right." He caught her hand in a forceful grip. "Would ye like to see the view from the point?"

Her low laugh ripped through him like fire. "More than I can say."

"Then come with me. And don't dawdle, *mo chridhe.*"

With a speed that left her breathless, Fergus whisked Marina out of direct view of the castle. Or perhaps that was excitement and anticipation—and still a few nerves about what she'd agreed to. No matter that she told herself she'd already cast her bonnet over a windmill, and it was too late for second thoughts.

He drew her into the shadows under a stand of Scots pines and glanced over his shoulder. "No watching eyes."

Warmth filled her. She was right to trust him with her reputation.

"Kiss me, Fergus," she said, no longer trying to conceal her yearning, a yearning that had eaten her alive for days. Today's interrupted kiss had only stoked her hunger. "Kiss me before I die of wanting you."

"Oh, my lovely lassie..." he said in a vibrant tone, as he drew her gently into his arms.

Marina had expected him to overwhelm her with passion. She didn't know what to do with this tenderness. It sought out the vulnerable spots in her soul that even now she fought to keep free of him.

This was the start of a short affair, not a lifelong commitment. When the liaison ended, she wanted to leave with a smile and a treasure chest of glorious memories. She didn't want to take away a broken heart as well.

His lips met hers and swift pleasure chased away her last misgivings. She sighed in surrender and curved into him, twining her arms around his neck and opening her mouth to his ardent exploration.

Perhaps because she no longer held back, the kiss was extraordinary, moving from sweetness to demand in a flash. His hands ran down her back to cup her buttocks through her gown and bring her hard against his body. She gave a hungry whimper when she met his arousal, a blatant weight against the soft flesh of her stomach.

With a groan, he eased away. "Tomorrow can't come soon enough. Although if we didn't have an audience, I'd carry you away now and have my wicked way with ye."

She touched his cheek. More care for her, although a reckless corner of her soul wanted to forget propriety and tell him to take her this very minute. "It will seem like forever."

"I promised to honor your good name. Trust me."

"I do," she said, surprised that she spoke without a scrap of doubt. As a woman making her way in a man's world, she'd learned to place her faith in few people. But Fergus was a man of honor. It was one of the qualities she most admired about him. That, and how he looked in a kilt.

"Thank you," he said, as if he understood the concession she made. "Now kiss me again, and I'll take ye back inside."

Her mouth turned down. "Bowing to public morality is going to become a nuisance."

"Och, the private pleasure will make it worthwhile."

He gave her another quick kiss. The seeking touch of his lips was a promise of joy to come, but it left her restless and unsatisfied. Her blood pumped thick and hot, and as Fergus drew back, her arms felt agonizingly empty.

"You'll arrange everything?"

His brief laugh was wry. "My sinful plans were set in place long ago."

"You were so sure of me?"

"Not at all. I still can't believe you said yes. Today ye were set to leave, and I wondered how I could endure it."

She liked that he didn't take her consent lightly. "You were right. I was afraid."

"I'll keep ye safe, Marina. I swear it." He caught her hand and raised it to his lips. Cursing the restrictions of propriety, she shivered in response. "We must go back."

"Anyone who looks at me must know something extraordinary has happened. I feel like I'm about to burst into flame."

"Oh, my dear..."

More dizzying kisses. This time, she pulled away. "We can't stay."

"No, we can't." Instead of shifting, he reached up to smooth her hair.

She forced herself to retreat a pace. The effort was painful. *Cielo,* so far he hadn't ventured past kisses. How would she bring herself to say goodbye, once she'd given him her body?

"I'll see ye at dawn?"

"Yes."

Marina wondered how he'd manage their rendezvous. Or did he mean to take her on the bare hillside? Excitement rippled through her as she imagined how they'd join together wild and free, with the sky above them and only the birds to hear her cries of ecstasy.

"Stop looking at me like that, or I willnae be responsible for my actions," he groaned.

"We must go in?"

His eyes burned through the dimness. "We must."

Fergus caught her up for one more kiss, then released her. She gave a shaky laugh. "Keep at least two feet between us."

"Three."

"I want you to myself." There was an intoxicating freedom in saying all the things she'd never dared to voice before.

"Soon."

"Yes, soon." Which struck her as a beautiful word, although "now" would be lovelier.

For a charged instant, she hovered on the verge of flinging herself into his arms. Then a bird called from the trees and reminded her that she lived in the real world, not a radiant bubble of passion where nothing else mattered but her craving for this man.

Reluctant to leave him, but knowing she must, she turned and picked her way back along the bank to the castle. True to his word, Fergus remained a few paces behind her. They didn't speak. He, like she, must know how close she was to yielding. One coaxing word, and she'd hurl her reputation to the wind.

Their circumspection went for naught because when they arrived back at the castle, the courtyard was empty.

Life was odd. When she'd had no intention of giving in to Fergus, Marina hadn't been self-conscious about his company. Now she'd promised to become his lover, she sensed spying eyes everywhere. She wrapped her arms around herself, and Fergus frowned as he caught up with her.

"I kept ye out too long. You're cold." He lowered his voice. "What I'd give to be able to warm you up."

"I'm so warm now, I doubt I'll sleep. I'm feeling rather bold being alone with you."

In the moonlight, his straight white teeth glinted white as he smiled. "Imagine how you'll feel tomorrow."

Imagine. Her heart performed a leaping skip that made her giddy. She raised a shaking hand to her chest, but nothing could calm her raging excitement. Her voice was unsteady as she spoke. "I don't think you should walk me to my room."

"Perhaps not wise."

She turned away, knowing if she didn't go now, she wouldn't. "Goodnight, Mackinnon," she said in a normal voice, in case anyone was listening.

"Goodnight, *signorina*," he said behind her, and as she climbed the steps to the massive doors, she heard him whisper, "Dream of me, bonny lassie."

CHAPTER SIXTEEN

he stone and wood structure huddled down into the landscape. With its sod roof, it looked like an extension of the hillside above it. Unless Fergus had pointed the small building out to her, Marina wouldn't have known it was there.

"A shepherd's hut?" she asked, as she drew her pony up beside his in the morning light. Today, no dogs trotted in their wake. Fergus had left Macushla and Brecon back at the castle.

She'd awoken, refreshed and brimming with anticipation, as the first lark started to sing. Having chosen to become a fallen woman, she'd had her best night's sleep since arriving at Achnasheen. Her lack of qualms about her forthcoming ruin proved she was wicked to the bone.

During the last couple of hours, she and Fergus had spoken about casual matters as he took her deeper and deeper into the hills, away from the coast. Anyone could have eavesdropped on their conversation and come away without a whisper of scandal to share. He'd hardly touched her, too. By now, she was in a fever to be in his arms.

He dismounted with the animal grace that always made her artist's soul soar. "You'll see."

"You're such a tease," she said, as he lifted her off her pony.

"I'm getting some of my own back." When his hands settled at her waist, she placed her palms flat against his chest.

This concord between them was so new, it felt daring to touch him. Today he wore traditional Highland dress, a loose white linen shirt and a kilt in the attractive red and black pattern.

"You look like such a wild and untamed Scot," she said, studying him. "I'd like to paint you like this."

His hands tightened, and that expressive mouth quirked. "Not right now."

"No, not right now," she echoed and leaned in to meet his kiss.

The world tilted, then tilted some more, as he picked her up and carried her over the rough grass to the strange little building. Her heart dipped and swooped like a swallow taking wing. Dizzy with excitement, she slid her arm around his neck, as he lifted the latch on the heavy oak door between two low-silled windows.

The dimness inside made Marina blink, but as her vision adjusted, she gave an exclamation of pleasure. "A shepherd with sophisticated tastes, *certo*."

"My father was mad for stalking the deer." Fergus strode across to the huge bed and set her carefully on the covers. "He had this built so he could stay up in the hills for days on end without sacrificing his comfort."

Her breath caught as what was about to happen suddenly gained a solid physical reality it had lacked before. Here she was in Fergus's bed, where soon he'd take her body. Today, her life would change forever.

The prospect was thrilling—and daunting. Until now, she'd managed to keep her nerves in check, but at this moment, she felt fidgety and far too aware of her lack of experience. She raised one unsteady hand to her throat, where her pulse performed a wild Scotch reel.

"So we're private here?" She took in her luxurious surroundings with the carved mantelpiece and leather sofas and elegant mahogany furniture, before her attention returned, as it must, to the man regarding her with brilliant gray eyes. She saw her excitement mirrored there in bright silver.

"Aye." He hauled off his boots and came down to lie beside her, raising himself on one elbow so he could look into her face.

How she hoped he didn't see her last-minute fit of collywobbles. She was disappointed in herself. Since she'd decided to become his mistress, she'd felt so brave and strong. She didn't feel brave and strong at this moment.

"Private and safe." His eyes glowed as he stared at her, and he brushed a few stray tendrils of hair back from her forehead. "This part of the estate is still given over to deer."

Her lips twitched, even as she trembled under the caress. "And my dear."

The warmth of his hand settled the worst of her jumpiness. His touch had always held such power over her.

"And mine." He leaned in to touch gentle lips to hers. The sweetness turned her blood to syrup and made foolish tears prickle at her eyes.

She lifted a shaking hand to stroke his face. How she loved the way the stark bones fitted together to form his striking features. How she loved the way his eyes glowed down at her, as if she were the most glorious creation on earth.

Fergus kissed her again with more heat, his tongue slipping between her lips to lure her into a sensuous game. She sighed with pleasure and joined the play, flicking her tongue against his and pulling away to nip at his lips.

He rolled over her, pressing her into the thick mattress. He nuzzled her neck, until she felt likely to melt. An insistent throb set up at the base of her belly, and she tightened her thighs around his narrow hips. Avid to touch him, she shoved aside the loose shirt. Insatiable fingers discovered his shoulders and chest; warm, smooth skin and a scattering of silky hair.

"I've imagined having ye in my arms like this since I first saw you," he groaned against her shoulder. "Yet now you're here, and reality is so much better."

"I wanted you, too," she responded just as unsteadily. "All the time."

"We have so much to discover." He sat up to tug his shirt over his head and toss it aside.

At this first sight of his naked chest, her eyes rounded, and her heart turned over in a somersault. She'd hoped the butterflies in her stomach had settled, but watching a man undress for the first time reminded her of her innocence.

She gulped for air, which suddenly seemed in short supply. "*Per l'amor di dio,* Michelangelo would weep if he could see you."

Her foolish heart turned over again, when she saw that her praise left him at a loss. The Mackinnon looked almost bashful, something she'd never have imagined possible. How delightful.

Cavolo, she'd better be careful. She expected to find passion in his arms, but this encounter tugged at her wayward emotions as powerfully as it stoked carnal hunger.

"Go on with ye, Marina," he said gruffly.

"*Si,* I will go on," she whispered, her confidence reviving as she sat up.

Nervous or not, she couldn't resist touching him. With a shaking hand, Marina traced a path from one broad shoulder, across to the dark red hair curling over his chest, and down across his flat stomach. Beneath her hesitant exploration, his muscles twitched and tightened. By the time she reached the barrier of the wide black leather belt, his stomach had turned as hard as rock.

How gratifying that her touch had power over him, too. With greater assurance, she retraced the path, brushing his light brown nipple on the way. He caught his breath on a hiss.

Interesting. He must like that. How fascinating his body was. How fascinating to discover ways to give him pleasure in return for the pleasure he gave her.

He caught her seeking hand and brought it to his lips. "Let me undress ye, lassie."

Marina summoned her courage. It wasn't as difficult as it would have been five minutes ago. "Yes, please."

She liked that he didn't fumble or rush as he released the buttons on her dark green jacket. With more of that mesmerizing care, he parted the lapels to reveal her fine lawn shirt beneath. When his eyes flared at the sight of her body under the sheer white fabric, her breasts swelled against her corset. Her very flesh longed for him.

"More buttons," he murmured.

Marina bit back a laugh, as the butterflies inside her fluttered down to rest. She even found the audacity to tease him. "You like a challenge."

"It seems I do, at that." With breathtaking efficiency, he undid the mother-of-pearl buttons down the front of her plain shirt. Her nipples tightened as his hands brushed them through the thin fabric.

Showing the same care, he spread the edges of the shirt to reveal her corset. His groan of frustration made her laugh. "Don't give up yet, Mackinnon. It's only a few hooks up the front."

"Easy for ye to say 'only.'"

With a patience that made her tremble, Fergus undid her corset. Her pale cream shift beneath was so transparent that it revealed the dark pink peaks of her nipples. When his heavy-lidded eyes leveled on the blatant display, he licked his lips as if he tasted something delicious.

"Italian lassies wear too many clothes."

His fingers busied themselves untying the blue silk ribbon that closed the top of her shift. More tantalizing glances of his hands across her skin.

The chemise fell open, and her breasts tumbled free into his palms. As he cupped her flesh, a flash of exquisite heat made her cry out. He squeezed again, and another shiver rippled through her.

The wonder in his expression as he stared enthralled at her naked breasts scored a rift across her heart. The sight of her bosom spilling between the parted edges of her shirt seemed almost more brazen than full nakedness. Against the dark green merino jacket, her skin appeared startlingly white.

As he touched her, a glow verging on reverence shone in his eyes. He bent to kiss the slope of each pale breast, and she combed her fingers through his thick hair as she held him to her. More unruly emotions. Already this affair took her beyond anything she'd ever imagined. She curved a shaking hand around his shoulder, feeling his sinewy strength beneath her palm.

"Show me more," he whispered, his breath making her skin tingle.

"*Si, caro. Con piacere.*" He sat back, as she wriggled out of jacket, shirt, and corset, pushing them to the floor in a tangled lump.

His breath caught, and he reached for her once more. "By God, you were worth waiting for," he said huskily, his thumbs brushing nipples already hard and aching.

He took one peak between his lips, drawing on the tip until she moaned and twisted upon the bed. When she was sure she could bear no more of this fierce pleasure, he shifted his attentions to her other breast. She was astonished to learn that desire knew no limit.

A swift frown darkened his features as he noticed the bruises on her arms from yesterday's fall. "To think, I came so close to losing ye yesterday."

He bent his russet head to kiss each dark mark on her skin. She shivered under his tender attentions, and overwhelming emotion tightened her throat, until her breath emerged in broken gasps. She'd expected him to lavish his sensual skills upon her, but this sweetness made her feel cherished.

Her fingers returned to tangle in his rich, red hair, and as his teeth scraped her nipple, she pulled on the straight, satiny strands until he grunted. By the time he raised his head, she was shivering with ascending need. The secret hollow between her legs turned slick and hot, and she met his kiss with open-mouthed desperation. His lingering attentions to her breasts made her crave the ultimate joining.

"Don't stop," she croaked in a voice she didn't recognize.

He dropped a kiss on the curve of her breast and to her dismay shifted to sit on the edge of the bed. Unable to bear even this much separation, she rose on her knees and pressed into his back. She twined her arms around him, feeling how he trembled. "Fergus?"

"You drive me right to the brink," he confessed unsteadily. "Give me a moment."

Snatching a choked breath, he caught her hand and placed it between his legs. Touching him where he rose hard and insistent under the soft wool kilt was extraordinary, as though she held the source of the world's power. Excitement and an echo of her earlier trepidation clenched in her stomach, as she imagined all that strength and potency sliding into her.

"I want you so much," Marina whispered, kissing a crooked line across the top of his naked back. The heat rising off his skin made her feel like she hunkered down next to a huge furnace.

"I want ye too much." His voice sounded like gravel.

The admission made her release his rod and slide her arms around his waist from behind. "Is that possible?"

His grunt of laughter held the familiar self-derisive note. "It is when I need to take my time and show ye what you've been missing, *mo chridhe*."

She couldn't imagine desiring him more than she did. "I'm ready for you now."

With a gentleness that set her blood moving in languid circles and soothed the upsurge of virginal fear, he stroked her arms. "Not nearly."

Cielo, there was more? She'd die of pleasure before he was done. "Don't make me wait."

"There's no rush, my bonny. I have all day to drive ye mad."

"You Highland laddies have high opinions of yourselves," she said.

"Aye, and well earned, as you'll soon see."

"I hope it's soon."

"Patience has its rewards," he murmured. "Trust me, Marina."

"*Si*, I trust you, Fergus," she said, and tried to ignore how closely her words resembled a declaration of love.

For a long time, he remained in her embrace. His erratic breathing settled. She'd wanted him to keep feeding her excitement. But as the seconds ticked by, the sweetness of this connection soon seduced her into a sensual dream.

"Lie back," he murmured. She stretched out on the bed, her limbs heavy with longing and her heart racing with anticipation.

He stood to slide her half boots and stockings off. He'd lulled her into quietness, but her lassitude melted away like dew in sunlight when he began to stroke her legs. He ran his hands up her thighs, approaching but never reaching the place where she throbbed with need. When she made a wordless sound of complaint, the brute had the nerve to laugh at her.

"Patience."

"I grow to dislike that word, *caro*."

"Whisht, lassie," he murmured, bending down to kiss her again. "We'll get there in the end."

He played with her mouth until she was shaking and panting. In a silent plea for more, she raised grasping hands to knead the hard muscles of his upper arms. When he brushed his lips over her instep, she jerked against the bed, although compared to what he'd done to her breasts, the kiss was almost chaste. She attained such a pitch of hunger, every touch sent heat exploding along her veins.

Fergus dropped a rain of kisses across her breasts before with impressive efficiency, he released her skirt and petticoats. He drew the garments down to reveal filmy drawers under the rucked-up shift. His eyes turned bright with hunger, as he undid his wide black belt and let it drop with a thud to the floor, followed by the soft rustle of his kilt falling away.

His nakedness transfixed Marina. "What a superb man you are," she sighed, her heated gaze tracing his powerful leanness, before focusing on the hard column of flesh rising from a nest of dark red hair between his legs.

Her hands closed on emptiness at her sides as apprehension stirred anew. He was so very big. *Per pietà*, how would all that male strength feel as it moved inside her?

"Thank you," Fergus said, and he bestowed his rare, full smile upon her. Whenever he did, she always felt like he gave her a wonderful gift. Her fleeting fear vanished as if it had never been.

Marina had imagined she'd feel nervous when a man saw her naked for the first time. She'd been nervous when he first joined her on the bed. But Fergus had built her responses inch by inch, until all she cared about was finding an answer to this endless craving.

She sat up and, hands clumsy with eagerness, she tugged her shift over her head. Now only her drawers remained. The transparent material did little to hide the dark patch of hair between her legs.

With glittering eyes, Fergus surveyed her body. Marina had a sudden memory of their first meeting when she'd wanted to spread herself before him and let him work his enchantment. The wanton thought had been a premonition.

"You're quite a sight yourself, lassie," he said in a hoarse whisper, kneeling over her.

Her skin tightened in anticipation as she waited for him to rip away her drawers and plunge into her, but there was just more of that tantalizing patience. His face stern with concentration, he explored her body, trailing fire across breasts and belly and flanks. Only when she was moaning and trembling against the covers did he touch her where she burned for him.

He found the slit in her drawers and cupped her mound. An uncontrollable surge of liquid heat welled to greet him. She gasped in surprise and bowed up, wanting more but not understanding what that meant. Fergus met her helpless response with a guttural sound of approval.

Per l'amor di dio, this encounter was a revelation. How she could burn to the point of immolation, then burn some more. How a man's hands on her bare skin made her blood rush in a hot tide of demand. How desire could tease and torture to the edge of pain, yet remain the most exquisite pleasure.

Fergus kissed her again. He'd kissed her so often today, and every time it was different. This was a passionate exploration, so that when he started to caress her between the legs, it felt like part of the same act. This bold exploration of her most private flesh should shock her, but his careful seduction had carried her far beyond shyness. Blindly she reached for his arm, seeking some stability in a reeling world.

Then thinking herself beyond shock, she discovered she wasn't at all. Subtle pressure, and one long finger invaded her body.

Marina shuddered at the intimate penetration, then cried out when he brushed his thumb over a place of tormenting sensitivity. A blast of pleasure shook her, then another and another, as he began to work his finger in and out. She was sleek with need already, but her uncontained female response to this invasion astonished her.

Fergus watched the way his hand moved on and in her with an unwavering concentration that fired her arousal to wildfire. There was something bewitching about having all that blazing masculine attention focused on her.

She shuddered anew when he stretched her with two fingers, then again when he curled the tips against a spot inside her and sent rivers of wild flame coursing through her veins. Her breath emerged in harsh sobs, and her hand clenched hard against his shoulder.

"Now," she said brokenly.

The eyes he raised to hers were black with hunger. "Soon."

"Mackinnon, stop torturing me." She dug her nails into his firm flesh. "I want you."

"Not enough."

"Any more and I'll explode."

"Och, you're nowhere near that yet," he said, and in her urgency, she hated his smugness, even as her body tensed toward some unknown end.

"I want..." she stuttered as sensation rose to inundate her. "I want..."

She expected him to smile, but he looked as if the fate of worlds hung on what he did to her. Still the powerful feeling swelled inside her. She was nearing some mysterious edge, when he eased his hand away.

"Kiss me, Marina," he said in a thick voice.

She lurched up, linking her arms around his neck and pressing her mouth to his. "Touch me again," she muttered against his lips.

Instead of returning to that delightful torment, *il cattivo*, he went back to squeezing and touching her breasts. She was in such a fever that every brush of his fingers made her quake. When he began to roll and pull the tips, fireworks exploded behind her eyes. All of her thirsted for him to take her. She bumped her hips up until her cleft met his arousal. Instead of providing any satisfaction, that only spurred her need.

"You want me, too," she said, sounding as if she accused him of a crime.

"More than my life, my bonny," he said, rubbing luxuriantly against her sex, lingering in the satiny folds. They were both shaking after that.

With unsteady hands, he untied her drawers and tugged them down her hips and off. She was in such turmoil, she barely registered that at last they were both naked.

Marina began to touch him, running eager hands over his arms and shoulders, down that strong, flexible back, pressing into the firm globes of his buttocks. He groaned and scraped his teeth along her neck until she moaned and bit his shoulder in retaliation.

He kissed her hard and pulled her knees up, opening her to him. She tilted her hips in immediate invitation, but he kept stroking her. Again and again, he brought her to the point where she was sure she must break apart, before he eased back.

Marina felt wrung out and exhausted, yet on edge and jumpy. She sucked in a breath that tasted of male musk and female desire and prepared to tell Fergus to stop teasing her. Then all conscious thought fled as the pressure between her legs became harder and hotter and more purposeful.

"Fergus..." she whispered in welcome, as her senses dissolved in a mixture of discomfort and delight.

He rose on his elbows so he could watch her face. The skin stretched tight across his chiseled features, and he struggled for every breath.

Cielo, without him inside her, she felt empty. Instinct made her lift her hips to take him. With a smoothness that astounded her, he shifted forward. She cried out at the sharp sting as he took her virginity, then forgot the brief discomfort when Fergus seated himself fully within her.

The experience ranged beyond her most extravagant imaginings. Fergus conquered more than her body; he claimed her very soul. Unashamedly possessive hands slid down his back, loving how the powerful muscles shifted under her caress. Her hungry gaze sought his. His gray eyes were dark and smoky and alight with joy.

"You're mine now." She couldn't mistake the masculine triumph in his words.

A week ago, she might have contested that statement, despite being so obviously at his mercy. Today she stared into that remarkable face and found it in her to smile. "And you're mine. Don't try and deny it."

His gasp of laughter quivered through her. Every time she shifted, he moved inside her. The raw intimacy of this connection thrilled her as nothing else, even her art, ever had. In silent affirmation of his possession, her body softened and settled around him.

"Aye, I think you might be right."

His muscles tightened under the hands she rested on the small of his back. With his slow withdrawal, she gave a long, reverberant moan. Her eyes fluttered shut as pleasure engulfed her. Then opened wide in amazement when he slid forward again, stirring every nerve to fresh sensation.

"Ooh," she said on a gasp of happy discovery. "There's more."

"Aye, much more."

"*Eccellente.*" She clenched around him in an instinctive attempt to keep him with her.

Fergus gave a broken groan, and the eyes gazing down into hers turned glassy. "Devil take you, do that again."

She tensed on purpose, relishing the way he trembled in response. How she loved the pleasure she gave him.

This time when he moved, Marina rose to meet him. Seduction exploded into a fiery dance of bodies meeting and parting. Anticipation surged anew, spiraling inside her like hot, twisting wire. It was the way she'd felt when he'd touched her to the point of torture, but now, nothing stopped her climbing the wave that towered higher and higher.

Her fingers dug into his back as he took her in long, deliberate strokes. Each glide of his body heightened the yearning after something she'd never known but instinctively sensed awaited. Her breath emerged in harsh gasps, and she pressed up toward him as the wild storm loomed closer and closer.

"Let go, Marina," he crooned, his Scots burr stronger than she'd ever heard it.

His breath against her ear as he rolled the 'R' in her name added yet another element to the whirling magic. She shivered, and her arousal soared higher yet, without sending her tumbling over into relief.

"I don't know what to do," she panted. "It's like running after something I'll never catch."

"You'll catch it." He lurched onto his knees and tugged her hips up. The change in position thundered through her. He plunged into her hard and high and slammed against some deep part of her that she hadn't known was there.

She convulsed into immediate climax. The world around her dissolved into white lightning, and she cried out Fergus's name in wonder as everything flashed into blinding light.

At last Fergus's control frayed. The relentless, driving rhythm of his thrusts became choppy, and his breath escaped in great groans of pleasure. For what felt like an eon, Marina remained suspended at a peak of rapture so pure it dimmed the sun. Then as she floated down, he jolted in her arms and went rigid.

With a guttural cry, he wrenched away to spill his seed in powerful spurts on her naked stomach. He clutched her hips, holding her in place as he found his release.

Marina stared up at him in a sensual daze, while reality called her back from the edge of transcendence. Stupid to regret that he didn't fill her. Stupid to feel empty and, despite all the pleasure that went before, disappointed.

He'd sworn to protect her from a child, and he'd stayed true to his word. She should be grateful that he'd justified her trust.

He drew a rasping breath, then another, and reached down to stroke her cheek. His tenderness had launched today's journey. Now after Fergus had changed her world forever, tenderness returned to his touch and his voice to remind her of that sweet beginning.

"You're astonishing, Marina Lucchetti."

CHAPTER SEVENTEEN

Through misty eyes, Marina lay on the bed and watched Fergus walk across to collect a towel from the pile on the washstand. He returned to her side and with more of that heartbreaking gentleness, he wiped away the sticky mess on her stomach. Then he bent to kiss her. The kiss contained no passion, but a wealth of gratitude. He lingered long enough for the sweetness to seep into her bones and turn them to honey.

She caught his wrist, running her hand down to his in a caress that communicated exquisite joy. What could one say after flying to the stars and back? Thank you seemed inadequate. What she'd experienced beggared description.

He moved away to clean himself and wrap his kilt around his waist. His action reminded Marina she sprawled naked across the bedcovers. She sat up and scooped up her shirt, hoping it might restore a shred of modesty. It was long enough to cover her to her thighs.

Fergus crouched in front of the fireplace and set the kindling alight. "I'll heat some water, so ye can have a proper wash."

"Thank you." This transition from paradise to the prosaic left her feeling tongue-tied and awkward. With unsteady hands, she started to button her shirt. Fergus must have shaved this morning, but her breasts and neck stung a little from his passionate attentions.

He tilted his head to observe her uncertain progress. "Did I hurt you?"

Ridiculous that she'd felt so free and bold when they'd made love, yet now she blushed to talk about what they'd done.

"No." At his arched russet eyebrow, she stammered the truth. "A little. At first." Even more unsteadily, she went on. "I didn't think it would be like that. I didn't think *you'd* be like that."

Frowning, he rose. "Damn it, did I let ye down, lassie?"

He was a man so confident, it verged on a fault. This hint of vulnerability touched her. She gave her head an emphatic shake. "There was no disappointment, Mackinnon. You were..." She struggled for words to convey that matchless pleasure. "...marvelous."

He sat on the side of the bed, taking her hand. Immediately she felt better, more at ease.

"So were you." He gave her one of those half-smiles that she cherished. "I hope before too long, you'll give me another chance to be marvelous."

Heat that had nothing to do with embarrassment flooded her. She was shocked at her reviving interest. *Per pietà*, how could she summon even a spark of arousal after what they'd done? "Really?"

"Aye, of course. If you're not too sore." He paused. "And if you'd like to do it all again."

Marina sent him a mock disapproving glance. "I don't trust you when you're accommodating."

"Take advantage of it while it lasts." The half-smile lingered. "What is your pleasure, my lady?"

You're my pleasure.

She bit back the words as too revealing, although after today, he must know that she couldn't resist him. "Perhaps breakfast."

Fergus kissed her with more intent this time. By the time he lifted his head, she lolled bonelessly against the pillows. "Och, you're a grand lass."

She summoned a smile, as her heart thundered fit to burst out of her constricted chest. "Just because I asked for breakfast?"

"Just because you are." The fondness softening his gaze was more dangerous to her equilibrium than his smiles. And they already made her as dizzy as a wheel. "Now tell me what ye meant when you said things didnae meet your expectations."

It was her turn to smile. "I'm not expressing any dissatisfaction."

"I'm pleased to hear it."

"After guarding my chastity so long, I imagined I'd rue the loss. But in your arms, it seemed so natural to let desire take its course."

Another purposeful kiss left her trembling. "So was that the surprise?"

She made a helpless gesture, as she struggled to express herself. "I assumed after the long pursuit, that you'd be..."

"Ah," he said softly. "You thought I'd fall on ye like Macushla devours a nice juicy bone."

A half-horrified giggle escaped her. "Perhaps not the comparison I'd choose, but all the same, I imagined you'd be more..."

"Voracious?"

"Yes."

"You were a virgin."

"So you were being considerate?"

He shrugged. "I've never been one of those greedy laddies who gobbles his food and misses all the fine flavors for the sake of filling his belly. Ye were a delicious meal indeed, lassie. I wasnae going to rush a moment of feasting on you." A sudden frown drew his auburn brows together. "Are you worried whether I wanted you? If you are, I'll never call ye an intelligent woman again."

"No," she said in a low voice. "I knew."

Indeed she did. His every action during that leisurely seduction had blazed with fierce desire.

"Good," he said shortly, before kissing her again. "Now let me look after you."

Independent, headstrong Marina Lucchetti nodded and lay back on the disordered bed. *Dio*, was she losing her spirit, now she'd discovered a man's touch?

Or was she learning a touch of humility at last and recognizing that sometimes there was no harm in relinquishing control to someone else?

Especially someone as competent as Fergus. She'd admired his graceful efficiency from the first, when he'd dragged her and Papa from the wrecked coach. Even when she wanted to give the Laird of Achnasheen a good shake, she credited him as an unusually capable man.

Now appreciation for his proficiency seeped through her, as she watched him fetch water and set it heating on the fire. He brought in the saddlebags and assembled an appetizing meal of bread with ham and cheese, cake and fruit on the gate-leg table in the corner near the hearth. She mightn't require someone to look after her, but it was agreeable to watch a man work so diligently for her comfort.

He raised his head from where he bent over the fire. "Ye look like the wee kitten who got the cream, lassie."

Marina smiled in unabashed delight. "Miaow."

He laughed in appreciation and rose with a cup and saucer in one hand and a small crystal glass in the other. "Some tea for you—and a wee dram to mark the occasion."

"Not that barbarous spirit?" She sat up and accepted the cup, while Fergus set the glass on the nightstand beside her.

Fascinating laughter lines deepened around his gray eyes. Her fingers itched to capture that expression on paper. But her portfolio was outside, tied to her pony's saddle, and for once in her life, she had something better than art to think about.

"Aye. Try it. You might like it."

"Papa has developed quite a taste for it. When we go back to Florence, he'll find our Italian liqueurs sadly tame."

For a chilling moment, the specter of the end of their affair hovered in the air. With an effort, she dismissed the unhappy prospect. She and Fergus looked forward to a few torrid weeks together. Why spoil today's joy by stewing on inevitable farewells?

"I'll give him a couple of bottles to take back with him," Fergus said easily, and she realized he'd already come to terms with her only sharing his bed until she went home.

Why shouldn't he? Her stay at Achnasheen was always going to be temporary, whether she gave herself to him or not. She had a career and a life in Italy. She couldn't throw it all away to play the laird's mistress until he tired of her.

Nonetheless, his easy acceptance of her eventual departure rankled a little.

"Thank you." This time, it took more effort, but she forced herself back to the present, when she'd just experienced incandescent joy and the prospect of further joy awaited. "Did you bring the china and glassware up with you?"

"No." He returned to collect his own glass. If he noted her brief disquiet, he didn't show it. "I told you, the lodge is kept set up for hunting."

"With only the finest." Her teacup was delicate and painted with birds and flowers. She sipped, unsurprised that Fergus had made the perfect brew. Once upon a time, she'd wanted to mock his endless self-confidence. Experience since then had taught her that everything he did, he did well.

Including use a woman.

She gave a voluptuous shiver, as incendiary memories of the morning's encounter rippled through her. If she had to fall, at least she'd chosen a man who knew how to catch her. Despite her inexperience, she recognized he was a lover in a thousand.

"Will ye no' drink a toast with me to an enterprise well begun, lassie?"

She set the teacup down on the nightstand and lifted the small, heavy glass filled with golden liquid. "I drink to the man who has shown me a new world. *Salute!*"

His eyes warmed. "I'll drink to the loveliest lass in the Highlands. Here's to your bonny black eyes, Marina Lucchetti. *Slàinte mhath!*"

She reached forward to clink her glass against his, and noticed the way his gaze dropped to the gaping neck of her shirt. She hadn't got far with the buttons. "You're not looking at my eyes, Mackinnon."

Another half-smile. "Aye, that's true. But then it's not only your eyes that are bonny, *mo chridhe*."

Through her gratification, she frowned in puzzlement. "What's that you call me?"

"*Mo chridhe?*"

"Mow cree?"

He chuckled at her hesitant pronunciation. "Something like that. It means 'my heart' or 'my darling.'"

"You've called me your darling before. When you saved me from the cliff edge and last night by the loch."

"Aye, I have." He sent her a searching look. "Don't ye like it?"

Like it? She loved it. The endearment transformed her heart into a great sugary puddle.

"Of course I like it," she admitted. "You know I do. You have a sweet tongue, Mackinnon."

"Let me prove it, my bonny lass." He leaned forward and kissed her with a thoroughness that left her breathless. On his lips, the local liquor was almost as delicious as his words.

When he raised his head, his eyes were dark. Feeling bold, she caught his free hand and slid it under her shirt and against her breast.

His touch was warm, and the slight calluses abraded her skin with delightful friction. The merest brush of his fingers set her head swimming. She shivered again, as her nipple hardened against his palm. A heavy, eager weight settled between her legs, where a pleasant ache lingered from his possession.

"Marina..." He spoke her name with such longing that she trembled.

When he squeezed her breast, her powerful reaction made her wriggle against the rumpled sheets. With each shift, she was breathtakingly conscious that her body had changed. She ached in places she hadn't known existed before today.

She lifted the glass to her lips. "Drink up, Mackinnon."

The liquor tasted strange on her tongue, but as it slipped down her throat, it warmed her on the inside the way his touch warmed her on the outside. The rich aftertaste almost convinced her she might come to enjoy the flavor. In about a hundred years.

Fergus surveyed her with a glowing admiration as restorative as any spirits, then swallowed his drink in a single mouthful. He set the glass on the nightstand.

"I didn't know desire could be like this." She blushed. "I think I'll like being your mistress."

"I'll do my best to make you happy, lassie." He scratched a nail across her beaded nipple, feeding her restiveness. "I ken what a gift you've given me."

When he said things like that, she couldn't resist him. "Oh, Fergus," she sighed, leaning forward for a kiss.

The kiss lasted far too short a time. He lifted his head and sent her a mocking glance. "Drink your whisky. It's bad luck to leave any in the glass. Then I'll pour ye some warm water for a wash, and we can have breakfast. You'll need your strength for what I'm planning."

Marina swallowed the rest of her whisky, surprised that the taste already became more palatable. "Curse your control and your common sense, Mackinnon," she muttered.

He gave a brief grunt of amusement. "You know ye dinna want a laddie who gives no thought for your comfort and seeks only his own satisfaction."

She sighed, although his consideration made her heart cramp with feelings she didn't want to examine at this precise minute. If ever. "You're still the laird, even now."

"Aye, always. And you're still the reckless *signorina* setting her will against mine." He spoke with no particular animus, so it was difficult to summon much pique.

"Do you mind?"

He shook his dark auburn head. "It's exciting. I've never held a woman in my arms, not knowing whether she'll bite me or kiss me."

She'd already done both, and she saw in his face, he shared the same thought. Her eyes narrowed on him. "Just remember that."

More of that devastating fondness lit his gaze. She found him madly attractive, but she also liked him more than any man she'd ever met. *Dio l'aiuti,* she even liked that she couldn't turn him to her will.

A woman might dare to consider herself Fergus Mackinnon's equal. She'd be a fool indeed to think herself his superior.

"You're such a bully," she said, without meaning a word of it.

A wry smile curled his lips. "Face it, lassie, you love it when I push you around."

"Only when you're right," she retorted.

He laughed aloud at that. "Aye, well, isn't that all the time?"

Before she could summon a suitable response, he dragged her into his arms for a kiss that promised passion. She could hardly wait.

CHAPTER EIGHTEEN

The sun was sinking low behind the Cuillins on Skye when Fergus rode away from his father's luxurious hunting lodge. As his pony ambled homeward, Marina rested in his arms, soft, warm and sleepy.

Pleasant exhaustion weighted his limbs, and his mind was at peace in a way it hadn't been since he met the lassie who leaned against him with such trust. Sweet memories of the day filled him with wellbeing.

Knowing he was this splendid woman's only lover moved him at a profound level. When he'd first seen her dishing out orders from that carriage window, he'd decided she was difficult and prickly—if damned attractive. But today she'd turned to him with such beguiling eagerness and generosity, that he'd come to recognize that her essence was passion.

Passion for her art. Passion for her life. Passion for...him.

He'd never known a day of such extraordinary joy.

His arms tightened, and with a drowsy murmur, Marina stirred from her doze to twist her head and kiss the side of his neck.

He'd taken her again after a long and thorough seduction that left them both shaking with need. Again he'd experienced that incandescent intimacy as he thrust inside her. As laird, he was used to being alone. Leaders often were. But when he held Marina, he found a home.

It had been a perfect day. Until now.

Reluctantly, he drew the pony to a stop. "I cannae go back to the castle holding you in my arms, lassie. Or the world and his wife will ken just what we've been doing all day."

She rubbed her cheek against his shoulder. "I almost don't mind, if it means I can stay here like this."

He'd wondered if having given him so much today, she might take fright and retreat behind her defenses. Instead she'd surrendered with wholehearted completion.

It made Fergus feel like a king. It made him feel unworthy of her.

"You will mind in the end," he said, wishing he could face the world and proclaim this woman as his. But he'd sworn to keep her safe from talk.

Dear God above, the agony of pulling away from her at his peak had come close to tearing him apart. Some forbidden, wicked part of him longed to flood her with his seed and know he'd planted his child inside her.

But he'd given his word to preserve her good name, and the Mackinnon's word was an iron-clad guarantee.

The sheer animal pleasure of what they'd done to one another during this unforgettable day overwhelmed him, and he buried his face in her silky hair. The second time he'd taken her, he'd lingered to release it from its pins, so it lay like an ebony cape around her bare shoulders, offering glimpses of that pretty bosom whenever she moved.

Och, what he'd have given then to possess an ounce of her artistic talent, so he could capture and keep that image. Even with only fallible human memory to rely on, he'd remember Marina's melting dark eyes at that moment until the day he died.

He inhaled, so when he was alone in his bed tonight, her scent would linger in his nostrils. She smelled of sexual satisfaction, and crushed flowers, and a musky hint of sweat. A bouquet fit for paradise.

She sighed. "The real world is dragging us back, isn't it?"

The aching regret in her voice echoed his regret at needing to pretend that nothing had changed, once he returned to the castle. Whereas in ways he had difficulty comprehending, after today, everything was different.

"Aye," he said without moving.

"I don't like it."

"I don't either."

"I wish we'd stayed in the lodge."

"We can go back tomorrow."

"Oh, yes." Her ready acceptance filled him with carnal anticipation. "But there's tonight in between."

Aye, there was. Having caught her at last, he was loath to let her go, even for a few hours.

"What I'd give to have ye in my bed. High up in my tower, you'd be queen of the glen."

Her laugh was weary, and not just because of all they'd done at the lodge, he guessed. "You know I can't. For your sake as much as mine. The Mackinnon can't take a mistress here where he rules."

No, he couldn't. He owed his people more respect than that. He suspected his father, for all his selfishness, had faced the same dilemma. The ostentatious fittings of the lodge had always struck Fergus as excessive to the needs of a man stalking the deer. As he'd grown to adulthood, there had been whispers about the previous laird trysting there with a crofter's wife or two. Warning enough that he and Marina needed to be careful. The hills might appear empty, but gossip could run through the glen at an astonishing speed.

"I don't want to let ye go." He was talking about more than the coming hours of separation, devil take it.

And wasn't that a terrifying revelation? They'd negotiated an affair, but with every minute, the connection strengthened between him and this extraordinary woman. Now the prospect of losing her felt like someone stuck a dirk between his ribs.

To his relief, Marina took his words at face value. "We have tomorrow," she said, repeating his reassurance.

"Aye," he responded, only just stopping himself from asking what happened when their tomorrows ran out and she went back to Italy.

"I dare not look at you tonight, or Papa will guess what we've done," she said.

"And if I look at you, I willnae be able to resist hauling you into my arms." He feared he wasn't joking, although he appreciated the way she tried to lighten the atmosphere.

"We'd scandalize Kirsty and Jenny."

He made himself laugh, although having to let Marina go felt like someone hammered on a bruise. He wasn't ashamed of what they'd done. It seemed more sinful to hide how he felt than it had to join his body with hers.

Reverend Angus in his kirk would find that thought utterly reprehensible.

"We must go back," he said. "It will be dark soon."

In the end, Marina was the one who shifted. He couldn't command his arms to release her.

"Fergus, it's been a day I'll always treasure." She slid to the ground and stared up at him, her eyes luminous in the gloaming. "Thank you for your care and your kindness. Thank you for the...pleasure."

Although her words were powerfully moving, they made him frown. "That sounds like goodbye."

Her lips twisted. "No, but I want you to know how precious you made me feel. There was desire, but there was friendship, too, and I loved everything we did."

"Marina..." Her name emerged as a choked mutter. "You are precious."

He dismounted and stepped up beside her. "Give me one last kiss."

To his surprise and regret, she shook her head. "No."

"No?"

Her smile was tremulous. "If you do, I'll be all starry eyed, and there will be no hiding what we've been up to." She bit her lip and despite her denial, the need to kiss her gripped him with talons of steel. "You go ahead, and I'll come behind and try and look as if I've spent the day innocently sketching the landscape."

Damn it, she was right, but he didn't like it. He wanted to shout the news from the mountaintops that this exceptional woman was his and that he dared heaven and earth to take her away from him.

Then as he stepped back, he remembered that she was going to leave anyway, that this was a temporary liaison, and that once her father could walk again, she'd be on her way back to Florence.

"I'll kiss you a thousand times tomorrow, lassie, to make up for it."

"I'll hold you to that." Bravely clinging to the smile, she raised her hands to her hair. "Am I tidy, or do I look like you've tumbled me six ways to Saturday?"

He smiled. "You look bonny."

Impatience flattened her lips. "That's no answer."

"But ye always look bonny to me."

Her eyes narrowed on him. "Don't use your Scottish charm on me, Mackinnon."

"It's worked so far." He tucked a few strands of hair back into her simple chignon.

"Fergus..."

"You look windswept but decent." He feared that her kiss-reddened lips and the somnolent satisfaction in her eyes were more likely to give her away to an observer than untidy hair.

"That's good."

"And your hair is often a rat's nest. You're always tugging at it when you work."

"You noticed that?"

"I notice a lot." He shrugged. "I love watching ye."

She shot him a cross look. "More Scottish charm. Stop it."

With a brief laugh, he caught her hand and carried it to his lips. "I'm only speaking the truth. Now we must go in, before I give in to my base urges and rush ye back to the lodge. I'm letting you sleep alone tonight under sufferance."

Her eyes softened to black velvet. "Blast you, Mackinnon, I'm trying to act as if nothing has happened, and you go and say that."

"Think about tomorrow, Marina," he murmured, then took mercy on her and lifted her up into her sidesaddle.

As he turned his pony down the hill, he suspected he, too, looked as if he'd spent the day in a heaven a thousand miles away from mundane life. He'd have to be careful, or his secret rendezvous with Marina would end up being no secret at all.

"I will. I'll also think about today," she said softly from a few paces behind him, and only with the greatest difficulty did he resist dragging her off that pony and kissing her until she couldn't stand up.

By God, it was going to be a long wait until the morning, when he had her to himself again.

CHAPTER NINETEEN

Who would imagine such an independent miss would settle with such ease into life as a gentleman's mistress?

The next few weeks flew by in such a haze of happiness and physical satisfaction that Marina regretted the passing of each glorious, golden day. She'd resisted giving in to Fergus for many reasons, not least her fear of subjugating her will to his. Two such determined personalities were sure to clash, but so far, he proved to be a more reasonable man than she'd thought was possible when she first set eyes on him. She was sheepishly aware that he might say the same thing about her.

There were differences of opinion, but to her surprise, he turned out to be willing to listen to her. On rare occasions, she even found herself coming around to his way of thinking.

There was one place where they always agreed. In the big, extravagant bed in the luxurious hunting lodge. The merest touch of his hands on her skin set her blood singing with delight. She often smiled to recall the day he'd pleasured her with his mouth, followed by his shocked gratification when she'd returned the favor.

Each day, she came back to the castle in a glow of sensual bliss. She was afraid it must show, but nobody, including Papa, had remarked on the change in her.

Which suddenly struck her as odd, given how well her father knew her.

"What is it?" Fergus asked from a few feet away.

Smiling in welcome, she raised her head from her drawing. "I didn't hear you arrive."

Marina was sitting on the hill, not far from where she'd challenged him about his dismissive attitude to the women in his life. She hadn't seen Fergus before she started work. These days, she knew the estate well enough to find her way to the places she'd decided to paint for the duke.

Fergus leaned in to kiss her with the casual affection that always made her heart stutter and stop. Her hand tightened on her pencil, and she made a false line that she brushed at with her thumb.

As he'd predicted, the good weather had held until the end of September. October had come in with squalls. She'd emerged from her lover's arms long enough to remember that she needed to return to Italy with preliminary work done on the duke's commission, and that her hundreds of sketches of Fergus wouldn't fit the bill.

So when fine weather blessed these most recent two weeks, she'd resisted Fergus's blandishments and worked. Autumn in the Highlands, she discovered, brought forth beauty to rival summer. The heather had faded from the hills, but the trees turned a magnificent red and gold, and bracken covered the slopes with a rich, rusty brown. Sunrise was magical, too, with the unreliable light sparkling on the frosty grass, portent of colder weather to come.

Fergus's duties as laird often called him away from her side, too. As the days went on, they settled into something like a life together. Their relationship began to feel oddly domestic, as if they shared something important and lasting, instead of the brief affair that she needed to remind herself was the reality.

Although she was wanton enough to appreciate the frequent bad weather, when a roguish Scotsman and his half-Italian mistress had no choice but to seek shelter in the hunting lodge.

"Did you decide where to put the new school?"

Fergus and Reverend Angus, the minister, had met today to discuss parish matters. Once she'd condemned her lover's lordly behavior, but she'd come to admire his endless care for the people in the glen.

"Aye," he said with a hint of mockery.

"Who won?" The minister hadn't much liked Fergus's plans to build the school on land he'd already earmarked for a new rectory.

One dark red eyebrow tilted. "Who do ye think?"

She didn't need an answer. She flicked over to a fresh page, and her pencil skimmed across the paper. "Stay like that."

He rolled his eyes. "Sometimes, lassie, I think ye only want me because you're short of an artist's model."

"Oh, you make a good subject." She cast him a teasing glance. "Not to mention your other uses."

"Naughty wench."

"That's me." Her heart leaped at the magnificent sight he made in his kilt, as much part of this wild landscape as the steep hills and the sky. "Turn your head a bit to the right."

"As my lady commands. How is your work going?"

"I'm surprised how well, considering what little attention I'm giving it." After she became Fergus's lover, her art changed. Even for someone as self-critical as she invariably was, she knew that these sketches were the best things she'd ever done. If she could transfer the magic to the finished paintings, His Grace would receive some extraordinary work from her.

"You were frowning when I came up. Is something wrong?"

She traced the line of his arrogant nose on the paper. "I often frown when I'm working."

"Aye, you do. This was different."

The close attention he devoted to her always surprised her. Nobody ever had before.

Most of the time, she liked it. Occasionally, like now, his keen perception made her afraid that she'd never hide anything from him. And she had a horrid feeling that something powerful took root in her heart, something she'd rather he didn't guess lurked there.

"I was thinking how the last time we came here, you disagreed with me about a woman's right to an opinion." For some reason, puzzling over her father's inexplicable blindness to his daughter's ruin seemed too revealing.

Fergus rolled his eyes again. "Don't tell me you're going to use that as a stick to beat me with."

"I wondered if your ideas had changed."

He cast her a knowing look. "Are things going so well that you're looking for trouble where there is none?"

Was he right? Her departure loomed closer and closer. Within a fortnight, her father should be walking, and once he was, she had no real excuse to remain at Achnasheen.

Fergus paused. "Or are ye really worried about whether I regard you as my equal?"

She closed the sketchbook on the half-finished portrait. "We've hardly disagreed at all since..."

"Since ye came to my bed. Scared you're getting soft, Marina?"

"That's one thing you don't have to worry about," she retorted.

His grunt was wry. "Aye. In fact..."

She shot him a startled look. "We're miles from the lodge."

He ran his hand through his red hair, ruffling it so a lock tumbled down over his broad forehead. *Santa pazienza,* he was so effortlessly attractive. No wonder she was besotted. "We dinna have to have a bed handy."

"I know. There was the armchair and the wall and..."

Amusement creased his eyes. "Aye. You don't have to list every one of them. And all grand places for a wee bit of pleasure."

Her lips twitched. "I don't remember anything being wee, including the pleasure."

"Glad to hear it," he said, and tilted his chin toward the space over her left shoulder. "There's a dip in the brae behind you that's covered in nice, soft grass. Unless ye fancy the trip to the lodge. I'm ready for you now, so it's a long way to go when relief is here at hand."

Her cheeks flushed, partly because she'd more than once imagined lying in his arms, with just the sky as their roof. "How are you so sure that the grass is soft, Mackinnon?"

He raised his eyebrows, and sly pleasure glinted in his eyes. "No need to be jealous, my bonny. You're the only woman I've had my wicked way with in this glen. I caught a wee nap or two there, back in the days when you wouldn't give me a second glance."

How she wished she could stay the only woman he had his wicked way with in the glen. Or anywhere else.

Diavolo, she was turning stupid over him, but she couldn't help herself.

"What if someone sees us?"

"It's a very private spot. Anyone who found us would have to be looking." He extended a hand. "Are ye no' tempted?"

Marina gave a delicate snort. "You know I'm tempted, curse you."

One of his rare, untrammeled smiles lit his face, and the restlessness she'd felt since he'd kissed her sharpened into desire. They had so little time left. She needed to seize every second of rapture she could.

Because tragically soon, she'd be alone again. There would be no more sensual pleasure, and no more sweet, shared laughter, and no more basking in the knowledge that she'd found the other half of her soul.

She set aside her sketchbook and accepted Fergus's hand, glorying in the firm strength of his grip. "Show me."

CHAPTER TWENTY

Fergus had once prided himself on his control as a lover. No more. He rushed Marina into the hollow and, once they were out of sight of the open hillside, dragged her into his arms for a ravenous kiss, wrapping his arms around her as if he'd never let her go.

They'd been lovers for a little over a month, and with every day, his need for her grew more powerful. As had his impatience with the restrictions this affair imposed.

At first, having to conceal their passion had been an annoying necessity, even while subterfuge added a tinge of forbidden excitement. Now he chafed against touching Marina only when they were alone. He wanted her with him all the time, not just when there were no curious eyes to take note of their attraction.

He was surprised that she consented to this tryst. But she'd agreed with a readiness that set his blood aflame. Marina's was a wild, free spirit. At first, that had taken him aback, but he'd come to appreciate the way her courage mirrored his.

Now she wrapped her arms around him and pressed her body so close that not even a breath separated them. Her lips burned against his, and her tongue darted into his mouth with a greed that made him mad for her.

Shaking with uncontrollable need, he fell to his knees before her and shoved up her skirts in a froth of petticoats. He buried his face in her belly, senses brimming with the rich scent of her arousal. She'd flared into need as swiftly as he had.

Over their time together, he'd spent hours exploring her silky cleft with his mouth. Today, he was too close to the edge to last through a slow seduction.

He fiddled with the tie on her drawers, until they fell to her booted ankles. He placed a kiss above the triangle of dark curls covering her mound. A silent promise that on the next occasion, he'd take his time.

Burying her fingers in his hair, she murmured incoherent Italian words of encouragement. As she stepped free of her drawers, she shifted against his mouth. He groaned into her satiny skin. Sometimes, he would spin out his desire by undressing her garment by garment, revealing each inch of her, until she stood magnificently bare to his admiring gaze. This wasn't going to be one of those occasions.

Unable to resist, he kissed her intimate curls, tasting the salty liquor of her arousal. She tilted toward him, then cried out when he caught her hips and pulled her down to face him.

Another kiss, a duel of teeth and lips and tongues, punctuated with gasps of pleasure. He fell back against the grass, taking her with him. "Ride me, Marina," he growled.

Without a word of protest—sometimes she could be breathtakingly obedient—she straddled him. "I do love it when ye wear the kilt, my braw Scots laddie," she said in a passable imitation of his Highland lilt.

"Because it's the dress of a proud Mackinnon?"

He cupped her breasts through the green jacket she'd worn the day they first came together. All those bloody buttons. He resisted the urge to rip the rag to shreds.

Sensual appreciation curled her lips. During the last weeks, he'd become a connoisseur of her smiles. This one had only appeared since they'd been lovers. He adored its gloating self-confidence. He adored its unabashed hunger. As their affair progressed, Marina's shyness had rapidly faded. This was a woman who reveled in earthy pleasure.

"No, that's not why." She tossed up his kilt to reveal his erection.

His hands slid under her skirts to shape her buttocks. Her naked skin was smooth and warm to his touch. "Then why?"

To his regret, she twisted out of his hold, then regret exploded to ash in a flash of blinding heat as she dipped her head to kiss the tip of his cock.

Mischief and desire lit her black eyes as she looked up from where she crouched over him. "It's because you're easy to reach. A most convenient costume."

"I wish you'd adopt it. I swear you're wearing this devilish cocoon to torment me."

She laughed, a low ripple of amusement that only made him want her more. "I like to make you work for your reward."

"Whereas ye don't have to?" he asked ironically, while his thundering pulse threatened to mash his brain to porridge.

"That's right."

With a sureness that shuddered through him like a blow, she took his cock in her hand and squeezed. By the time she rose on her knees and sank down to take him inside her, he was tensing every muscle and grinding his teeth to hold back from spilling.

His sight dimmed, until the sky and the hillside became a blur. All he could see was light-speckled darkness and the beautiful woman rising above him like a queen. Then he closed his eyes and yielded to glorious sensation.

Heat. Darkness. Pressure.

As she rose and fell against the bright blue sky, he opened his eyes to watch. How he loved the way her face changed when she strove after ecstasy. He caught her waist, the subtle shift of muscles under his palms echoing the subtle shift of the muscles holding him snug inside her.

She descended with voluptuous slowness, and he groaned as he verged closer to losing himself. Be damned if he'd let this end so fast. He tightened his jaw to the edge of agony and dug his fingers into her hips as he strove to restrain himself.

The taunting smile on her lush mouth told him she recognized his struggle. "Not yet, *caro*."

"Not yet," he grated out, as she clenched and almost shot the top of his head off.

With shaking hands, she undid the row of buttons down the front of her jacket, then the buttons down that saucily masculine shirt. He had a sudden powerful memory of their first day as lovers when she'd worn nothing but that shirt over her nakedness.

Panting with excitement, he ran his hands up the thighs framing his hips. With each move, she set off thunderclaps of pleasure. He hoped to hell she didn't intend to take her time, or he couldn't answer for the consequences.

At last the shirt parted to reveal breasts pushed high by her corset. The sight of that sumptuous flesh pressing against her sheer shift made him groan and bump his hips higher.

"Have you any idea how much I want ye?" he asked hoarsely.

Marina gave a wiggle that drove him closer to the brink. "I think I just might."

Clumsy hands shoved aside the material covering her chest. When he began to tease the hard pink nipples, she spasmed around him and cried out.

Fergus bowed up and closed his lips around one hard peak, while his hand continued to torment the other. By the time she slid back to take him inside her again, she was lusciously hot and slick.

She moved on him, circling her hips, varying the rhythm, sweeping him to the doors of heaven. He tightened his balls against the clamoring need to fill her. While he couldn't doubt her enjoyment, she hadn't yet reached her peak.

He cupped and stroked the breasts on wanton display. "Don't wait too long, *mo chridhe*," he groaned.

She flattened her palms on his chest, her touch hot through his shirt. "I love having the upper hand."

"Remember I'm only human."

"You?" She gave a choked laugh. "Never. You're the Mackinnon, great Laird of Achnasheen."

Until he'd met Marina, nobody had teased him. Over the last six weeks, he discovered he rather liked it. "Not so great, when he's a slave to a slip of a girl who's too clever for her own good."

"Ooh, I like that even better."

"I thought you might." He smiled at her in delight. "Now put me out of my misery, lassie, and take your pleasure so I can take mine."

"So considerate," she said, and he marveled that she had the cheek to mock him when he was so far inside her that he felt like they became one being.

"Aye, well, that's the great laird for ye."

She laughed low in her throat. "One thing about him is great."

His grunt of laughter did nothing to steady his slipping control. He seized her by the hips and caught the flare of thrilled astonishment in her eyes as he rolled her over.

Fergus rose above her where she lay on the crushed grass. "It's time to show ye who's in charge."

When he plunged into her, she gripped him tighter than a fist. Dear God above, he really wasn't going to last.

She curled her hands over his shoulders. "Is that so?"

"Aye, it is." He kissed her hungrily, then began to move, glorying in how she met every thrust. "Hold on, and pray for mercy."

She quaked and moaned as she crossed into rapture. Being inside Marina as she found her shivering climax was so magnificent, he only remembered at the last moment to pull free.

With a guttural groan, he withdrew and turned to pump his seed into the grass beside her. Hell, they'd had a few close calls, but this was the closest yet.

He collapsed onto his back and stared unseeing up at the cloudless sky. Satisfaction and exhaustion coiled lazily in his veins. "I'm never going to move again," he said, his voice gruff.

He felt her hand seek and find his. "That was wonderful," she said, and he was shocked to hear her voice was thick with tears.

Weariness forgotten, he sat up to look at her. She was an unforgettable sight, spread-eagled upon the rich green grass, her breasts bare, and her skirts rucked up to reveal spectacular legs.

He took a second to appreciate the view, then focused on her face. She was flushed, and her features were soft in the way he loved after a tumble. But her generous lips turned down, and there was a sheen in her eyes that betrayed unhappiness.

"What is it, Marina?"

She avoided his questioning gaze. "I'm being silly."

He squeezed her hand. "Tell me."

She bit her lip, then spoke in a rush. "Everything's coming to an end. Papa should be up and around next week, and winter's almost here, and I have to go back to Florence. I know all of that is true. It's been true from the beginning. After what we just did, it seems cruel that our time together is so short." She turned away. "You'll think I'm a fool."

Tenderness as intoxicating as fine wine engulfed him. He turned her face toward his. After brief resistance, she gave in. Her eyes were dark pools of misery.

"I'd never think you're a fool."

"I am, to fret like this when I know I must go."

"Must ye?"

"You know I must." She frowned in bewilderment. "We've escaped discovery so far, but our luck won't last forever. And I can't stay at Achnasheen indefinitely as your mistress. You must see that."

He did. He'd seen it for weeks. Since they'd first come together in such a blaze of passion.

"Then don't stay as my mistress." He sucked in a fortifying breath and spoke with a conviction that caught him by surprise, although this was the obvious solution. It had been from the start. "Stay as my wife. Marry me, Marina."

CHAPTER TWENTY-ONE

Marina stared into Fergus's face, while his astounding words echoed in her mind. For one mad second, she let herself imagine what life would be like if she said yes.

Nights of Fergus in her bed with no need for sneaking around. Day after day in this beautiful glen, watching the seasons change in all their beauty.

Having Fergus's babies.

For a fleeting instant, four small Mackinnons filled her imagination. A pair of daughters and a pair of sons. Two redheaded like their father, two dark like her. The thought made her empty womb contract in yearning. How she'd love to bear this magnificent man a brood of strong and spirited children.

Then deliberately, she tucked those alluring images away and buried them deep in her heart. So deep that with any luck, she'd never have to look at them again.

She sat up, keeping a careful distance from Fergus, and tugged her hand free.

"Marina, did ye hear me?" he asked, and she'd come back to reality enough to register the vulnerability in his expression and to regret that she was going to hurt him. "I asked you to marry me."

"You know it's impossible, but thank you for asking," she said, surprised at how composed she sounded.

Baffled anger darkened his features. "You speak as if I invited you for afternoon tea, not asked you to share a lifetime with me, lassie."

With calm movements, she began to restore her clothing to decency, tugging her shift into place and doing up her shirt. Her hands weren't even shaking. Everything seemed to happen at a great distance. It was an eerie sensation, as though her body no longer belonged to her. Doubly eerie when mere minutes ago, she'd basked in a sated daze that had felt like the sun's embrace.

"Fergus, we both knew this couldn't last."

He surged to his feet and glared down at her. "So why were you blethering on about not wanting to leave me?"

That had been her soul crying out for the unattainable.

Her hands weren't quite as steady as they had been. When the buttons on her jacket defeated her, she decided to keep it open. "I wasn't being practical."

A furious swipe through the air dismissed her answer. "To Hades with practicality. I dinna want ye to go."

She scrambled up to face him, ignoring the hand he stretched out to help her. If he touched her, she feared she'd weaken. His touch held such power. It had always held power. She should have seen the dangers long ago.

What was she saying? Of course she'd seen them. She'd just been too greedy to have this glorious man in her arms to heed the warning signs.

"Marriage between us would be a disaster. We're too different."

"Are ye sure about that?"

She shrank away from those searching gray eyes. "You know we are."

"I believe we're remarkably similar, which makes it a miracle that we've found one another." He sighed and ran his hand through his hair with a gesture of frustration. "Be damned if I mean to let ye leave me without a fight, Marina."

"Fergus..." she said, stepping back. Her knees felt like blancmange.

She didn't underestimate what he was saying. This was a declaration of war.

Marina fell back on stale arguments, even as she admitted what she said wasn't true now, had probably never been true, not really. "Stop trying to push me around. You're such a bully."

She expected—hoped—that he'd take offense and either stomp off and leave her alone, or act badly enough to confirm that her decision to refuse him was the right one.

He did neither. Instead, he subjected her to another of those penetrating stares that made her feel like he sliced her heart open and read every word she battled against speaking. "Why are ye so frightened of admitting that you want to marry me?"

"Don't be absurd." Stiffening, she cast him a contemptuous glance. "I'm not frightened of anything."

"Aye, you are." He stepped close enough to take her hand and despite her attempts to pull free, he kept it. "You're terrified. I want to ken why."

Santo cielo, she'd been right to fear his touch. And his perception. The urge to fling herself against him and say yes rose to smash against the boulder jamming in her throat. The boulder, blast his knowledge of her, composed entirely of panic.

"I've said no," she choked out. "Can't we leave it at that?"

"You know we can't." Compassion and affection softened his features. "Come and sit beside me. Let's talk about this."

"You mean you'll try and persuade me to agree." Her tone was tart.

He gave an unapologetic shrug. "That, too."

She sighed and at last curled her fingers around his. "You're wasting your time, Mackinnon."

But she let him lead her out of the hollow where she'd found such transcendent bliss and where now her heart threatened to split in two. He brought her back to where her sketchbook waited, forgotten. That was warning enough that what she dreaded would come to pass, surely.

Marina released his hand and scooped the sketchbook up and pressed it to her chest, as she had when Fergus carried her home after saving her life. Although it held no more secrets from him, except perhaps the final, unspoken one. And she had a queasy feeling that her last secret was already in his possession, despite frantic efforts to keep it from him.

"Armor again?" His tone was dry.

Sheepishly, she loosened her death-like grip. "Do I need armor?"

"Not against me, *mo chridhe*. Never against me." She slumped onto the tussock where he'd found her drawing an hour ago. She felt like she'd lived through a lifetime since, until she became an old and bitter woman with nothing left to look forward to.

Oh, grow up, Marina. This isn't a grand Shakespearean tragedy. It's a mere difference of opinion that won't matter a fig in ten years.

If only she could believe that.

With wary eyes, she watched Fergus lean against a tall rock a few feet away. The fact that he wasn't touching her warned her that he believed he could win this argument by appealing to her intellect rather than her physical weakness for him.

She hated that he was so reasonable. She hated that he was so generous. She wanted an excuse to flounce off and he, blast him, was clever enough to deny her the opportunity.

He folded his arms across his imposing chest and took a moment to study her. That piercing inspection made her shift with discomfort.

"Do you want to know why I asked ye to marry me, Marina?" he asked in a gentle voice.

She frowned. She'd expected him to continue attacking her position, not invite her to understand his. "Because we can't keep our hands off one another," she said in a sour tone.

"Aye, that's one reason. Is it a bad one?"

"You can't base a future on fleeting passion," she said, far too primly for someone who had been heaving all over him a few minutes ago.

He arched one of those expressive eyebrows. "Are ye so sure it's fleeting, lassie?"

Surprised, she met his eyes. "Aren't you?"

He shrugged again. "I suspect over time, my desire might change, but I cannae see it fading."

She gulped and closed her eyes, as she fought against the lure of a lifetime sleeping beside this man.

"I'd never have said you were a romantic." *Porca miseria*, she meant to sound snide, but she just sounded needy.

"I'm telling you what I believe. If it's romantic to think that something as strong as the passion between us is likely to last, then I'm a romantic."

"You're a romantic to think we wouldn't murder one another," she forced through stiff lips, as the sweetness of what he said coalesced into a giant hammer that battered against her closed heart. Because she, too, was in thrall to this bond between them, and leaving him was going to slice her to ribbons.

He didn't smile. "Of late, we havenae fought much at all."

"That doesn't mean we won't."

"A fight isn't necessarily a bad thing."

"It is, if you're always the winner," she retorted acidly. "You're stubborn and used to getting your own way."

Another tilt of a russet eyebrow. "And you're not?"

"Well, that alone promises disaster."

"You don't think you're strong enough to hold your own in an argument? That doesn't sound like you." No, it didn't, curse him. "By God, Marina, you underestimate yourself, if that's the case. Or is it that ye don't think I'm capable of seeing reason?"

She was being unfair. They both knew it. He was arrogant and sure of himself, but she knew him well enough by now to admit that there was a reasonable man hidden inside the all-powerful laird. His motives were generally good, even if at times, he was a little too blunt in expressing them.

Marina twined shaking hands together in her lap. "You don't like to compromise."

"Nor do you. That doesn't mean I cannae compromise when I have to." He paused. "I'm compromising right now, in fact."

"How?" The word was a challenge.

A grim smile twisted his lips. "You're speaking to a man whose ancestors grabbed what they wanted and asked pardon later. Do you think I've never considered stealing you away like Bonny Mhairi and locking you in my tower until you consent to stay with me?"

Despite everything, forbidden excitement tore through her at the idea of Fergus forcing her hand. "Then why don't you?"

He narrowed his eyes, and she had a shameful inkling that he guessed her wish to have the decision wrenched away from her. "Because I respect ye too much. And because I ken that unless you come to me wholehearted, this won't work, magnificent as the battle between us will be if I defeat you in bed."

Oh, *Madonna santa,* that would be a magnificent battle indeed. One he'd lose in the end because, while some reckless part of her thrilled to the thought of him snatching her away like a maiden of old, her independent soul would eventually revolt at the coercion.

"You seem to have come to know me well." That terrified her, too.

"Aye, lassie. That's why I'm not touching you right now."

"If...if you touch me, I'm lost," she admitted, the few feet between them bolstering her courage enough for honesty. At least about this.

When his long body tautened, she braced for him to take her in his arms. He was right. If he kissed her, she couldn't hold out. And she'd never forgive him.

She was almost sorry when he subsided back into that watchful readiness.

"I know. But that willnae win me what I want." He paused. "Marina, we can overcome whatever divides us. Tell me why you're so set on running away. Tell me what's really frightening ye about marrying me. I won't believe you're afraid of a few clashes of opinion."

"You think you know." Her voice was unsteady.

"I can make a guess." When she didn't speak, he went on. "Your talent has singled ye out, mostly from other women. You're Marina Lucchetti, the great artist, raised high above the rest of her sex because you paint like an angel."

She flinched away from an accusation that she resented, perhaps because it held enough truth to sting. "You make me sound so conceited."

Fergus shook his head. "It's not conceit to recognize your worth. But ye fear if you stay here with me, you'll dwindle into a mere wife. You'll lose your art."

She sucked in a breath that combined shock and relief. When he'd asked her to marry him, the urge to flee had been instinctive. She'd hardly understood it herself. Now the sick dread coiling in her stomach eased, and the painful tension drained from her shoulders.

"I suppose you condemn that as unwomanly."

For the first time, a trace of temper lit his gray eyes to flaring silver. "Stop putting words in my mouth, lassie."

Odd this should annoy him when until now, he'd been remarkably even-tempered about her refusal. He went on before she could object to his tone. "You've succeeded in the world you inhabit by laying claim to a freedom like a man's. You're afraid you'll betray your talent if you stay."

She licked dry lips. "Then you must understand why I say no to your proposal."

"I understand." He went on before she could claim victory. "That doesnae mean I agree."

Startled Marina met his eyes and recoiled from the adamant purpose shining there. "You must see it's impossible."

"You once said an affair between us was impossible."

She shot him a look of dislike. "I'm beginning to think I was right."

"You dinna mean that."

God help her, she didn't. These last weeks had given her a joy beyond anything she'd ever imagined. But they were a bubble, ready to burst to nothing when she returned to reality. Reality was her life as a painter. Reality was going home to Florence.

She made a helpless gesture. Now that her panic subsided, pure misery remained. It wasn't an improvement. "My patrons are in Italy. My life is in Italy."

He looked unimpressed. "You can paint here. You can make a life here."

"With painting as a hobby."

"With patrons seeking you out. Never doubt that I'm in awe of your exceptional talent. It would be a sin for ye to stop painting. Anyway, Scotland has rich men enough to rival Florence. If you're seeking people to buy your work, I can introduce you to my friends."

"As a favor to you," she said savagely. "I have no reputation here."

"Don't belittle yourself." A muscle worked in his lean cheek. "I never have."

No, he hadn't. She'd challenged his ideas about what a woman should be, but he'd always treated her as a worthy adversary, even in the early days when they'd disagreed more often than not.

Marina decided to attack this lunatic idea from another angle. She wasn't getting anywhere from her current position. "*Per pietà*, you wouldn't want to be married to me. I'm not at all a proper Scots wife for the great Laird of Achnasheen. When I'm caught up in my painting, I disappear into another world. If my work isn't going well, I'm evil tempered and morose. You'll start to resent that I'm not paying you proper attention."

"For God's sake, woman, how shallow do you think I am?" Fergus straightened away from his boulder so he stood tall facing her, his expression uncompromising. "Do ye believe me so spineless that I'll turn tail at the first sign of trouble? If you do, you don't know me at all. Do you imagine these dire warnings about how difficult you can be are any great revelation? Credit me with some perception. When something's worth the effort, I'll go to the ends of the earth to achieve it."

Oh, *per l'amor di dio,* when he said such things...

"I'll be a dreadful mother." She fought once more to banish that poignant vision of the sons and daughters they'd never have. "You'll have to rear the children."

A growl of disgust escaped him. "Marina, there's a bloody castle full of people ready to keep an eye on the bairns. If you're worried that I want ye to be a nursemaid for the rest of your life, you're a fool. Anyway in my experience, all that bairns really need, as long as they're fed and housed, is love. Are you saying you wouldnae love the children we have?"

She bristled under his impatient tone. "Of course I'd love them."

Satisfaction filled his expression. "In that case, you'll make a good mother."

Marina lurched to her feet. She started to feel at a distinct disadvantage sitting on her tussock while he towered over her. "You're trying to make everything sound easy."

"No, I'm trying to make everything seem possible, if we have the will to make it so."

She swallowed to shift the lump damming her throat. "What about Papa? He and I have traveled together since I started work as an artist."

"He can live with us. He can go back to Florence, and visit us when he feels like it. We can visit him." Fergus spread his hands as if her objections were mere nonsense. She felt like clouting him. She felt like throwing her arms around him and begging him to let her stay. "Don't ye want to marry me, Marina?"

"It wasn't what we planned." *Diavolo,* what a pathetic answer.

"Plans can change." His stark attention peeled away her skin to reveal the cowardly, needy creature lurking within. "Do you want me?"

In dumb misery, she surveyed him, taking in the intense, austere face, the powerful body, the sheer *everything* of him. "Yes, I do," she mumbled, knowing there was no point lying.

"As a lover, but not as a husband." The bitterness in his voice made her wince.

"I've never thought of taking a husband."

"Perhaps it's time ye did."

She made a violent gesture with one hand, as though she tried to disperse all his arguments. "I don't understand why on earth you want to marry me."

His gaze didn't shift from her. "Yes, you do. I told ye."

"That you want me. It's not enough."

"Aye, well, ye could be right at that." He drew himself up to his full impressive height and spoke with a resonant certainty that vibrated in her bones. "Is it enough if I love you? Because by heaven, I do, Marina. I love ye, and I want you to be my wife."

CHAPTER TWENTY-TWO

Fergus watched Marina jerk back as if he'd struck her instead of telling her that he loved her. The terror returned to her eyes.

She was so heartbreakingly afraid of relying on anyone but herself. He understood why she felt that way. He even understood how it had helped her become the proud, independent woman she was today.

But her resolve to forge her own path stood in the way of ultimate happiness. For him—and for her. Somehow he must convince her that they were stronger together than they could ever be apart, even if right now that seemed impossible.

It hurt like hell that she was so determined not to have him. He'd expected an argument, given he was dealing with Marina, but he'd also imagined she'd relent, given time, because she wanted to stay with him as much as he wanted her to stay. For God's sake, after they made love in the hollow, she'd been crying about leaving him.

But so far, all his persuasion had proven most unpersuasive. Nor had his confession of love produced any softening. That hurt, too.

"You...you can't love me," she stammered, raising one shaking hand to her throat and retreating a couple of paces across the grass.

"I can." He paused, knowing he was about to take a risk so much greater than confessing his feelings. "And I believe you love me."

She went so white that her eyes turned into huge black pools in her ashen face. "I never said so."

Interesting she didn't deny it. Interesting and revealing. "Actions speak louder than words."

"You're reading too much into desire."

He shook his head. "No, I dinna think so. Or are ye going to tell me I'm wrong?"

He watched her consider lying. Then it was as if she were a marionette and someone cut her strings. In some obscure way, she collapsed in on herself. "You devil, Mackinnon."

Fergus didn't smile, although he wanted to. "So you do love me?"

"How could I do otherwise?" She made a defeated gesture. "I was in love with you when I agreed to become your mistress. I must have been, or else I'd never have said yes."

Her admission fell on his troubled soul like rain on parched ground, and he drew his first full breath in what felt like an hour. "Is it such a huge step from mistress to wife?"

Those fathomless eyes studied him, before she shook her head. "No, you won't win against me, just because I'm stupid enough to love you."

Impatience had him growling again and running his hand through his hair. "Can't you see that if you say yes, we both win?"

She subjected him to more of that ruthless stare, then her shoulders slumped and she turned away to gaze across the empty hills. "I can't accept a man's dominion, Mackinnon."

"Even though you love me?" God almighty, despite everything, had he lost her? Was all their passion to end in a parting? How could he bear it?

The weight of sorrow in her voice crushed him like a rock fall. "Most of all because I love you. It's too easy for you to gain the advantage over me."

"Not so far," he said sourly.

That made her face him. Her eyes had turned dull as he'd never imagined they could. He always thought of Marina as a creature of fire, but the woman who regarded him now looked as if every ounce of life and vigor had been sapped from her.

"I'm sorry, Fergus. I can see I'm making you unhappy, and I hate that."

She sounded utterly exhausted. An hour ago, he'd have taken her in his arms and offered to comfort her. Now he could tell that his touch was the last thing she wanted.

He loathed that she rejected his proposal and his love. But the thought that she'd never let him touch her again made him want to smash something priceless into dust.

But he could see that haranguing her further would be cruel. She looked close to disintegrating. He had a brief, piercing memory of the gloriously vital and sensual creature who had brought him to shattering release such a short while ago. That seemed like a different woman.

He loved that woman for her passion and her strength. He loved this wounded woman, too. Her vulnerability was so raw.

Marina needed him as much as he needed her. All he could hope for was that she'd come to see that before she returned to Italy.

Noting the stubborn line of her jaw, he couldn't be optimistic.

"Let me take ye home. I won't push this now."

Bleak amusement turned her lips down. "Now."

He spread his hands. "I told you I willnae give you up easily."

"I know that's true." She raised her chin, and he watched her gather her strength around her. It was impressive, even if she used that strength against him. "But I won't stay here to become your satellite, Mackinnon. Please accept that while I'm honored by your proposal, I can't accept it."

And that, he thought grimly, seemed to be that.

Dinner was an ordeal for Marina. Her father's leg had healed to a point where he could come downstairs using a stick, and he was in a mood for celebration. She couldn't blame him. He'd chafed under the restrictions of his long recovery.

With her hours in the hills, trying to finish the duke's commission, she'd rather neglected him over recent weeks. She told herself she'd make it up to him, but that didn't stifle a pang of guilt. Nor could she put all the blame for her absence on hard work. During a lot of those hours when she was ostensibly sketching, she'd been lying in her lover's arms.

Although her father's mobility meant her departure from Achnasheen loomed closer, she struggled to appear happy for him. After this afternoon's tribulations, she should be glad that her torment wouldn't spin out indefinitely.

Fergus's proposal had changed everything between them, but not so drastically as his declaration of love. Refusing him had come close to killing her, but she knew if she yielded, he'd end up subsuming everything she was and everything she'd achieved.

Right now, watching Fergus with her father—he hid his perturbation better than she did, but she knew him well enough to discern the turmoil beneath the Highland charm—she wondered whether her artistic calling was worth the sacrifice of his happiness. In forty years, would she regret giving up his love, and his friendship, and his company, and his kisses, and his children, and...

Santa pazienza, if she kept this up, she'd start howling like a lost puppy.

"Marina, *per favore*, walk me to my room," her father said. "I'm still uncertain on my feet."

"As you wish, Papa." She rose from the table.

"*Grazie, figlia mia.*"

"Goodnight, Mackinnon," she said without looking at Fergus. Thank God this interminable *purgatorio* of an evening would soon be over, and she could shut herself in her room and cry her eyes out for the rest of the night.

Fergus stood when she did. "Goodnight, Ugolino. Goodnight, Signorina Marina. I might take a stroll outside."

His statement startled her enough to make her look at him directly. "But it's pouring."

As they'd come down the mountain, the weather had closed in. By the time they reached the castle, the wind blew a gale and the gusts carried sleet. The elements conspired to reflect her bleak mood.

Now she saw that the self-control that had sustained Fergus so far tonight was fraying. He looked drawn and unhappy, and that betraying muscle twitched in his lean cheek. He struggled for a smile, but she couldn't even call the result a half-smile. "Och, just a wee Scotch mist."

A wee Scotch tempest, more like. But she'd lost the spirit to argue.

She crossed to help her father out of his chair. "How's your leg, Papa?"

Marina was sharply aware of Fergus leaving the room behind them. She wanted to call him back and say she was sorry for making him so unhappy. What was the use? She'd told him no this afternoon, and he'd refused to accept her answer. If she betrayed any weakness now, she'd forsake all hope of resisting him.

"It's weaker than I'd like, but I'm so pleased that I can use it again. We have much to thank Fergus and his people for."

"Yes, we do," she said without enthusiasm. Not because she disagreed, but because the last thing she wanted right now was to participate in a discussion about her host's generosity and all-round perfections. "Should I call Jock to help you up the stairs?"

"No, *grazie.* I can manage with your arm."

Marina and her father didn't talk much as they climbed to his room. His leg had healed well, but after all the enforced rest, his vitality soon waned.

"Please stay while I change into my nightshirt," he said in Italian, once she got him inside his room.

Per pietà, was she never to find a minute to herself? She curled her hands so tightly that her nails dug into her palms. The sting helped keep her tears at bay. She knew she owed Papa some attention, but she felt stretched to the limit of endurance. "Can I help?"

"No, this I can do for myself." He limped behind the screen and eventually emerged ready for bed. Despite her misery, Marina was glad to see him moving about.

"You'll be dancing before you know it," she said, then feeling like she cut herself with broken glass, she went on, "A good dose of Italian sun will have you back to yourself before you know it. It's time we went home, Papa."

"Yes, I miss Florence. It will be good to be back in my own house, kind as everyone has been to us here."

Marina bit her lip and tasted blood. She turned to go before she started to cry. A few more minutes, and she wouldn't have to pretend anymore.

Except her dear Papa didn't understand that.

"Help me into bed, then stay and talk to me."

Could she bear much more? "I'm very tired." Unshed tears thickened her voice. "I've been working hard on the duke's commission, and it's another early start tomorrow."

"A few minutes, *cara*. Surely you can spare that."

Surely she could, if she hadn't been concealing a broken heart all night and the effort was becoming too much. Struggling to hide her reluctance, she crossed to perch on the edge of the bed. "It's nice to see you up and about, Papa."

"Tcha." He made a dismissive gesture that matched the dismissive response he gave to her comment about his recovery. "The work, it goes well?"

"Very well." She dared speak the words that superstition had stopped her from saying aloud until now. "I think these pictures will be the best I've ever done."

Papa smiled. He'd never understood her talent the way her mother had, but he'd always supported her. "Marvelous. You've found the scenery here inspiring?"

"Any artist would love it. To think, I'm the first to capture it in paint."

"And the laird of this glen, you find him inspiring, too?"

For a moment, talking about her painting, she'd almost forgotten what had happened this afternoon. Her father's sly question brought all the anguish flooding back.

To evade his searching gaze, she stared down at the hands linked in her lap. She struggled to keep her voice steady. "While the Mackinnon has been very good to us, I imagine he's looking forward to his chance-met visitors going home."

"I doubt it. Tonight when he saw I could walk again, he looked like a hound whose master had died."

Startled, she glanced up. "Papa..."

"Marina, I've struggled to hold my tongue." His expression was serious as it rarely was. "After all, you're no longer a little girl, you're a grown woman. But I can't see you as you are tonight, ready to snap into pieces like a dry twig, and stay silent."

A sour stew of shame and misery churned in her belly. "You know?"

Her father's smile was kind, and he caught her hand. "That you've at last met a man who makes you think of something other than pigments and paintbrushes? Of course I know. For the first few weeks here, you're like a cat whose fur is rubbed the wrong way, all arched back and claws and hissing. Then in the space of a day, the cat is purring. While

Fergus, he stops acting like a man on the rack and can't keep his eyes off my daughter. When he looks at her, his face says he's caught in a spell."

Santa Madonna, was that true? She supposed it must be.

Fergus hadn't told her when he'd fallen in love with her. Perhaps it was weeks ago. She remembered how hungry he'd been for her before she went to his bed.

And afterward.

"You don't mind?"

"That he takes my daughter as his mistress and not as his lawful wife, so she can celebrate her love in the sunlight? I mind it very much. But I also remember what it was like to be young and in love." His eyes were sad, and she knew he was thinking of her mother. "Then tonight. Ah, tonight, the hissing cat and the mournful hound are back, eyeing one another off over the dinner table, and they're giving me indigestion."

"I hardly said a word," she protested.

Her father shrugged. "You were hissing in your heart."

Despite everything, a grim huff of amusement escaped her. "That's not a very flattering description of either of us."

Her father rolled his eyes. "Imagine how I felt having to look at you both." He paused. "What's happened? Has Fergus decided he no longer wants a mistress? The young can be fickle, but he doesn't strike me as a shallow man. And he still looks at you as if he wants to gobble you up like a bonbon. No, I don't think he's tired of you. Perhaps you've tired of him. If you have, you don't seem happy about the end of the affair."

She shifted in discomfort. Her father was a worldly man, but she remained his daughter. "Papa, I'm not sure I can talk to you about this."

He made a sound that indicated how asinine he considered that remark. "If you're old enough to go to a man's bed without benefit of marriage, you're old enough to speak about what you've done."

She winced. "You are upset."

"Well, I'm your father. Now, tell me what's happened, because I've held off giving you advice so far, but you look so woebegone tonight, I might be able to help."

He'd been compassionate and perceptive, and better to her than she deserved. Anyway, he was right. She was making a horrid mess of things. She couldn't forget how stricken Fergus had looked this afternoon when she'd told him she couldn't marry him.

Marina looked down to their linked hands. The view became mistier by the second. "It's all hopeless."

Her father squeezed her hand. "He doesn't love you?"

A tear trickled down her cheek. "He says he does."

"So you don't love him?"

"Of course I do. Do you think I'd have..."

"No, I didn't think you would." A prickly pause. "So he wants you as his mistress, not as his wife?"

Marina shook her head and more tears escaped. She lifted her free hand to wipe her eyes, but it didn't help. "He asked me to marry him."

Her father said slowly, "I'm not sure I see the difficulty."

She drew a constricted breath and made herself meet his eyes. "Don't you really?"

"You're both in love. He's proposed marriage. He's a fine young man. You're the best girl in the world—and don't accuse me of being biased. Why are you crying your poor heart out to your papa, instead of announcing the good news to the world?"

Since the day her mother died, Marina had missed her. She'd never missed her as much as she did at this moment, when she realized her father didn't understand her at all, despite their long years together. The knowledge made her feel more alone than ever.

She tugged her hand free and fumbled in her pocket for a handkerchief. "You must see that marriage is impossible."

Her father frowned in dismay. "Now I've upset you, when you're already so unhappy." His voice softened. "Tell your old papa why you won't marry Fergus."

She made a defeated gesture. They seemed to be becoming a habit. "I'm an artist, not a wife."

"Can't you be both?"

"I don't know," she said unsteadily. "I doubt it. The Mackinnon is a demanding man. He'll ask a great deal of the woman he weds."

"You have a great deal to give."

"He's stubborn and opinionated."

"So you don't think you're strong enough to stand up to him?"

Fergus had asked her the same question. "I'm not," she admitted, and blew her nose.

To her chagrin, her father laughed. "*Cara*, you've established a reputation as an artist in a world that disdained you as an amateur and even worse, a woman. If you can do that, handling a mere laird should be easy."

She sniffed. "He isn't mere at all."

"No, he's not. Neither are you."

"And what if we have children? What about my painting then?"

"You don't want children?"

"Yes, I do. But can I be a mother and an artist?"

Papa's smile was fond. "I believe you can be anything you want, Marina. So did your dear mother. If Fergus is willing to work with you, why can't you have the things other women have, and still be an artist as so many other women can't be?"

She began to tear at her damp handkerchief and spoke in a rush. "It's more than that. It's the practicalities. My life and work are in Florence. My patrons are in Florence, or traveling through it. And what happens to you? You don't want to spend the rest of your life in Scotland. You and I have had such a partnership."

He sighed and sent her a sheepish glance. "No, I don't want to live in Scotland, although if I have grandchildren here, I'll visit you often. This wet, gray country is too cold for my old bones. I want to go back to Italy."

For an instant, she'd started to hope that perhaps she overestimated the barriers to a new life with Fergus. Her father's answer, however expected, hurled her back into despair. "There you are, then."

"There you are not, my girl," he said. "I've wanted to tell you for a long time, Marina, that I grow tired of this endless traveling. Bad roads. Bad food. Bad inns. Short-sighted coachmen who can't see bridges in front of their noses. Breaking my leg is the last stick."

"The last straw," she said absently, as she regarded him in shock. "I'm so sorry, Papa. I thought you enjoyed the travel."

He shrugged. "I did at first, but I'm a dozen years older than I was when we started out together, and the excitement has gone. I want to go back to

Florence and find a nice comfortable widow to marry. Nobody will ever replace your mamma in my heart, but this is a lonely life, *tesoro.* I'd like the chance to stay in one place for a while."

Marina stumbled to her feet, guilt joining the mix of unpleasant emotions already tormenting her. "I've been so selfish."

He shrugged again. "You're my daughter, and I love you, but to the ignorant, even a great artist like you is a fragile woman first. You needed a man to chaperone you and protect your good name. You've won so many battles, *cara*, but that weight of propriety, you couldn't vanquish. Now, if you marry Fergus..."

"You can go back to having a life of your own."

His lips turned down. "Don't you dare think of marrying him, if you're only doing it so that I can give up all this moving around."

She shook her head. "Not even for you, Papa. But I wish you'd said something earlier. We could have paid a companion to travel with me, some woman to lend me respectability."

"Tcha," he said again. "Some pudding-faced spinster? At least Ugolino Lucchetti added dash to your progress."

She managed a shaky smile. "He did at that."

"So you'll marry Fergus?"

She went back to ripping at her handkerchief. "My work is back in Florence. I paint Italian scenes for the English gentlemen who visit the city on their grand tour. You know that's my bread and butter, not exotic ducal commissions that come out of the blue."

Her father's smile was bemused. "If your paintings here are as good as you say, I'll wager you can paint anything you want anywhere you like and people will buy it. And at this time, Scottish scenes please the popular taste. If you're worried about your Florentine connections, I can continue to act as your agent there. If I know about anything after all these years, it's selling art."

"You make it all sound so easy," she said, as she'd said to Fergus.

Her father shrugged. "If this is what you want, you can make it come to pass. You have to decide that, Marina. Nobody else."

"I always imagined when I chose art, love wouldn't be part of my future."

"But now you're in love."

"Yes."

"And he loves you."

"Yes," she said, all of a sudden feeling much more cheerful.

"Isn't that worth trying for, then?"

Her hands settled loosely in her lap, and she frowned into the distance. Was her father right? "I need to think."

"Yes, you do, my darling daughter." Her father's smile was approving. "Now give your old papa a kiss goodnight. It's tiring work, advising young lovers."

This time, her laugh held a note of conviction. "Thank you, Papa. You're a wise man."

Again he shrugged, but she could see her compliment pleased him. "I don't know why this surprises you, *cara*."

She put her handkerchief in her pocket and stepped forward to give him a fervent hug. "I don't know either."

CHAPTER TWENTY-THREE

Wearing only his kilt and shirt, Fergus slumped in front of the blazing fire in his tower room. A half-full glass of whisky dangled from his hand. Liquor wasn't helping to alleviate his suffering. He had a bleak suspicion that the only thing that would help was the woman he loved turning up at his door and saying she'd marry him.

Which wasn't likely to happen any time soon.

He cringed to recall his disastrous proposal. He'd hoped Marina loved him, too, and that she'd agree to marry him with joyful alacrity. They could work out the complications later.

Instead, she'd turned him down flat. That had felt like a punch in the guts, and made him realize quite how much she'd come to mean to him over these weeks.

Even hearing she loved him hadn't provided balm to his wound, because her love paled in comparison to her dedication to her bloody art.

He wasn't being fair, he knew it. She'd worked hard for her reputation as a painter, and it was a tribute to her talent and determination that she'd carved out a successful career.

But God damn it, he loved her. He wanted her in his arms, not back in blasted Italy, impressing the connoisseurs. He wanted her beside him as they grew old together. He wanted her to bear him a brood of children, who would no doubt take after their headstrong mother and prove to be a string of wee hellions.

These weeks of having her as his mistress had been glorious, but more and more frustrating. They'd shown him that he wanted a wife. And not any wife, but Marina.

He didn't want to skulk around and hide what he felt, when he had a woman he was proud to show off. He didn't want to sleep alone in the big bed looming out of the shadows behind him, the bed where every laird of Achnasheen had been conceived and born for the last two hundred years. He didn't want to listen to the wind howling like a banshee around his tower eyrie, without having Marina cuddled close in his arms. Spectacular as the sex between them was, he wanted more. Want. Want. Want.

It all boiled down to wanting a life with Marina.

And that life remained as out of reach as the moon.

He tightened his grip on the glass and hurled it into the fire. It shattered and the whisky caught fire. The sudden roar of the flames meant hc almost missed the tentative knock on his door.

Who the devil was it? Everyone in the castle should be in bed. It was well after midnight. He'd been up here brooding for hours.

He almost told his visitor to go to hell. But duty, rusty but persistent, kicked in. Somebody might need help.

Stiffly, like an old man, he staggered up onto his bare feet and crossed to fling the heavy oak door wide. "To Hades with ye, what do..."

The rest of his rough greeting died unspoken. He swallowed to ease his constricted throat, and continued in a different tone altogether, one that combined surprise with endless longing. "Marina?"

Under her spectacular crimson cape, she wore a long white nightdress. Her black hair hung loose and shining around her shoulders. With a shock, he realized he'd often seen her naked, but he'd never seen her ready for bed. The everyday intimacy of this meeting struck him like a blow. They'd shared so much, but there were many things, mundane yet important, that remained a mystery.

The elegant hands twisting at her waist betrayed apprehension, and her voice was husky with uncertainty when she spoke. "Fergus, can I talk to you for a moment?"

He burned to drag her into his arms, but after today he wasn't sure he still had that right. Odd that now they'd both declared their love, he felt more awkward with her than he ever had before.

"Come in, *mo chridhe*." He stepped back to let her enter, then wondered if he'd lost the right to call her his heart, too. Although she was and always would be his heart.

After a hesitation, she crossed his threshold. So often he'd imagined having her here in his tower, but his mind had focused on passion, pounding into her like thunder, high above the glen he loved, and feeling her tighten around him as she found her pleasure.

Would he ever do that again?

He gestured to the second armchair beside the fire. "Would ye like to sit down?"

"No. No, thank you." She paused. "Are you all right?"

He frowned. "Are you here to find out how I'm feeling?"

"No. Well, yes." He wasn't used to seeing her so unsure. "I heard something break."

"A fit of childish theatrics." Damn him if he didn't blush. "I threw a glass into the fireplace."

"Oh."

A bristling silence crashed down, then they both spoke together.

"I'm glad you came to see me. I wanted to…"

"I talked to Papa after dinner, and he said…"

They both faltered into silence. He supposed if she'd talked to her father, that meant she'd decided to leave Achnasheen. "May I speak first? I have something to say to ye."

A tiny wrinkle of worry appeared between her eyebrows. "If you wish, but I'd like—"

He spoke before she could finish. "I've been going over everything ye said this afternoon."

"So have I."

He raised a hand. "Please, lassie, let me say my piece."

"But, Fergus—"

"Mo chridhe."

With a mulish expression, she folded her arms over that lovely bosom and nodded to indicate he had her permission to continue. He supposed it was an improvement on looking like she faced the guillotine, the way she had when she'd first appeared at his door.

"I ken what it's cost ye to build your career. I understand that you don't want to sacrifice all that, just as you're reaching the pinnacle of success. The woman I'm in love with is an artist. She's unconventional. That's one of the reasons I love her. So I suggest an unconventional marriage."

Fergus paused, because she looked like she was about to interrupt him again. But as she uncrossed her arms, she didn't speak. She was listening so intently, he felt like her very skin soaked up his words.

He prayed to God that when she'd listened, she'd agree. If she said no to this, he had nothing more to offer.

"Your patrons are in Florence, and your subjects are in Italy, so I'll come and live with ye there."

Marina made a choked sound and went as pale as hawthorn blossom. "Do you mean that?"

"Aye, with all my heart."

"But you love Achnasheen." She spread her hands in bewilderment. "You're the laird."

He shrugged, although they both knew how much it would pain him to abandon his home. Before he reached this decision, he'd taken the time to consider its full cost. "I'll still be the laird, but I'll be the laird who lives in Florence with his beautiful, talented wife, and who runs his estate through a capable bailiff. It's not as if half the estates in the Highlands dinna have absentee landlords."

"Not this estate." She shook her head. "You'll miss it."

"Aye, I will." He made a sweeping gesture. "Not as much as I'll miss you if ye leave me. And we can visit. I suspect that once the duke has his pictures on display, your patrons are going to want more Scottish scenes."

"You'd do this? Leave Achnasheen?" When she blinked, he caught the glitter of tears in her eyes. "For me?"

"And for me." He gave a heavy sigh and ran his hand through his hair. "I love you, Marina. I've never been in love before. Devil if I'll lose ye just because we cannae decide where we'll live."

Her lips tightened, and a tear trickled down her cheek. Now that he took a closer look, her eyes were already pink with weeping. He hated to think he'd made her cry. Still made her cry.

His gut knotted with anguish as he realized her lack of response didn't bode well for his proposition. Could he lose her yet, despite making this sacrifice to keep her?

After a long pause, she spoke in a tight voice. "You'd come to hate me."

"Never." He meant it.

Her delicate throat moved as she swallowed. "Then to hell with you, Mackinnon."

Startled, he staggered back. "What?"

"You heard me." Marina summoned a shaky smile, although Fergus's offer came close to shattering her heart. Unchecked tears poured down her cheeks. "Because I came here to say that I'd stay, that I'd try and overcome any qualms I have about losing my identity as an artist, because I love you too much to leave you. Then you go and turn everything around with this incomparable act of generosity."

He made a gesture as if to dismiss his extraordinary self-sacrifice. "I ken what I want, and it's you," he said seriously. "You must know I'd go to the ends of the earth for ye."

Surely she must burst with joy and gratitude. She'd come so close to losing him. "Even Florence?"

The eyes he leveled on her were alight with love. "Even Florence."

She raised her hands in a futile attempt to dash away her tears. Silly to cry like a rainspout when she was so happy. "Although I'll always treasure your offer, you don't have to live in Florence, *amore mio.*"

Even after all that soul-searching in her room when she realized that she was a fool to forsake a once-in-a-lifetime love, she'd feared Fergus's autocratic tendencies. Hearing him say he'd give up the life he was born for told her everything that she needed to know about how dearly he valued her.

He was ready to compromise and make sacrifices. He did, indeed, love her. More than she'd ever imagined, if he'd decided he could live in Italy for her sake. The sheer magnanimity of his gift left her awed and humbled.

He looked confused. "I don't?"

"No, I want to live here. With occasional visits to Papa in Florence."

"He's going home?"

"Yes. It turns out I didn't need to worry about him after all. He approves of you—or he will, if you make an honest woman of me. We weren't quite as clever at hiding our affair as we hoped."

Fergus frowned, as she wondered why he didn't sweep her into his arms and tell her he loved her. He must know she'd laid down all her defenses, and she was here to deliver her willing capitulation. This subdued reaction to her declaration troubled her.

She stepped closer. "Why don't you kiss me, Mackinnon?"

He spread his hands. "I need ye to tell me straight out what you want." His voice lowered, and the raw emotion in his expression made her heart ache. "I dinna want to make any more mistakes, like I did this afternoon."

He'd said something similar, the night she promised to come to his bed. "I'm sorry." Remorse pierced her like a knife. How she'd hurt him today. "You took me by surprise when you proposed, and you're right—I reacted in blind fear."

"Are ye saying you're no' frightened anymore?" Somber gray eyes studied her. Still he didn't touch her.

Marina was now close enough to take his hand. She licked dry lips and met a gaze that asked for everything she had to give. Was she brave enough to answer yes? "I'm saying that I might suffer a few collywobbles, Mackinnon. But I'm ready to entrust my future to you."

"Tell me, then."

She raised his hand to her lips and kissed the knuckles. His grip tightened, and she wondered if he'd haul her up against him then, but he remained quiet and watchful.

"Unconditional surrender?"

He nodded without smiling. "Unconditional surrender."

She gulped in a shuddering breath and tangled her fingers in his, drawing strength from the warm certainty of his touch. "First, let me say that I love you more than I can ever say. I didn't tell you that this afternoon, or not in the way I should have. I've never been in love before either. I had no idea..."

"How love sweeps everything else before its path?"

"Exactly. It's like you're part of me." She mustered another smile. "No wonder I wanted to run a mile."

He didn't smile back. "Do you still?"

"No." Again with more emphasis, "No. It would be like trying to escape my soul." Then in a low voice, she went on, "You're everything to me, Fergus. The sun in my sky."

His eyes darkened. "Marina…"

Her free hand made a shaky gesture. "I'm afraid you're stuck with me."

"I'll take that." His grip tightened to the edge of pain. "I'll take you."

This smile was a little more secure, although emotion still clogged her throat. Her voice cracked when she spoke. "And I'll take you. As my husband, and the father of my children. I'll take this extraordinary place you live in and make it my home. I'll paint it in every season. I'll show you sides of Achnasheen not even you have seen before. I'll live with you in your castle, and we'll grow old together, and your strength will feed my strength, and nothing will ever divide us." She paused and took a tremulous breath. "Now, do you understand what I'm asking for?"

When he raised his head, the candlelight caught the rich red of his hair. Triumph and joy shone in his silver eyes. So much joy that her breath jammed in her chest and she felt dizzy.

The rare, unconstrained smile lit his face to brilliance. How she'd always loved that smile. "I understand, and I accept, my beloved."

"Fergus…" she whispered, folding forward as her knees gave out. With the stumble, her Venetian cloak slipped to the floor. "Kiss me."

At last, at last, he wrenched her up against his body and swooped down to capture her lips with his. She sighed in relief and lashed her arms around him, crushing him into her.

Heat flared and passion ignited, but beneath the powerful physical reaction, there was love, steadfast and eternal.

"I love ye, lassie," he murmured against her lips.

Before she could respond with an avowal of her own, he lifted her and carried her the few steps to the ancient four-poster bed in the corner.

CHAPTER TWENTY-FOUR

he abrupt change from despair to elation left Fergus reeling. When he'd come upstairs, he'd wondered if this one last roll of the dice would win him the prize. Now he struggled to comprehend that everything he'd dreamed of having was within reach.

The lassie he loved. The life he relished. The chance of creating a family with this exceptional woman.

Fergus stepped back from the bed and ripped off his shirt and kilt with clumsy hands. Marina rose far enough to tug that alluringly prim white nightdress over her head, leaving her lavish cascade of hair to tumble over her breasts and shoulders. When she lay back against the pillows, he sank down to bury his face in the warm fall of silky hair. He breathed deep, drawing in her essence. Lilies and love and Marina.

This willful lassie was his at last. He could hardly believe it.

"Don't make me wait, *tesoro*." With a tender gesture that made his blood pulse heavy and sweet, she ran her hands down his back. "I came so close to losing you."

"Never." Through her wealth of hair, he kissed her neck and delighted in her shivery response. "It took me my whole life to find you. I wasnae going to let ye go for the sake of a small geographical disagreement."

"I can't tell you what it meant when you said you'd come to Italy." Marina arched up until her breasts brushed his chest and sighed when his hands trailed down her flanks to settle on her hips. "Now I know you really love me."

He groaned and grazed his teeth across the curve of her shoulder. Their legs tangled against the cool sheets as he settled on top of her. "I die for love of ye, lassie."

Her fingers dug into his shoulders, her touch as fiercely possessive as his. "Don't die, *amore mio*. Live. Live for me, as I'll live for you."

Fergus rose on his elbows so he could see her beautiful face, noting the signs of will and intelligence and passion. What a wife she was for a wild Highland laird. "I meant it when I said I'd go to Florence."

"I know you did." Her smile was incandescent. "But I'm also sincere when I say we'll make a good life here. We have everything we want in Achnasheen. We can visit Florence now and again, to see Papa and meet my patrons. I'd like the children to know about their Italian heritage as well as their proud Scots blood."

He arched an eyebrow at her. "Children, is it, *mo chridhe*?"

"Aye, my braw laddie, I've got plans for four bonny wee bairns, two boys and two girls."

His laugh rang with delight. He loved it when she imitated his accent. "Och, there's no time to be lost, then."

Mischief sparked in the flashing black eyes that had intrigued him from the first. "No reason to delay at all."

He kissed her with all the love overflowing in his heart. She was a thousand miles from the wife he'd ever imagined himself taking, yet she was the absolutely perfect choice.

He started to stroke her, touching breasts and thighs and belly and sex, but neither he nor Marina was in a mood to linger.

"Fergus, I need you now. Please," she said in a husky voice, cradling his hips between her knees and raking her nails down his back. The sting only stoked his need.

He tightened his loins and thrust. With a long sigh, she stretched up to take him deeper.

"I love you, Marina," he groaned, raising his head.

Her eyes, heavy with arousal, burned into his. "And I love you, Mackinnon. I love you, Laird of Achnasheen." Then with an aching tenderness that made his heart cramp, she said, "I love you, Fergus."

"My darling..."

"Let's try for a child. We don't need to be afraid anymore." When she squeezed around him, the blast of heat almost incinerated him. "I want everything life and love can give us."

Her grip on his shoulders tightened, and he realized that while he might claim her, she claimed him just as adamantly. Why not? This woman was his equal, the balance to his soul.

"I give ye everything I am." The words were a vow, as his soul expanded to contain all the joy he felt.

She lifted her hips in encouragement. "And I give you everything I am."

Fergus could hold back no longer. With deep, purposeful strokes, he plunged into her. She moaned her pleasure and rose to meet him.

He heard Marina cry out as she reached her peak, then hot darkness crashed down over him. For the first time, he lost himself inside the woman he loved and found a radiant welcome that would sustain him all his life. With a broken groan, he slumped over her, spent and knowing that he'd found his destiny.

Fergus stirred, sensing that Marina was no longer beside him in the bed. After that first swift, miraculous joining, they'd made love again, lingering to share tenderness and passion, before they'd both tumbled into sleep.

The room was dark. The candles had burned down to nothing, and the fire needed stoking. As autumn closed in, the nights grew colder. He looked forward to holding his bride close and snug in his arms all through winter. What a life stretched ahead of them.

Marina stood at the window in her white nightdress.

Drowsily, he pushed up against the pillows. "Is all well, my bonny love?"

She turned toward him, a graceful twist of her slender body and a drift of midnight hair. "All's well, *amore.*"

He rolled out of bed, hooking up his kilt from a chair and wrapping it around his nakedness. "What's got your attention out there?"

"I was thinking how beautiful your glen is, and how lucky I was to find this place—and you," she said in a dreamy voice.

Och, she was the lassie for him.

He added some wood to the fire, before he padded up behind her and slid his arms around her waist. When she leaned back to rest her head on his shoulder in perfect trust, his heart performed another besotted somersault.

He dropped a kiss on her crown and tightened his embrace, while he stared out over his domain. This side of the tower faced the loch. The weather had cleared, and in the sky, the stars shone like fire.

"How lucky I am, you mean, *mo chridhe,*" he murmured. "I always wanted to have ye up here with me, you know. Say we'll marry as soon as we can call the banns."

"I'd marry you right now, if I could."

"Aye, well, you might have just got your wish, lassie." He smiled into her rumpled hair. "Have ye heard about the old Highland tradition of handfasting?"

She tilted her head. "Another barbarian custom, *caro*?"

"You'll like this one. In the eyes of God, we're already husband and wife. If a man and a woman hold hands and promise to stay true to one another for the rest of their lives, they're wed. It's a very solemn vow, you ken."

She drew away and turned to take his hand. "Fergus Mackinnon, Laird of Achnasheen, I promise to be your wife and love you until the day I die."

He stared down into eyes lustrous in the firelight. After all the turmoil and unhappiness, her pledge moved him beyond words. "Marina Lucchetti, formerly of Florence, I swear to protect and love and cherish ye for all our life together. From this moment forward, I'm your husband."

Catching her up against him, he kissed her with all the adoration he felt. Their lips met in a passionate promise for the future.

By the time he raised his head, he was trembling. So was she.

Marina lifted an unsteady hand to touch his cheek. "We're married now, *caro*?"

His smile was wry. "In spirit at least. However for the vows to be binding, we need to make them before witnesses, and I'm no' sure a court of law will uphold the contract, even then. We still have an appointment with the Reverend Angus ahead of us."

Her lips turned down in disappointment. "So we need to be respectable?"

"For a mere three weeks, lassie."

She caught his hand where it rested at her waist and kissed it. "*Dio mio*, it will be a long three weeks."

"Aye, that it will."

"I feel married," she said softly.

"So do I."

"And I suppose I have to sneak back to my room before the sun comes up."

"Aye, that, too." He kissed the side of her neck and felt her shiver. "But in late October, the sun doesnae rise until late, and it's nowhere near dawn yet. You don't have to leave me for hours."

"I think I might come to like these dark Scottish winters." He could tell from her voice that she was smiling.

"It's no night to wander around barefoot, so ye should stay here as long as you can." He lifted his head to look down into her face. "I'm only thinking of your health, you ken."

She laughed. "You're all consideration, Mackinnon."

"You have no idea." Then in another tone altogether, "Will ye no' come back to bed and warm up the last hours of the night with me, *mo leannan*?"

She rose on her toes and kissed him briefly but with purpose. "It will be my pleasure, laird of my heart."

EPILOGUE

Edinburgh, April 1819

*E*dinburgh's high society gathered en masse at the George Street Assembly Rooms to view the new Highland paintings by noted artist Marina Mackinnon, Lady Achnasheen. A few connoisseurs even abandoned the London season to venture north and see what all the fuss was about. The critics from London and Edinburgh had also turned out in force, and so far seemed bowled over by the artwork on display under the line of crystal chandeliers that lit the magnificent ballroom.

"Are ye over your nerves, *mo chridhe*?" Fergus asked, coming up behind Marina and curling his arm around a waist that was no longer as slim as it had been. The fashionable high waist of her dark gold silk gown concealed that she was expecting their first baby in late August.

His touch warmed her as it always did, and she rested back against him for an instant before standing straight as befitted a laird's wife in company. "Not until I see the reviews."

Fergus's laugh was fond. "You and your artistic temperament." He glanced around the packed room. "All I've heard is the most extravagant praise. People must have told you how much they love your work. I've certainly had trouble getting near ye all night."

She cast him a seductive smile. For an instant, the busy crowd disappeared, the noise faded to nothing, and she became just a woman standing beside the man she loved.

He looked superb in elegant evening dress. Nobody seeing him would guess at the wild, kilted Scots warrior who strode the hills and braes of Achnasheen like a king.

"Once we go back to the glen, we'll have plenty of time alone, *caro*. Have patience."

His silvery eyes dropped to her lips, and she knew he thought of kissing her. She gave a shiver of wanton anticipation. "Not here, Mackinnon," she whispered.

"Och, why did I marry such a troublesome wench?" he said in mock despair. "A good Scots lass would kiss her lord and master when he asks."

"Whereas your Italian bride retains some grip on decorum."

"Blast decorum," he said, sliding his arm free of her waist and catching her gloved hand.

"I promise to be very indecorous later, *amore*."

"I cannae wait," he murmured, brushing his lips across her knuckles.

"Marina, you're a grand success. Congratulations."

She shook herself out of the daze she always tumbled into when her husband set out to beguile her and turned to greet Fergus's friend, Hamish Douglas.

"Good evening, Hamish." When she kissed his cheek, she had to stretch up to reach him. He was as large as a small mountain, and as fair and handsome as a young Viking. "When did you arrive?"

"An hour ago. Diarmid is here, too."

"Oh, I hope I see him."

Since her wedding, life at Achnasheen had proven more convivial than she'd expected. Diarmid and Hamish were regular visitors, as were Fergus's sisters and their families.

Poor Mary and Clarissa. They'd never recovered from their shock at how casually Marina treated their brother's authority. She could see where he'd picked up the wrong-headed idea that women were fragile flowers who needed a male to protect them from life's harsh winds. She was glad she'd disabused him of that notion.

Eighteen months of marriage had witnessed the occasional clash, but she and Fergus had both learned to compromise, or even upon occasion lose a battle. With each conflict that found its resolution, their trust in one another grew stronger and more certain.

And there were benefits to their infrequent arguments. Marina and her husband had marked the start of each truce with some spectacular encounters in the laird's tower bedroom.

"I've asked Signor Lucchetti to save me one of the waterfall pictures, and I believe Diarmid means to buy the painting of the Cuillins." Hamish gestured to where his lean, dark-haired cousin was chatting to Marina's father. "I hope he's in time. Soon the only pictures that haven't sold tonight will be the ones that the Duke of Portofino lent for the exhibition."

As Fergus had predicted, Marina's move to the wilds of Scotland hadn't damaged her burgeoning career. His Grace, the duke, had been delighted with the twelve pictures she sent him and had commissioned more. From the moment the first suite of Achnasheen paintings went on show at the ducal palace, his aristocratic friends had clamored for views of Scotland to decorate their own fine houses. She and Fergus had since traveled across the Highlands, seeking out beautiful places for her to paint, although nothing in her opinion could compare with the glories of her home.

Marina's fears that Fergus might resent her dedication to her art proved unfounded. He was proud of her talent. Not only that, he was delighted that because of her work, the world learned to admire his beautiful homeland.

Life was grand. Now they expected a child in late summer, it promised to become even better. She felt blessed beyond what anyone could deserve.

Diarmid and her father approached. Since breaking his leg, Ugolino had visited Achnasheen three times. On his last trip, he'd brought Giulia, the plump, easygoing widow he'd married not long before Christmas.

Giulia was here tonight, charming potential purchasers with her broken English and flashing green eyes. Much of Papa's spectacular record as Marina's Italian agent stemmed from her new stepmother's skills in persuading older gentlemen to buy the artworks.

"*Dolcissima,* you're a wild success," Papa said, once Marina and Diarmid had greeted one another. "The Prince Regent's secretary has just bought two pictures, and the fellow says His Royal Highness will likely want more for Carlton House. You're under royal patronage now, *figlia mia.*"

"Papa, you amaze me," she said.

Fergus scowled at his father-in-law, stouter and more cheerful than ever since he'd settled down with Giulia. "That fat pretender is lucky to have a painting by my supremely gifted wife."

"Hush, *caro*," she said. Her husband was no lover of a Hanoverian Royal family he dismissed as mere usurpers on the throne that rightfully belonged to the Stuarts. "Once His Highness has paid for his pictures, you can harangue me about the Jacobite cause to your heart's content."

"*Brava ragazza.*" Her father's glance was admiring. "I've taught you the worth of a shilling."

"And a florin, Papa," Marina said with a laugh.

"That's what a Scotsman needs, a thrifty wife," Diarmid said.

Fergus's half-smile had been much in evidence tonight. It reappeared now. "Nice to hear ye thinking about marriage, laddie. Does that mean you've got a lass in mind at last?"

"Not me, my friend." The shadow that passed across Diarmid's dark, intense features sparked Marina's curiosity. "The lassies can sleep easy. I willnae trouble them with a wooing just yet."

Before she could probe further, Papa was clapping his hands and requesting silence. She and Fergus had appointed him master of ceremonies, not only because he was Marina's business representative, but also because his theatrical nature thrived on being the center of attention.

"*Attenzione, attenzione! Prego! Prego!*"

Gradually the hubbub subsided, allowing Papa to begin a fulsome speech about Marina and her work. When Fergus caught her hand, she twined her fingers about his. It was lovely being feted and receiving such accolades for her art, but her unshakable love for her husband was the source from which all her other happiness flowed.

"He's enjoying himself," Fergus whispered in her ear. "Do ye think we'll get out of here before Tuesday?"

"Shh," Marina said, stifling a giggle. Her father had been speaking for ten minutes already, and he was only up to the day Marina started at art school.

At last Papa became aware that his audience grew restless, and he stepped aside to gesture to a shrouded easel that the waiters had carried in while he meandered on. "My brilliant daughter has one more surprise for you, a final painting that she tells me is a gift to her most distinguished husband, the Mackinnon, Laird of Achnasheen. The man I am honored to call my son-in-law. Fergus Mackinnon."

Fergus's grip tightened, and he turned to her baffled. "What the devil..."

Marina smiled up at him, as uncertainty coiled in her stomach. It was possible he mightn't appreciate her offering, even though she'd worked harder on it than she had on any other painting in her life. "It's a surprise."

"Aye, it's that, all right. Is it a picture of the castle?"

"Wait and see," she said, pulling free and crossing to stand at the easel.

More applause broke out and an occasional cheer, which she would have thought beneath the dignity of this high-born audience.

Ladies didn't make speeches, so she'd been informed, and while she had few qualms about standing up to Fergus in private, she had no wish to shame him in public by having the world say he'd wed a hoyden. So she curtsied and murmured her gratitude and waited for the acclaim to die away.

Fergus stepped up to her side. "What in heaven's name have ye been up to, *mo chridhe*?"

"Look and see, *tesoro*." Without any more hesitation, she caught the blue silk cloth and flung it away from the painting.

The room fell silent, then fresh applause broke out, even more fervent than last time. Half-afraid of what she might find in Fergus's face, Marina lifted her chin and met his eyes. "What do you think, Mackinnon?"

"Marina…" When he breathed her name, it sounded like a prayer. His features were stark with astonishment, and that little muscle in his cheek began to jerk and dance, always a sign of strong feeling. "You've made me look like a hero."

She glanced at the full-length portrait of Fergus in his red and black Mackinnon kilt, set against the view across the sea to Skye. He stood proudly in the place where she'd started to fall in love with the glen—and with its laird. In the dramatic landscape, he ranged tall and straight. A breeze rustled through his auburn hair, and the gray eyes burned with steadfast and invincible power.

Marina had worked like a demon on this painting, although keeping her project secret from an attentive husband had presented its problems. She'd chosen to paint Fergus in oils, hoping the rich colors would do him justice. There had been some false starts before she grew proficient in the unfamiliar medium.

"But of course I have, *amore mio*." She turned back toward her beloved laird, who was so much more vivid and potent than any painting could ever be. "Because you are a hero. You're my hero."

As she watched his slow, radiant smile light his features, all her nerves vanished. She couldn't doubt that he liked her gift.

"I love you, lassie, and I thank you from the bottom of my heart. It's a masterpiece." He swooped in and kissed her, without sparing a thought to their watching audience. "I was a lucky man the day I rescued ye from a cold dip in the burn."

Marina couldn't resist kissing Fergus back, although she was blushing by the time she drew free. "You once told me that if you save someone's life, you keep a vested interest in that person forever." Her voice was thick with emotion.

Her beloved husband's smile told her he hardly credited his good fortune. "I'd have it no other way, my bonny lassie."

ABOUT THE AUTHOR

Australian Anna Campbell has written 11 multi award-winning historical romances for Avon HarperCollins and Grand Central Publishing. As an independently published author, she's released more than 30 bestselling stories. Right now, she is working on a new series called A Scandal in Mayfair, set amidst the glamour and sensuality of Regency London. Anna has won numerous awards for her stories, including RT Book Reviews Reviewers Choice, the Booksellers Best, the Golden Quill (three times), the Heart of Excellence (twice), the Write Touch, the Aspen Gold (twice), and the Australian Romance Readers' favorite historical romance (five times).

Anna loves to hear from her readers. You can find her at:

Website: www.annacampbell.com

facebook.com/AnnaCampbellFans

twitter.comAnnaCampbellOz

bookbub.com/authors/anna-campbell

The Laird's Willful Lass:
The Lairds Most Likely Book 1

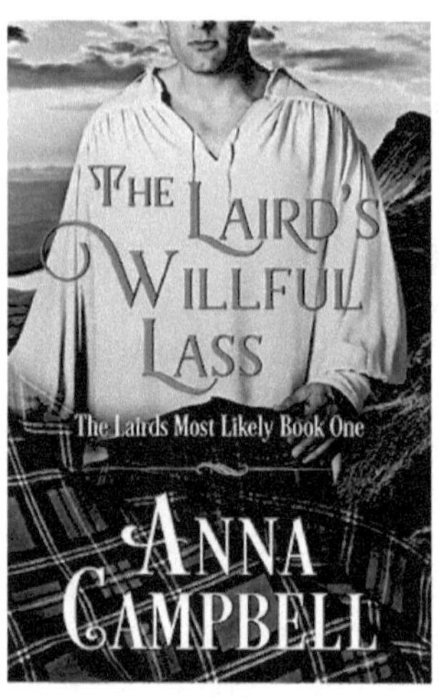

An untamed man as immovable as a Highland mountain...

Fergus Mackinnon, autocratic Laird of Achnasheen, likes to be in charge. When he was little more than a lad, he became master of his Scottish estate, and he's learned to rely on his unfailing judgment. So has everyone else in his corner of the world. He sees no reason for his bride—when he finds her—to be any different.

A headstrong woman from the warm and passionate south...

Marina Lucchetti knows all about fighting her way through a wall of masculine arrogance. In her native Florence, she's become a successful artist, no easy feat for a woman. Now a commission to paint a series of Highland scenes promises to spread her fame far and wide. When a carriage accident strands her at Achnasheen for a few weeks, it's a mixed blessing. The magnificent landscape offers everything her artistic soul could desire. If only she can resist the impulse to smash her easel across the laird's obstinate head.

When two fiery souls come together, a conflagration flares.

Marina is Fergus's worst nightmare—a woman who defies a man's guidance. Fergus challenges everything Marina believes about a woman's right to choose her path. No two people could be less suited. But when irresistible passion enters the equation, good sense soon jumps into the loch.

Will the desire between Fergus and Marina blaze hot, then fade to ashes? Or will the imperious laird and his willful lass discover that their differences aren't insurmountable after all, but the spice that will flavor a lifetime of happiness?

The Laird's Christmas Kiss:
The Lairds Most Likely Book 2

Down with love!

Ever since she was fifteen, shy wallflower Elspeth
Douglas has pined in vain for the attentions of
dashing Brody Girvan, Laird of Invermackie. But
the rakish Highlander doesn't even know she's
alive. Now she's twenty, she realizes that she'll
never be happy until she stops loving her brother's
handsome friend. When family and friends gather
at Achnasheen Castle for Christmas, she intends to
show the world that she's all grown up, and grown
out of silly crushes on gorgeous Scotsmen. So take
that, my gallant laddie!

Girls just want to have fun...

Except it turns out that Brody isn't singing from the
same Christmas carol sheet. Elspeth decides she's

not interested in him anymore, just as he decides
he's very interested indeed. In fact, now he looks
more closely, his friend Hamish's sister is pretty
and funny and forthright – and just the lassie to
share his Highland estate. Convincing his little
wren of his romantic intentions is difficult enough,
even before she undergoes a makeover and
becomes the belle of Achnasheen. For once in his
life, dissolute Brody is burdened with honorable
intentions, while the lady he pursues is set on
flirtation with no strings attached.

Deck the halls with mistletoe!

With interfering friends and a crate of imported
mistletoe thrown into the mix, the stage is set for a
house party rife with secrets, clandestine kisses,
misunderstandings, heartache, scandal, and love
triumphant.

The Highlander's Lost Lady:
The Lairds Most Likely Book 3

A Highlander as brave and strong as a knight of old...

When Diarmid Mactavish, Laird of Invertavey, discovers a mysterious woman washed up on his land after a wild storm, he takes her in and tries to find her family. But even as forbidden dreams of sensual fulfillment torment him, he's convinced that this beautiful lassie isn't what she seems. And if there's one thing Diarmid despises, it's a liar.

A mother willing to do anything to save her daughter...

Widow Fiona Grant has risked everything to break free of her clan and rescue her adolescent daughter from a forced marriage. But before her quest has barely begun, disaster strikes. She escapes her

brutish kinsmen, only to be shipwrecked on
Mactavish territory where she falls into her
enemies' hands. For centuries, a murderous feud
has raged between the Mactavishes and the Grants,
so how can she trust her darkly handsome host?

*Now a twisted Highland road leads to
danger and passion...and irresistible love.
But is love strong enough to banish the
past's long shadows and offer these wary
allies all that their hearts desire?*

The Highlander's Defiant Captive:
The Lairds Most Likely Book 4

Peace in the glens means war in the bedchamber!

Scotland. 1699. In a time of heroes, the greatest hero of all is Callum Mackinnon, Laird of Achnasheen. Brave, reckless, canny, and handsome enough to turn any lassie weak at the knees, Callum is a legend in the wild corner of the Highlands where he rules. Now the young laird is determined to choose a new path for his clan and end the violent feud with the Drummonds, a conflict that has painted the glens red with blood for centuries. This means taking Bonny Mhairi Drummond, the Rose of Bruard, as his wife. When negotiations with her pig-headed father break down, Callum seizes matters into his own hands and kidnaps the fairest maiden in Scotland, swearing to make her his own.

Bonny Mhairi is the adored only child of Clan

Drummond's doughty chieftain and she's inherited
all her father's courage and stubbornness. Not to
mention his undying hatred for anyone called
Mackinnon. When the Mackinnon chieftain steals
her away from her home and vows to woo her into
accepting him as her husband, she swears that
she'll never consent to be his bride. But trapped
inside her foe's castle, Mhairi finds it hard to cling
to old certainties. She detests her arrogant jailer,
even as he sparks a fierce, forbidden hunger in her
soul.

Loving the enemy...

As Callum and Mhairi wage their passionate war of
hearts, danger, treachery and desire circle closer
and closer. When her father's army masses at the
gates of Achnasheen, will Mhairi prove herself a
Drummond now and forever? Or will new
allegiances trump ancient hatred, as the desperate
laird battles to win the lass he loves more than his
life?

The Highlander's Christmas Quest: The Lairds Most Likely Book 5

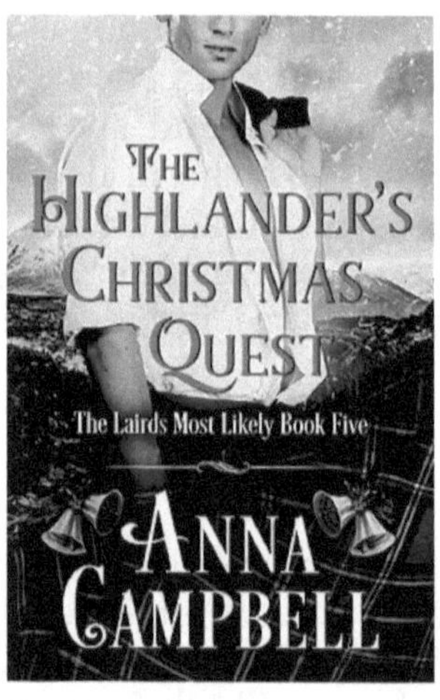

She's found the man for her, but he has no plans to stay on her island. Perhaps it's time to try a little sabotage!

Scotland. 1725. The moment she sees handsome Dougal Drummond, Kirsty Macbain tumbles headlong into love. A chance storm a few days before Christmas has blown the gallant Highlander off-course to her father's isle of Askaval, but once he's repaired his boat, Dougal is determined to continue on his way. His bright blue eyes are firmly fixed on valiant deeds and a distant horizon. What does he care for a smart-mouthed, independent lassie who forms no part of his plans for his future?

Kirsty is convinced that if only she can keep Dougal on Askaval, he'll see how perfect they are together. With his boat out of action, he's trapped in her company. Some surreptitious midnight destruction with a drill and a hammer might help true love to win out. On the other hand, if Dougal discovers what she's been up to, there will be the devil to pay.

Will this madcap Christmas deliver Kirsty's heart's desire – or will her scheming see Dougal sailing away to a life without her?

The Highlander's English Bride:
The Lairds Most Likely Book 6

An impossible pairing…

Hamish Douglas, the mercurial Laird of Glen Lyon, has never got along with independent, smart-mouthed Emily Baylor. Which wouldn't matter if this brilliant Scottish astronomer didn't move in the same scientific circles as Emily and if her famous father wasn't his mentor. But when Emily looks likely to derail the event which will make Hamish's career, he loses his temper with the pretty miss and his recklessness leaves her reputation in ruins.

A marriage made in scandal…

Emily has always thought her father's spectacular protégé was far too arrogant for his own good. But what is she to do when the only way she can save her good name in society is to wed the unruly laird? Reluctantly she accepts Hamish's proposal, but only on the condition that their union remains chaste. That shouldn't be a problem; they've never been friends, let alone potential lovers – except that after they marry, Hamish reveals unexpected depths and a host of admirable qualities, and he's so awfully handsome, and now the swaggering rogue admits that he desires her...

From the ballrooms of London to the grandeur of the western Highlands, a battle royal rages between these two strong-willed combatants. Neither plans to yield an inch – but are these smart people smart enough to see that sometimes the greatest victory lies in mutual surrender?

The Highlander's Forbidden Mistress:
The Lairds Most Likely Book 7

A week to be wicked…

Widowed Selina Martin faces another marriage founded on duty, not love. When notorious libertine Lord Bruard invites her to his isolated hunting lodge, he promises discretion – and seven days of hedonistic pleasure before she weds her boorish fiancé. All her life, Selina has done the right thing, but this no-strings-attached chance to discover the handsome rake's sensual secrets is irresistible. She'll surrender to her wicked fantasies, seize some brief happiness, then knuckle down to a loveless union. What could possibly go wrong?

In a lifetime of seduction, Brock Drummond, the dashing Earl of Bruard, has never wanted a woman the way he wants demure widow Selina Martin. When Selina agrees to become his temporary lover, he soon falls captive to an enchantment unlike any other. He sets out to slake his white hot desire until only ashes remain, but as each day of forbidden delight passes, the idea of saying goodbye to his ardent mistress becomes more and more unbearable.

When scandal explodes around them and threatens to destroy Selina, Brock is the only person she can turn to. After so short a time, can she trust a man whose name is a byword for depravity?

Will this sizzling liaison prove a mere affair to remember? Or will their week of passion spark a lifetime of happiness for the widow and her dissolute Scottish earl?

The Highlander's Christmas Countess: The Lairds Most Likely Book 8

The new stableboy has a secret!

Kit Laing is a genius with Glen Lyon's horses and a favorite with his employer's family, but he isn't all he seems. In fact, the shy stablehand isn't a he at all. Kit is actually Christabel Urquhart, Countess of Appin, on the run from a greedy, violent stepbrother with designs on her fortune.

And the laird's handsome nephew has worked out just what it is.

Quentin MacNab, the dashing heir to Cannich, has had his suspicions about the new stable lad from the first. Kit is far too pretty to be a boy – and far too well spoken to be a servant.

Now passion and danger combine to create a Yuletide like no other.

When a snowstorm traps Kit and Quentin overnight in an isolated hut, the discovery of her true identity sparks a rushed marriage to stave off a scandal. But can the Christmas Countess learn to trust her charming new husband's promises of protection? Or will their fragile alliance fall victim to the evil forces assailing her?

The Highlander's Rescued Maiden: The Lairds Most Likely Book 9

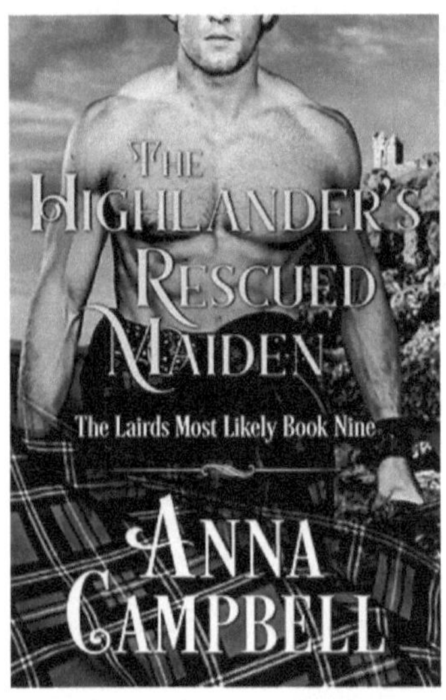

The myth of Fair Ellen of the Isles.

Across the Highlands, people recount the legend of a beautiful lassie in a tower, locked away from her clamorous suitors by a tyrannical father. Any person of sense dismisses the story as a fairy tale, no more substantial than a wisp of Scottish mist.

Rogue or hero? Or a little bit of both?

Dashing Highlander Will Mackinnon is a devil with the ladies, disinclined to fall for such romantic nonsense. But one day, his storm-tossed boat washes ashore at a rocky island dominated by a stone tower. Inside the tower, he discovers lovely, gallant Ellen Cameron and a passion that eclipses anything he's experienced before in his reckless life.

Danger and desire...

This brave adventurer vows to rescue the captive
maiden and make her his own forever. But dark
shadows gather about the lovers and threaten to
destroy all their hopes for happiness. Will has
found the love of a lifetime – but will it end up
costing him his life?

The Highlander's Christmas Lassie:
The Lairds Most Likely Book 10

Young love torn apart.

As teenagers, Malcolm Innes and Rhona Macleod
fell passionately in love. But Malcom's parents were
horrified to think of the aristocratic heir to Dun
Carron marrying a humble crofter's daughter.
Desperate to crush the affair, they locked Malcolm
up and exiled Rhona to London where she
disappears. But Malcolm is faithful and stubborn
and devotes his life to searching for his beloved and
the child she was carrying when they were cruelly
separated.

A chance to mend two shattered lives.

On a snowy Christmas Eve, Rhona opens the door
of her isolated farmhouse to find the man she never

thought to see again, the man who betrayed her. When she was pregnant with his son, Malcolm abandoned her to find her way alone in a cold, heartless world. Now she discovers that her long-held hatred is based on lies and that he's been true to her. Yet surely after all these years, it's too late to awaken the love that once united them.

As Christmas Eve turns into Christmas Day, Malcolm and Rhona discover that their mutual desire has never died. Will this Yuletide reunion lead to a lifetime together? Or has old tragedy ruptured their bond forever?

9 781925 980097